# A Novel Death

## by

## Suzanne Rossi

**A Novel Death**

Cover Art by *RJ Morris*

The Wild Rose Press, Inc.
PO Box 708
Adams Basin, NY 14410-0708
Visit us at www.thewildrosepress.com

Publishing History
First Crimson Rose Edition, 2015
Print ISBN 978-1-5092-0161-7
Digital ISBN 978-1-5092-0162-4

Published in the United States of America

**An inner voice begged Anne not** to climb the stairs. Dorie was often thoughtless, but Nancy was right. With her first sale in four years, Dorie would want to crow.

A chill skittered along her arms causing the hair to rise. She wanted to dismiss it as a reaction to air-conditioning on overheated skin, but intuition suggested something was off key. They trooped upstairs and stopped in front of the closed office door.

Candace didn't bother to knock, but opened the door to the sacred chamber. The room was dark thanks to the black walls and draperies covering the window. The only light source emanated from the computer screen.

Isadora Powell lay slumped over the keyboard, her head, complete with headphones, rested against the monitor, and her fingers, trapped beneath her torso, continued to send the cursor across the screen in never-ending rows of the letter "k." A wine glass lay on its side. The iPod dangled off the edge of the desk.

Anne followed Nancy into the room.

Candace trailed, saying, "Oh for Pete's sake, she's sound asleep or dead drunk."

Nancy stepped forward. "Dorie?" she said with a catch in her voice, and then leaned in closer.

Anne flipped the light switch. Nancy yelped and leaped back. The monitor, desk, and the back of Dorie's head were covered with blood.

Nancy turned, her eyes wide, and said gasping, "She's not drunk—just dead."

## Dedication

People sometimes ask why I'm a writer. My answer is the love of words was instilled in me at a young age by my father. He traveled a lot when I was a kid, but when he was home, he always read to me before I went to bed at night.

I was in my teens when I discovered he also wrote short stories for a newsletter related to his occupation—selling supplies to circulation departments of newspapers. While in Europe during WWII he started a newsletter of his own titled, "Bottom Man in a Foxhole."

I think it was his influence that grounded my love of reading and, eventually, writing. So, Daddy, I know that even though you are gone, you're smiling at my accomplishments. Thank you for all you did.

Chapter One

Anne Jamieson jammed her finger on Isadora Powell's doorbell for the third time and tapped her foot.

"Did she forget we were coming?" she asked her friend, Nancy.

"Knowing Dorie, she's writing a scintillating scene and ignoring us." Nancy fished her cell from her purse. "I'll give her a call. She might answer."

"If she's ignoring the doorbell, she'll ignore the phone, too, unless it's her editor or agent. Oh, this is ridiculous," she protested when the door remained closed.

Anne was hot, sticky, and had better things to do than be ignored by the temperamental author. Her slacks, a sensible choice an hour ago, added to the heat quotient and her discomfort level.

*I should have worn shorts or a skirt like Nancy.*

Nancy disconnected and dropped her phone back in her purse. "Not answering her phone either. I still say she's ignoring us. Dorie doesn't forget anything, especially good news. She'll want to crow she's sold another book."

Nancy spoke in an even tone, but Anne sensed the underlying anger. She sighed with uncharacteristic exasperation. "Well, it's silly to stand in the sun waiting for her to make an appearance. Dorie's world revolves around Dorie and if she deems something more important than a critique meeting, then I guess we can go hang. Why do we allow ourselves to be used like this?"

"Because we all like having a New York Times bestselling author's advice." Nancy glared at the front door. "It wouldn't be the first time she's stiffed us. Who else is supposed to be here?"

"I don't know. When I talked to Dorie she was contacting everyone, but I have no idea who accepted."

A car door slammed. The women turned and saw another member of the group, Candace Warren, making her way up the front walk.

"Hi, am I late?" she asked, pushing her blonde bangs out of her eyes.

Anne detected the faint odor of breath mints, and wondered if Candace had been drinking again.

"Dorie said to be here by eleven o'clock sharp," Nancy replied, glancing at her watch. "It's after that, but she isn't answering either the doorbell or her phone."

Candace frowned, stepped forward, rang the doorbell, and then knocked, calling out in a loud voice. "Dorie, are you in there? Come on, open up."

Anne wiped a trickle of sweat from her temple. Did Candace think they'd been standing on the porch without having rung the bell?

She pulled her blouse away from her damp back. Even this tiny bit of exercise made her long to relax with a good book in the air-conditioned comfort of her bedroom.

Candace drew a sharp breath. "You don't suppose there's been an accident, do you?"

Uneasiness prickled Anne's scalp. Candace's

words conjured up a lot of nasty thoughts.

*Don't be an idiot. Candace is being melodramatic, spurred on no doubt by generous shots of vodka.*

Nancy leaned on the doorbell again. A few seconds later, Candace grasped the doorknob and turned. The door swung open. Anne stared.

"Why didn't we think to do that?" she asked.

Nancy raised her eyebrows and shrugged.

"Dorie," Candace called. The three women entered the foyer. No one replied.

Anne noted not a smidgeon of dust spoiled the surfaces of the highly polished furniture in the immaculate living room. The scents of lemon and pine hung in the air.

"Looks like the maid's been here," Nancy commented.

Anne walked through the room and into the kitchen. A huge crystal punch bowl filled to the brim with Hershey's Kisses stood on the counter.

"I'd say she was expecting us," Anne said, recognizing the usual post-meeting treat.

Candace fumbled with the lock on the back door and jerked it open. She exited, crossed the patio, and halted at the edge of the pool, gazing into the clear, blue water.

Anne held her breath. Had Dorie taken a late night swim and drowned? No, if she had, the maid would have found her. *If the maid had gone out back.*

"At least she isn't floating," Candace reported when she returned.

Anne released the breath and swallowed. *Thank goodness.*

Nancy inspected the laundry room and the garage.

"Car's here."

"Dorie?" Candace called heading back through the living room and into the foyer. "Maybe she's in her office and has the iPod plugged in."

An inner voice begged Anne not to climb the stairs. Dorie was often thoughtless, but Nancy was right. With her first sale in four years, Dorie would want to crow.

A chill skittered along her arms causing the hair to rise. She wanted to dismiss it as a reaction to air-conditioning on overheated skin, but intuition suggested something was off key. They trooped upstairs and stopped in front of the closed office door.

Candace didn't bother to knock, but opened the door to the sacred chamber. The room was dark thanks to the black walls and draperies covering the window. The only light source emanated from the computer screen.

Isadora Powell lay slumped over the keyboard, her head, complete with headphones, rested against the monitor, and her fingers, trapped beneath her torso, continued to send the cursor across the screen in never-ending rows of the letter "k." A wine glass lay on its side. The iPod dangled off the edge of the desk.

Anne followed Nancy into the room.

Candace trailed, saying, "Oh for Pete's sake, she's sound asleep or dead drunk."

Nancy stepped forward. "Dorie?" she said with a catch in her voice, and then leaned in closer.

Anne flipped the light switch. Nancy yelped and leaped back. The monitor, desk, and the back of Dorie's head were covered with blood.

Nancy turned, her eyes wide, and said gasping, "She's not drunk—just dead."

Anne's first thought was to run like hell. With her heart hammering and knees weak, she whirled running blindly for the door before bumping into a small table. The statuette on it rocked and fell. Nancy was right behind Anne. Together they made a grab for the object, held it for a moment, and then let loose at the same time. It fell to the carpet with a thud.

"Oh God, oh God," Nancy mumbled. "Let's get the hell out of here."

Candace stood rooted to the spot with her hand over her mouth, her eyes bugged out and breathing loudly through her nose.

"Candace, come on!" Nancy said.

Their friend backed away in slow motion and kicked the statuette. She bent, picked it up, and stared.

"It's her Campbell," she said. "And I think there's blood on it."

Anne swallowed hard, her hand gripping the doorjamb. Someone had used the most prestigious award given out by the Writers Association of America as a murder weapon? Waves of cold rolled over her.

"Well, put it back and let's go. The killer may still be here," Anne said through chattering teeth. She grabbed Candace's arm and pulled. The Campbell fell once again and bounced.

"No way," Nancy said in a shaky voice. "That blood was like jelly. She's been dead for hours."

They stumbled down the stairs to the foyer where Nancy searched her purse, finally finding her cell, and called 9-1-1 with trembling fingers.

"I want to report a—a murder, I guess…My friend, Isadora Powell…Oh, shit, I can't remember. What's the address?"

"Fifteen-fifteen Winchester," Anne replied rubbing her arms, hoping the action would restore some warmth. Strange, ten minutes ago she'd been sweating.

Nancy relayed the information. "It's in the Manatee Cove subdivision east of U. S. 1...I have no idea, but there's blood all over the place...Of course I'm sure she's dead...Right...Nancy Carlyle."

Nancy hung up. "They're sending someone."

Anne nodded, and not trusting herself to speak, swallowed the rising nausea. She'd never considered Dorie a good friend, but no one deserved to die like that. Had she felt pain or was the first blow the killing one?

Candace's gaze swung from one to the other. "God Almighty, did you see the back of her head? It was all bashed in."

The words did nothing to stem the nausea. Anne clapped a hand over her mouth and hurried to the front door, mumbling, "I'm going to be sick."

She barely made it to the bushes along the side of the porch where she lost her breakfast. Wiping her mouth with a tissue, she turned. The others had followed her onto the porch.

Candace sat on the front steps tugging at the small gold cross on a slender chain around her neck, her breaths still coming in short gasps. Nancy lit a cigarette. Her tall, lanky frame slouched against the stucco wall of the house. Her hand trembled as she inhaled, and Anne wondered what she was thinking. Nancy had sometimes been brutally blunt in her opinion of Dorie's character.

After what seemed an eternity, two police cars arrived. The officers emerged and hurried toward them.

Anne welcomed the look of crisp, clean uniforms as opposed to the chaotic horror in Dorie's office.

The first policeman approached asking in a brusque voice. "What's going on?"

Anne licked her lips. He sounded calm and competent in contrast to the obvious tension the women exhibited. She tried to gather her tattered nerves.

"Our friend, Isadora Powell is upstairs in her office. Dead. Murdered," Anne replied, amazed she sounded so normal.

The second cop drew his gun and entered the house with cautious steps. The other two policemen did the same and followed.

"Your name?" the first cop asked.

"Anne Jamieson."

"Address?"

"Seventy-four fifty-nine Hamilton Avenue in San Sebastian."

San Sebastian, a dull, medium-sized city in South Florida, was known for its beaches and easy-going lifestyle. Murder didn't happen here. That was reserved for places like Ft. Lauderdale and Miami.

The policeman took the rest of their names and addresses before asking, "Why are you here?"

"We were expected for a critique session."

"Excuse me, could you repeat that, Ms. Jamieson?" the policeman asked.

"We're romance authors. We meet every two weeks at someone's home to discuss our work," Anne told him.

"And why are you here?"

"Dorie called a few days ago. She'd sold another book and wanted to celebrate. We sometimes suspend getting together during the summer. What with vacations and all, we occasionally found it hard for all of us to assemble. This was a special occasion."

Her gaze strayed to the others. Candace stared back, her eyes wide with a blank expression. Her fingers tightened around the necklace until the chain snapped.

Nancy stubbed her cigarette out on the sole of her shoe, flicked the butt into the grass, and then pulled another from the pack. The aroma of North Carolina's finest drifted toward them.

She took another long drag and flicked the ash from its glowing tip. An unfelt breeze tumbled the feathery gray powder across the front porch and over the edge into the caladiums.

"Ladies, let's move out to the curb," the cop suggested.

Nancy extinguished her half-smoked cigarette and tossed it, then pushed her body away from the wall. She immediately lit up again, shoving the pack along with the lighter into her skirt pocket.

Anne leaned down to help Candace to her feet. "Come on, Candace. Are you all right?"

Candace opened her purse and dropped the mangled necklace inside. "Yes, I think so. Just a little shook."

*Probably wanting a drink. Not a bad idea. I wouldn't mind a shot myself.*

More police cars arrived along with paramedics and fire rescue. The latter two were useless, but Anne assumed it must be standard procedure. Some entered the house, while the rest strung yellow crime scene tape around the yard. Neighbors stood across the street, gawking.

At the curb, the critique group lounged against Nancy's car parked in the shade of a tree while the police turned their attention to the house and its grisly contents. Candace couldn't hide the trembling of her hands.

Anne slung her arm around the woman's shoulders. "Calm down."

Anne feared Candace Warren was a woman on the brink of a meltdown. Recently divorced after thirty years of marriage, the past year had been hell. And while she tried to be supportive of a friend, the two-hour phone calls from Candace bitching about her ex-husband and his new girlfriend interfered with her own writing.

Not for the first time, she marveled at Candace's determination to be a writer. The woman boasted more rejections than Kurt Vonnegut. The sad truth was she just didn't have the talent, but persevered anyway.

The fact someone had killed Dorie didn't surprise Anne. Her blunt opinions with little constructive criticism had more than one of them near tears on several occasions causing her to suspect the bestselling author enjoyed being nasty. She'd often wondered why Dorie had bothered to remain in the group.

*Big fish, little pond? Well, the pond just dried up.*

The same policeman, the light blue of his shirt deepening his Florida tan, approached and looking at her said, "Describe the events of the morning."

Anne told him what had happened.

"And the room was dark?"

Nancy nodded. "Dorie was a night owl and could only work in the daytime if the room resembled a cave, hence all the black. We saw Dorie slumped over her keyboard. Then I moved closer, saw all the blood and called nine-one-one."

"And your name, please."

"Nancy Carlyle."

"Thank you, Ms. Carlyle."

"Will this take much longer? I have a deadline, and I should be at home working."

A man wearing khakis and a knit shirt stood nearby talking with the uniformed officers. He must have overheard for he glanced in their direction and walked over.

"If you're so busy, why are you here?" he asked.

"Who're you?" Nancy demanded, her hand on her hip.

"I'm Detective Gil Collins. I'll be working this case. And you are?"

"Nancy Carlyle." A hint of irritation crept into her voice.

"I repeat, why are you here?"

"I took time out of my busy schedule to help a friend celebrate. She'd just signed a contract for another book."

"So, you're all writers? What do you write?"

"Dorie wrote romantic suspense. I write historical romance. Anne does paranormal."

An eyebrow arched. "Like in ghosts?"

"More like vampires and werewolves."

"Vampires and werewolves?" He cast an amused glance toward Anne. "And it sells?"

*No, stupid. I write for the fun of it.* Anne wanted to say it in the worst way, but didn't. His attitude pissed her off. However, this wasn't the time or the place to take him down a notch.

Of medium height with graying sandy hair, the man didn't look like a detective, but then her only experience with detectives was through *Law and Order* or *CSI*.

Nancy answered for her. "Of course, it sells. Just ask Angela Mason."

"Who? Is she a member of your group?"

"Angela Mason is a bestselling paranormal author and, no, she isn't a member of this group," Anne told him.

He directed his gaze to Candace. "And what do you write?"

"Romantic suspense. I'm not published yet."

"Any idea who'd want Ms. Powell dead?"

*Anyone who ever met her, I imagine.* Anne didn't say that either.

"None whatsoever," Nancy replied.

Detective Collins smiled. "Thank you for your time."

He walked away to re-join the cops and compare notes.

Nancy fumbled in her pocket, grabbed a cigarette from the rapidly diminishing pack and lit up. Candace still trembled and ran her hand through her hair every few seconds.

Anne gazed back toward the house as the buzz of conversation rose from the spectators across the street. The sound reminded her of snakes hissing. She figured that even now, Isadora Powell, queen of the suspense writers, was enjoying the attention. Well, the queen was dead. Anne tried to summon up a few tears, but her eyes remained dry.

She moved away from Nancy's constant chain of cigarettes. The breeze brought the smoke in her direction.

"Nancy, would you please put that out? It stinks and while you may not care if you die from lung cancer, I don't want to be on the wrong end of secondhand smoke."

Nancy heaved a sigh and moved downwind. "Yes, I mind. It's my way of dealing with stress. You shred paper. I find that annoying, so allow me my vices."

Anne bit her tongue. It had taken ages to get used to Nancy's blunt talk. She didn't mean to be rude, but frequently spoke her mind. And even though she'd known the woman for quite some time, Anne didn't know much about her other than she'd been divorced for many years and with no children, and had devoted herself to writing. Coupled with a nice settlement from her ex-husband, she made a living from it.

*Wish my ex was as accommodating.*

Kenneth fought every child support increase she sought, yet showered the kids with gifts and money on visitation weekends. At fifteen and twelve, Ken, Jr., and Lisa didn't understand why Mom wasn't as generous.

A man emerged from the house and presented a large plastic bag for Detective Collins's inspection. Anne moved closer.

"Looks like the murder weapon. Some kind of statue. An award I think. There's blood and hair on the base."

"Excuse me, but it's a Campbell," she informed them.

"A what?" Detective Collins asked.

"A Campbell. That's a yearly award given by The

Writers Association of America to the best book by a published author. It's named after Charlotte Campbell, our first president. It's highly coveted. Dorie won three times in the Romantic Suspense category."

"She was good?"

"Her first three books hit the New York Times Bestseller list. That's quite an accomplishment."

"Was anyone jealous of her success?"

"I don't know about jealous. Envious perhaps."

"Envious enough to kill?"

Anne hesitated, choosing her words carefully. To admit she didn't like Dorie could cast suspicion on her. And the last thing she needed was to become a suspect.

"Dorie wasn't the easiest person to get along with, but I can't see anyone clubbing her over the head because they were envious."

Candace walked up and added, "Anne's right. Dorie could be very temperamental, but we just accepted it as part of her personality. She was always pleasant to me. Helped me a lot with my books."

Anne looked away, afraid the expression on her face would tell a different story. Dorie had subtly belittled Candace's work, and she wondered if Candace had ever picked up on the insults. Dorie had been a genius at giving jabs with a smile. And her friend, eager to improve her stories, had nodded and smiled back.

"May I have your name and address?"

"Oh, Candace Warren. I live at seventeen-twelve Bedlington Avenue."

"Thank you, Ms. Warren," Detective Collins replied writing the information in his notebook.

"Oh, by the way, Detective, I think you should know something," Candace said, pointing to the plastic bag. "I touched it."

"What?"

"The Campbell."

"You touched the murder weapon?"

"I'm afraid so. We all did." Candace explained how they'd come to handle the statuette. "My fingerprints will also be on the front and back doors, and the office door."

"You'll find all of our prints," Anne said. "I'm not sure what we touched in the house."

"The downstairs looked to have been recently cleaned."

"Dorie had a maid in once a week. I'd say late yesterday or early this morning, since she was expecting us."

"The upstairs doesn't look touched," Collins said.

"Dorie had two rules concerning maids—they had to speak English, and if the office door was closed, they left the upstairs alone. And they never entered her office, not even to clean. She hated being disturbed while working and didn't trust them not to screw with her stuff. She kept a lot of notes and papers on her desk," Anne replied.

"The maid could have come in this morning and cleaned downstairs, never realizing her client was dead," he mused.

"Any time of death yet?" she asked.

"Won't know until after the autopsy."

While Anne hadn't gotten a good look at their late critique partner, Nancy said the blood had been congealed. For some reason, the spilled wine staining the pages of a manuscript deep red stuck in her mind. It had appeared dry. Plus, Dorie had looked horribly stiff.

How long did it take for rigor mortis to come and go? Twelve hours? Twenty-four? She'd research later.

Nancy, lighting another cigarette, wandered over.

"Ladies, since you admit touching things, we'll need to take your prints. We'll also need statements from each of you regarding your whereabouts last night."

"Last night?" Anne asked.

"Just routine," he replied.

"Sure, no problem," Candace said.

"As soon as possible, if you can. This afternoon or tomorrow morning down at the station will be fine. By the way, any significance to the enormous bowl of candy?"

"That was the chocolate rewards," Nancy said.

"The what?"

"Whenever the group meets, we set aside a few minutes for every member to tell her accomplishments or sorrows of the last few weeks. You get a chocolate prize if you sold a book, won a contest, or received a rejection letter," she told him.

"It was my favorite part of the meeting," Candace said, her tone melancholy. "We use any excuse for eating chocolate."

"Dorie sold a new book. The majority of it would have been hers." Anne stated, then wished she hadn't made Dorie sound greedy.

*The fact that she was a greedy, duplicitous witch isn't something he needs to know.*

Anne opened her mouth to ask another question when a car careened around the corner and screeched to a halt at the curb.

Chapter Two

The sunny glare bouncing off the windshield made Anne squint. Still, she had no problem recognizing the car as belonging to Jennifer Swanson, another critique partner.

The last member of the group, Rose Bennett, exited the car as though grateful to have arrived unscathed. Riding with Jennifer was always an adventure. Jennifer also bailed out and jogged over to them.

"Oh, gosh, I'm so sorry I'm late, but you know me. I hate the interstate, and naturally I went the wrong…" she paused, taking in the crime scene tape and police activity with ever-widening eyes.

Rose also stared. "Good grief, what's going on? Did Dorie have a burglar or something? And this is such a nice neighborhood, too."

"Jennifer, Rose, Dorie is dead. Murdered," Anne said in a somber tone.

Jennifer's mouth dropped open and her green eyes bugged out.

Rose inhaled a sharp breath and clasped a hand around her throat. "No," she said, gasping.

"But how? Why?" Jennifer asked.

"She was apparently bludgeoned with one of her Campbells," Candace said.

"We don't know why yet," Nancy added, giving the newcomers the details of events so far.

Jen's eyes widened further while Rose clapped a hand over her mouth as though about to be sick. Anne related to that.

"And you found her?" Jen asked. "That must have been gruesome."

Rose moved her hand to over her heart and swallowed hard.. "Oh, my God." Her voice had a breathless quality.

"Are you all right?" Anne said, concerned by her friend's pale face and shaking knees. "Come on, sit down on the curb."

Rose straightened her back and waved a hand. "I'm fine. Just...just..."

"We feel the same," Nancy finished.

Detective Collins walked over. "Hello, ladies. Are you friends of Ms. Powell?"

"Detective, this is Rose Bennett and Jennifer Swanson, members of our group," Anne told him, indicating each woman.

"I see. May I have your addresses and phone numbers?" Both women supplied the information while he wrote in a notebook. "It's after noon. I thought the meeting was supposed to start at eleven."

"Oh, that was my fault," Jennifer said, launching into an involved story about interstate highway signage and slow moving freight trains.

Anne waited until the detective's eyes glazed over before calling a halt to her friend's non-stop monologue.

"I'm sure the detective doesn't care why you were late, Jen."

Jennifer stared for a moment before backing off. "Oh, of course, he doesn't. How silly of me. But there really should be a law about those damned trains."

Anne sighed. Jennifer was a great gal and one of the most talented in the group, but never knew when to shut up. A simple trip to the grocery store turned into a thirty-minute description of the frozen food section. Luckily, her penchant for excess verbiage translated well into her romantic comedies. Anne didn't like to stereotype, but maybe it was a blonde thing.

Anne cast her gaze on Rose who hadn't said much since learning the news. She was twenty-eight years old and had four children under the age of seven. As a result, she was harassed and disorganized, which no doubt explained the shoulder length brown hair in serious need of a trim, total lack of make-up, and chipped nail polish. The only peace and quiet she received was at her part-time job processing insurance claims.

*I don't know how she does it. I'd be a candidate for the asylum.* Yet amid all the turbulence of her life, Rose was an excellent writer. That first contract was close.

"Uh, thank you, Ms. Jamieson. Do either of you have any idea who could have wanted Ms. Powell dead?" Detective Collins asked.

"I haven't a clue," Jennifer answered. "She wasn't always the nicest person around. I mean, she could be a real bitch at times. She'd sometimes judge contests and really let the entrants have it."

"What contests?"

"Writing contests," Nancy said before Jennifer wound up again. "Unpublished writers send in their first chapter or something and win prizes. In return, the judges give a critique with suggestions on how to make it better. It's supposed to be constructive."

"But Ms. Powell wasn't?"

"Not always," Candace replied. "In fact, she could be downright hateful. I know she's been banned from judging by several chapters."

"Chapters?"

Anne explained. "The Writers Association of America has almost a hundred and fifty chapters. For instance, we all belong to the Southeast Florida Writers. Some chapters hold a contest as a way to raise funds. Dorie was banned from judging ours a few years ago."

"So, it's possible someone she judged harshly sought revenge?"

"I doubt it," Anne said. "Judges are anonymous. Besides, we all develop thick skins in this business."

Candace shook her head. "Dorie always signed the score sheet. She got off on having people know a bestselling author was giving a free critique, while at the same time ripping the work to shreds. Takes real talent to do that, but Dorie managed it."

"I think it's ironic that she got whacked with her own Campbell," Jennifer mused.

"Why is that, Ms. Swanson?"

"Well, rumor has it that she won her last one by buying off one of the judges, which I wouldn't put past her. When it came to contests she was highly competitive. I remember the year she lost. She stole a bunch of the winning author's books from the conference bookstore and spent the rest of the night tearing them up."

"Are you saying a disgruntled loser killed her?" the detective asked with raised eyebrows.

"Certainly not," Anne replied, her heart thumping. "Jen, those are rumors, and I don't believe them for a moment."

"Oh, I don't know," Candace said. "I can see her doing it. Campbell's are for published authors. I don't suppose finding out who's judging would be all that hard. And Lord knows Dorie was good at research. A few martinis here, a couple of dinners there with the right people, and voila, you know the judges' names and are awarded another Campbell."

"It's true about the books," Jen insisted. "I was at the conference and saw the books in her tote bag. She was in the bar, drunk as a skunk, and in a foul mood. When I asked why she had so many books, she said something like, 'I'm gonna burn the sonsabitches. Fucking hack won't make a dime.' Dorie didn't like losing."

Anne wanted to smack both Jennifer and Candace. The detective didn't need gossip and innuendo. He needed facts to solve the crime.

"I don't think it's very nice to talk about Dorie this way. After all, she's dead," Rose said. "And I don't think anybody in WAA would stoop so low as to accept a bribe."

"That's absolutely right," Anne answered. Rose had been so quiet Anne had forgotten she was here. "Detective Collins, can we go? I don't know what else of a factual nature we can tell you."

He snapped his notebook closed and smiled. "Yes, you can go." He handed them each a business card. "If you think of anything else, please call."

Anne sidled toward her car in the driveway. Nancy followed, still smoking.

"I'm hungry," Anne said. "Should we ask the rest to join us for lunch?"

"Might as well, but only if we gag Jen," Nancy replied, crushing her cigarette under her foot.

"Would you like to come with us for lunch?" Anne called to the others. "How about the Imperial Dragon?"

"God, no," Candace said with a shiver. "The red interior reminds me of blood, and I've seen enough of that today."

"Good point. Any suggestions?"

"Let's go to Casa Grande. I could use a giant Margarita," Nancy said.

"We'll meet you all there. Jen, follow me. Candace, you follow her. Maybe that way, she won't get lost."

Anne backed out of the driveway, and they moved down the street like a convoy. With her eyes on the rearview mirror, Anne watched as Jen tried to turn right instead of left. She bit back an oath at her knuckleheaded friend, hoping Rose knew the way.

****

The five of them slid into a large corner booth and ordered margaritas all around. Anne supposed the main topic of conversation would be Isadora Powell. She wasn't wrong.

"You know, I should be crying or showing sorrow about Dorie, but all I feel is, well, surprise," Rose said.

"The only thing surprising me is that it took so long for someone to kill her," Nancy replied.

"Nancy!" Jen said with a gasp.

"Well, it's true. Can any of us at this table say we enjoyed being around the great Isadora Powell?"

"Nancy, you're being harsh. Dorie may have been a little curt at times, but that was just her way. You're blunt and sometimes hurt people's feelings," Candace said.

"You just got through telling the police what a bitch she was. How can you defend her? She made fun of your stories and on more than one occasion reduced you to tears with her assessments." Nancy pulled a cigarette from the pack and lit up.

"You're not allowed to smoke in here," Anne reminded her.

"Damned laws," she muttered, crushing it out.

Anne remembered a meeting where Dorie had sliced and diced one of Candace's offerings. Everyone had squirmed with embarrassment for both women. Unfortunately, she agreed with Dorie. Candace's writing never improved, and she insisted on sticking to a genre she just couldn't handle. Romantic suspense required discipline, an eye for detail. Candace had neither and little imagination. She liked the woman and had known her for years, but at some point in time every unpublished writer had to face that the talent wasn't there, even though the dream lingered.

The waiter brought their drinks along with a couple of plates of complimentary chips and salsa. Rose grabbed a chip, scooped a mound of salsa, and popped it into her mouth.

"Oh, God, why do they tempt us like this? I can't say no and will end up ordering the SuperDuper Burrito. There must be a million calories in one of those," she lamented. "I really have to go on a diet. My clothes are getting tight again and Jack will go ballistic if I buy new."

"Order the Taco Salad instead," Nancy told her.

"Establish a routine," Anne suggested grateful the table talk had veered toward food and away from Dorie.

The less said about her, the better. "A light breakfast followed by some exercise would be a good start."

"You try it with my brood," she stated, shoving another salsa-laden chip between her teeth.

"Who do you think did it? I'm sure the cops think it was one of us," Jen asked, before taking a sip of her drink and gazing around the table with wide eyes.

Candace choked on her chip. "Good God, Jen, what makes you say that?"

"Well, it had to be someone who knew her. If it was a burglar, the downstairs would have been trashed, and the maid would have seen it. Plus, even with her headphones on, Dorie would have heard it and come down to investigate."

A creepy chill slithered down Anne's spine. Leave it to Jen to supply more drama to an already drama-laden morning.

"Which means she wouldn't have been murdered at her desk. Lord, you could be right," Rose said with a thoughtful look.

"Oh, for Pete's sake, be reasonable," Anne replied. *Lord, don't let that be true.* "Can you honestly see any of us doing it, and what would be the motive?"

"Well, it had to be someone who knew she'd be in her office," Rose insisted. She turned to Nancy. "You made no bones about your feelings for Dorie. Where were you last night? Where were any of us?"

"That's insulting," Candace said in a sharp tone.

Nancy shrugged. "I've got nothing to hide. I have a deadline in three weeks and worked like a demon to make it. I didn't get to bed until three. I almost called Dorie this morning and cancelled. Since you brought it up, Rose, where were you?"

"I made dinner, cleaned up afterwards, did three loads of laundry, and gave the kids their baths. Then, I actually wrote five pages on my work in progress. I crawled into bed around midnight."

The waiter returned to take their orders with Rose caving in to the SuperDuper Burrito as prophesized.

When he left, Nancy continued. "Anne? What about you? Where were you last night?"

Anne's heart hammered and she swallowed, not wanting to answer, but knowing it would look odd if she didn't.

"The kids are spending the week with Kenneth. I used the opportunity to sit and read with no interruptions for a change. Come on, Candace, you may as well tell us about your evening."

Candace scowled and chugged her Margarita. "I did what I always do—ate alone. Took Bruno for a walk in Sunshine Park alone, watched TV alone, and went to bed—alone. Your turn, Jen."

Jen grinned and sipped her drink. "This is fun. Just like being real detectives. Let's see, it was Little League game night, which screwed up dinner, but since it was just me and the kids, it didn't matter. Carl worked late again and didn't get home until nine. I stayed up until almost two working on a new story. Oh, and by the way, my agent sold *The Whole Nine Yards* to Bear Press."

Everyone stared for a moment until Rose finally blurted, "Oh, my God! Jen! That's fantastic." She leaned over and hugged her.

"Jen, that's terrific!" Anne cried, truly happy for her friend. She'd worked hard for this.

"Congratulations," Nancy said, grinning. "I'm glad

to see you finally broke the barrier. This calls for another round of drinks." She signaled the waiter who nodded and headed for the bar. "Make it a pitcher," she called. "Did Dorie know?"

Jen shook her head. "No, I was going to surprise everyone at the meeting."

"That's wonderful," Candace said with a smile. "When's it coming out?"

"Don't know yet. Have to do the revisions and all that, but I'm over the moon. I still can't believe it's happened. Sometimes I wake up in the middle of the night and wonder if it's all been a dream. Then, I look at a copy of the contract and realize I did it. Maybe it'll be a bestseller."

"I think success is going to your head," Rose laughed.

Jen drained her drink. "If Isadora Powell could do it, there's no reason why I can't either."

She sat back, twirling the stem of the glass in her fingers, then hiccupped and laughed.

Anne laughed along, all the while shredding her cocktail napkin. She had a sour taste in her mouth that had nothing to do with the margaritas. Nancy's comment about no one liking Dorie had struck close to home.

Why had they put up with her for all these years? Anne knew why she stayed. She liked the others and refused to let one tart-tongued person drive her away. She should have jettisoned her cruel and opinionated critique partner years ago, but had been afraid of a vindictive Isadora Powell. And Candace's statement about the dead woman's penchant for research also brought a chill of uneasiness.

One of the reasons for Dorie's success was her ability to gather every particle of information about a subject before committing anything to paper. Police and forensic procedures, the law, poisons, weapons, it didn't matter—Dorie researched it. Technically, her books were brilliant and if she had any writing flaws, it was a tendency toward weak characterization.

Isadora Powell was a natural born snoop, which was why Anne had lied to both her friends and the police concerning her whereabouts last night.

"Will you stop with that damned napkin?" Nancy said, bringing her out of her thoughts.

"What?"

"The napkin," she repeated. "You're making a mess. Sheesh! And you climb all over me for smoking."

Anne gazed at the pile of paper strips in front of her. A nervous habit developed in college—one she should work on correcting.

"Sorry," she said in a calm tone. Her companions had no idea how her stomach churned. "I was thinking."

"What about?" Rose asked.

"What did you guys think of Detective Collins?"

"He's a cop. What's to think about?" Nancy replied.

"Seemed nice enough," Candace said.

"No, I mean, does he seem competent?"

"You mean at finding the killer? I guess so. He does it for a living," Rose stated.

"Yes, but he doesn't understand writers or the business. I could tell from his questions. We know the first forty-eight hours are crucial to any investigation. If you don't have a suspect by then, you may never have one," Anne said.

"What's your point? We may never find out who killed Dorie?" Nancy asked.

"That's a possibility, but what I'm thinking is maybe we could help the police. We all knew Dorie, and some of us know her other friends."

"You mean, play detective?" Candace said with a frown. "I'm not sure that's a good idea."

"It's a great idea," Jen answered, bouncing in her seat. "Candace, think of it as research for your next book."

Candace shrugged. "I suppose, but won't the cops get pissed at a bunch of amateurs horning in and asking questions?"

"So what? Dorie's friends and acquaintances may be more willing to talk to us than to the cops," Rose said before transferring her gaze to Anne. "Were we her only critique partners?"

"No. Dorie critiqued online with several people and had at least one more group within the Southeast Florida chapter. They may add something about Dorie we didn't know."

The waiter brought the pitcher. Nancy poured another margarita and sipped, her forehead wrinkled in thought. "The police will review phone records and confiscate Dorie's computer to check the hard drive for any threatening e-mails. They'll also go through her files, but you know Dorie—she could be secretive as hell. They might miss something that's clear to us."

"In other words, the slip of tissue paper bearing the secret code is stuck between the pages of a book and we find it, thereby solving the mystery?" Candace questioned, draining her glass, and reaching for the pitcher.

Anne looked at her friend in surprise. Candace wasn't usually sarcastic. She cleared her throat.

"I think what Nancy means is, yes—we could come up with something the police might miss because they don't know what to look for."

"Let's face it," Nancy said. "Isadora Powell lived for two reasons, to write and be a pain in the ass. She was successful at both. Her only friends were in the publishing world."

"That we know of," Rose interceded. "Her death was violent. Lots of hate, if you ask me. Could a man be involved?"

Jen snorted. "Isadora Powell and a male of the species? Get real. I mean, she liked men, but as long as she owned a vibrator and had a supply of batteries, she didn't need a man."

"Jennifer!" Rose admonished while the others laughed.

"Well, it's true." Jen sipped her drink. "And why are you so shocked? You write erotic romance, for God's sake."

Rose's reply was cut off by the waiter delivering lunch. Anne paid little attention to the food. Her mind was busy searching Dorie's house, especially the office.

"So, how do we help?" Candace asked.

"We need to search Dorie's office to see what the police may have missed," Anne replied.

Candace drank a generous portion of her margarita. "And how do we accomplish that? Even I know the place will be sealed."

"Not forever. As soon as they're done collecting forensic evidence, they'll release it," Anne said.

"I suppose she may have left a spare key outside for emergencies, but I wouldn't count on it," Nancy mused.

"We'll cross that bridge when we get to it," Rose said digging into her SuperDuper Burrito.

"And we'll have to dodge any family members Dorie may have had," Jen added. "If she left a will and they inherit, then we'll be trespassers. We could end up in the clink. You know, that might not be such a bad experience. I've often thought that if you're going to write about certain things, you should experience them firsthand, you know like when…"

Anne tuned out Jen's rambling. Her mind raced and her hands shook. How would they get in? She'd think about it tonight.

*If Dorie hid incriminating evidence, I have to find it before the cops.*

Chapter Three

Candace lay on the sofa in her family room watching an old movie and crying. She did a lot of that, especially the crying part. Between Eric's leaving her for a younger woman and everything that had happened with Dorie, she couldn't stem the flow. A friend had suggested therapy.

*Might make sense.* She'd bottled up a lot of anger. Maybe it was time to let it go. *And speaking of bottles...* She grabbed the Grey Goose from the coffee table, poured some into her glass, and drained it.

She'd done little in the past three days since finding Dorie's body. The booze helped her forget. She shuddered and refilled her glass. She knew her friends thought her an idiot for letting Dorie humiliate her, but in the back of her mind there lurked a hope that one day the bitch would say, "Nice job, Candace."

But Dorie's words had hurt, cutting deeply, and she had retained a stoic face, a calm demeanor, not wanting the others to know, preserving her pride. Over the years, resentment had built. Now, Dorie was dead, and Candace didn't really care.

The ringing phone dragged her from the pity party. Tempted to ignore it, the caller ID showed it was Anne. She hadn't heard from any of the group since Dorie's death.

She pushed the accept button. "Hello?"

"Dorie's house has been released. Let's do it. Tonight at nine-thirty. You in?"

Candace sighed. "So, you're really going through with this crazy idea?"

"Of course. The forty-eight hours are up. The police haven't made an arrest. I think we can help."

"Have you considered just asking Detective What's-his-name if they would like our assistance?"

"He'd say no. All that amateur sleuth business is for books and television. It doesn't happen in real life. So, are you in?"

Candace wanted to say no in the worst way, but was afraid if she did the rest of them would make *her* the main topic of conversation.

"Yes, I'm in," she said hiccupping.

"Good. I'll pick you up at nine-fifteen."

*Typical Anne, everything timed down to the last nanosecond.*

"All right." She hiccupped again and sniffed.

"Are you okay? You sound like you've been crying."

"Old movie—*An Affair To Remember*," she replied, wiping her cheeks with the back of her hand.

"Not a good subject matter. Watch a comedy. I'll see you tonight."

Candace hung up and switched off the TV. Watch a comedy. Yeah, right. Like that would make a difference.

She rose from the sofa and grabbed the vodka bottle, splashing a generous amount into the glass before climbing the stairs to her bedroom. She'd moved the computer from her office when Eric had left. It was more convenient for writing during sleepless nights.

Taking a long gulp, Candace opened the bottom drawer of her desk, extracting a manuscript. She removed the large rubber bands holding it together and cradled it to her chest, then fed it page by page into the shredder.

She was calling it quits. No more writing. This was the best she'd had in her, and it would never see the light of day. How many rejections had she gathered over the years? How many bad contest scores had come her way? How many times had she lied about those scores to her friends? Well, it didn't matter. Nobody would belittle Candace Warren anymore.

The shrill whining of the shredder brought tears coursing down her cheeks again. She drained the glass and poured more vodka. Maybe it would lessen the pain. She fed three more pages into the blades and sobbed.

*Dammit! All I wanted was one stinking book. One fucking novel I could point to with pride and say, this is mine. Something even Eric would be forced to acknowledge as an accomplishment.*

The gloating face of Isadora Powell, her twenty-three novels, three Campbells, and the framed accolades from reviewers covering the walls of her office floated in front of Candace's vodka-laced eyes.

Dorie had often mocked Candace's heroines as too stupid to live, including this latest that was slowly being turned into confetti. Well, in her opinion, Dorie's heroines had no depth, no soul. *How dare she judge me?* Anger bubbled from the pit of her stomach, through her chest, and exploded in her brain.

"Damn you," she screamed, ripping several sheets of printed paper by hand. "You didn't deserve another contract."

Candace grabbed her glass from the desk and held it to her lips, sobbing, her tears mixing with the liquor.

"You didn't fucking deserve anything!"

She bolted the rest of the vodka and tossed the glass onto the carpet, and then tilted the bottle to her mouth. Still sobbing, she fed the best manuscript she'd ever written into the jaws of the beast.

****

Anne hung up, tempted to call Candace back. In spite of her friend's protestation about watching an old movie, she suspected otherwise. The words had sounded slightly slurred. And it was barely noon. Should she intervene? Unsure, Anne dialed in the first three numbers before stopping.

"No, wait until you see her face to face. The phone is no way to tell her you're concerned about her drinking habits," Anne muttered out loud, and then started at the sound of her own voice.

She entered the kitchen, poured a glass of iced tea, and tried to bring her shaking hands under control. The past few days had been stressful not knowing what the police had uncovered at Dorie's. And did they understand all the writing related material?

Sitting at the table, she called Nancy.

"Am I interrupting?" she asked.

"I'm on the deadline from hell and have been sitting at this damned computer since six. At least I'm at the halfway point. Could be worse. What's up? Any news about Dorie?"

"No, but tonight's the night—nine-thirty," Anne said. "Are you coming?"

A moment of silence followed her question before

Nancy answered, "I guess. They've released the house?"

"I drove by this morning and the tape is gone."

"So, how do we get in?"

"The obvious choice would be to look for a hidden key, but just in case, I went online and did some research. Most of it's technical, but I think I may have hit on a solution. I remember seeing it once on an old TV show."

"Oh, swell, we're working from an ancient episode of *The Rockford Files* or *MacGiver*. Hollywood always over-simplifies things, but then they deal with a simple audience."

Anne didn't need sarcasm. "You don't have to come."

"I'll come. Why are you so anxious to get into Dorie's?"

She didn't have a good reply. "Well, don't you want to know who killed her?"

Nancy sighed. "Suppose we find something. Then what? We'll have to turn it over to the police, which means they'll know we were in the house."

"Let's see what we find. Maybe we can do the investigating on our own."

"You mean withhold evidence."

Anne wiped a bead of sweat from her upper lip. That's exactly what she meant. "Just at first. A couple of days won't make a difference."

Silence once again greeted her statement. She could almost hear the gears meshing in her friend's mind.

"I think it will make a damned big difference to the cops, but I wouldn't mind getting a look at Dorie's office myself. Do I meet you there?"

"No, the fewer cars, the better. I'll pick you up at nine, and then swing by to get Candace."

"Anne, I refuse to synchronize my watch, but I'll be ready."

"Good. Don't forget to bring a flashlight."

Anne said goodbye and hung up, drumming her fingers on the tabletop. Nancy, a very private person who rarely asked about the lives of her colleagues, had surprised her at lunch the day of the murder by making suggestions on how they could pull this off. It was out of character. And now she admitted to more than idle curiosity, too. *Why is Nancy so interested in Dorie's office?*

Maybe this shouldn't be a group project. Maybe she should call the whole thing off and go alone. *Too late now. Might as well go through with it.*

Shrugging, Anne dialed Rose's number.

"Have you got a minute?" she asked when Rose answered.

"Barely. It's been a chaotic morning. Make it fast before crisis number fifteen pops up."

Anne gave Rose the news and her intentions. "Nancy and Candace have agreed to go. How about you?"

"Nine-thirty? Why so late?"

"Well, I don't think it's a good idea to go slinking around sleuthing in broad daylight, do you?"

"I didn't think of that. What am I going to tell Jack? I'll have to have some kind of excuse for leaving at that time of night."

"You're a writer. You'll come up with something. Don't forget to bring a flashlight. Oh, and I think it's best if you pick Jen up. I don't want to stand around for two hours waiting because she got lost again. Okay?" Anne asked.

"Check. I'll be by her place at nine-fifteen."

A sharp cry in the background on Rose's end interrupted the conversation.

"What now?" She didn't bother to cover the phone. Anne heard a whining voice. "Of course the dog growled at you, Rory. You pulled his tail. How many times do I have to tell you to leave him alone? And Bethany, I see you. Put those Oreos back. You've had enough sugar this morning. And don't give me that look."

A pause ensued which led Anne to assume Rose's oldest was negotiating. She tapped her foot impatiently and waited.

"All right, I'll put *The Little Mermaid* on as soon as I'm finished here. Just sit down and be good for a change. Sorry about that, Anne," she said when she resumed the conversation. "What do you expect to find?"

"I don't know. Fan mail, hate mail. She's still got our last chapters all critiqued. I'd like to have that back. Who knows what we'll uncover? Maybe something the police will have overlooked."

"I could use my latest chapter, too. Any ideas on how we get in?"

"A couple. Look, do you know of…"

"Oh, crap! The baby's awake already. I hear him wailing through the monitor. Damn, I also hear the toilet flushing over and over upstairs. I swear if Jason's shoved a whole roll of toilet paper down it again, I'll kill him. Took me hours to clean up the mess last time.

Sometimes I wish I was childless. I've gotta go. I'll see you at Dorie's." She hung up without bothering to say goodbye.

Anne did the same, shaking her head. Poor Rose. She had her hands full. Four kids, none of whom had much discipline, a huge house, and a husband who rarely helped with anything.

She drained her glass of tea and poured more. Three calls down and one to go. She dialed Jen's number. Her friend answered on the third ring.

"Hi, Anne. What's up?"

"Game on. We're going to Dorie's tonight at nine-thirty."

"So, we're really going to do it? That's fabulous. I can hardly wait. This is going to be so much fun. We'll be just like Jessica Fletcher and solve the crime. Want me to pick you up?"

"Uh, no, Rose will pick you up at nine-fifteen, and for God's sake, don't be late or tell Carl where you're going."

"I'll make up a good story. Don't worry. What time did you say?"

"Nine-fifteen."

"Got it. What are you going to wear?"

"What?" Only Jen would ask that question.

"Never mind. Do you think we'll find any clues?"

"I have no idea."

"Well, whether we do or not, it's going to be fun. I can't wait to paw through Dorie's things looking for secrets. Dorie once told me she documented everything, especially money matters. I've never done anything like this before, have you? It's exciting and scary all the same time. I'll probably have heart palpitations and pass out or something. Is there any…"

"Jen, I've got to go," Anne said, cutting her friend off.

"Oh, sure, I understand. See you at nine-thirty."

"Nine-fifteen, Jennifer!"

"Right. Nine-fifteen."

Anne hung up, hoping Jen wore a watch with big numbers. And she swore if the woman fainted, she'd leave her lying on the ground. She liked Jen, but God, the woman could be a total ditz at times. She suspected her newly contracted friend babbled out of nervousness. Sometimes being unable to shut up had its advantages. People tended to tune her out after a while—like Detective What's His Name the other day.

Then something Jen said hit her like a bomb. *Dorie documented everything, especially money matters.*

Anne dropped her phone on the table and covered her mouth. *Oh, dear God, I have to get into that house.*

\*\*\*\*

Anne parked on the street in front of Dorie's next-door neighbor's house, switched off her headlights, and cut the engine.

"Do we look suspicious? Is anyone watching?" she asked.

"Everything looks quiet, but then the floodlights in the neighbor's backyard are bright enough to illuminate Yankee Stadium," Nancy replied in a dry tone.

"We'll just have to hope nobody thinks to look over the fence. Candace, are you all right. You're shaking," Anne said. She caught the scent of peppermint on her friend's breath.

"I'm fine. I had a long nap after you called, and I can't help shaking. That's the way I always react to breaking and entering."

Anne sighed and checked the gently glowing display on her cell before shoving it into her pocket. Nine thirty-five. Rose and Jen were late. She should have told them nine-fifteen to make up for Jen's lack of time sense.

She glanced at Candace again. The poor woman looked on the edge. The divorce had only been final for a few months. Anne remembered how signing those papers and flinging away years of her life had felt. Candace's ex-husband, Eric, was an investment banker making beaucoup bucks, so she knew the settlement had been a whopper. Still, she suspected the slight slurring of her friend's words when she'd called had nothing to do with an old movie.

Nancy opened the window and pulled out a cigarette.

"Not in the car," Anne warned her.

Nancy shot her a bored glance and jerked open the door, then got out and slammed it.

"Why not pick up a bullhorn and announce our presence?" Candace snapped in a hushed tone.

Nancy leaned against the front fender and lit up. The smoke drifted in the window. Anne doubted it was an accident. Her friend's subtle statement hit home. *I guess we can all be bitchy at times.* She knew she could.

Headlights slashed through the rear window as a car pulled in behind them. Anne and Candace exited with Anne stopping to pull a small plunger from under the seat.

"Sorry, we're late," Rose said in a low voice. "I had to get the kids settled down and break it to Jack that he'd be alone with them tonight. I told him we were meeting to plan a memorial service for Dorie."

Jen bounced out from behind the car.

"Aye-yeah!" she cried, taking a karate stance.

"Quiet!" Rose hissed.

"Good God, what the hell are you made up for?" Nancy asked crushing out her cigarette.

"Geez, Jen, I didn't know it was Halloween," Candace commented.

Anne stared in disbelief. Jen wore a pair of black leggings, a long-sleeved black T-shirt, and black ballet slippers. Her medium-length blonde bob was tucked up under a stocking cap—black, of course. Everybody else in the group was dressed in jeans and tops.

"Jennifer, you look like a commando," she stated. "And what's that stuff all over your face?"

"Shoe polish," Rose told them.

"Hey, we're sleuthing. I'll blend in with the shadows."

They moved down the sidewalk and trod softly up Dorie's driveway. Next door, someone turned on the floodlights over the garage. The women froze. Anne sucked in a deep breath, held it, and listened through the hedge separating the properties to the sounds of Dorie's neighbor emptying the trash. A minute later, the door closed and the lights went out.

Anne blew out her pent up breath.

They continued on to the wooden privacy fence surrounding the back yard.

"All right, since you dressed the part, Jen, you can be the one to go over the fence." Anne handed her the plunger. "Here, take this. Push it up against the window in the back door. Then take this." She pulled a small pencil shaped object from her pocket. "Cut the glass around the edge of the plunger and pull. It should just pop out."

"Oh, isn't this cute," she said. "It has a little wheel, just like a pizza cutter." She ran her finger over the circular head. "Ouch! That's sharp."

"Works much better for cutting glass than a dull one," Nancy said.

Anne sighed. "Nancy, knock it off. Now, Jen, we'll boost you over the fence. When you get to the back door, pop the glass, reach in, and unlock it. We'll meet you on the front porch. Now hurry."

The tallest in the group, Nancy cupped her hands. Jen placed her foot in the finger cradle and grasped the top of the fence as Nancy lifted. Her lithe body had no problem clearing the gate.

She disappeared around the corner with the plunger and glasscutter, her flashlight bobbing.

On the front porch, the rest of the sleuths stayed in the shadows and waited, and waited—and waited.

"What the hell is taking so long?" Candace whispered.

"Maybe she's having trouble getting the glass out," Rose suggested.

"Maybe she's having trouble drawing a circle around an already circular object," Nancy said.

"That was unkind. I should have gone," Anne stated.

"I agree," Nancy replied with a shrug.

Anne took a deep breath and counted to ten. Over the years, she'd learned Nancy reacted to stress with sarcasm and barbed comments.

Finally, Jen opened the front door.

"What took so long?" Nancy asked as she entered, switching on her flashlight and cupping the beam with her hand so only a fraction of the light escaped between her fingers.

"How did the glass cutter work?" Rose questioned.

"I didn't try it. I looked for a key and finally found one taped under the cushion of a patio chair."

"Okay, we're in. Let's get started. The office is the best bet," Anne said.

One by one they mimicked Nancy's actions with their flashlights.

"What are we looking for?" Rose asked, climbing the stairs.

"Anything. Papers, an address book, files the police might not have realized were important," Anne told them.

"A list of names under the heading 'people who'd like to kill me' would be nice," Jen said.

"I doubt if we'll have that kind of luck," Nancy returned.

Anne opened the door to Dorie's office and they stepped through. She allowed the full beam from her torch to sweep the room. As expected, Dorie's monitor and keyboard were on the desk, still covered with blood, but the CPU was missing. The cops had the hard drive.

"Let's make this as quick as possible. Nancy, you and Jen take the desk drawers and the credenza. Candace, you and Rose deal with the file cabinets. I'll go through the bookshelves."

For the next several minutes the only sounds in the room were drawers being opened and closed, and the rustling of papers.

The silence was broken by Rose. "Has anybody found anything yet?"

"Nothing," Nancy stated. "Not even an address book. Now *that* would have been useful."

"Probably the first thing the cops confiscated," Anne reminded her.

"I'm coming up dry, too," Candace said.

"I wonder where her cell is," Rose mused.

"I'd guess the cops have that also. It's not in or on the desk," Nancy said. "And Dorie never had her phone any more than an arm's length away."

"What about her other cell? She had two, you know," Jen informed them.

All noise ceased as the women stopped to stare.

"I never knew that," Rose said.

"Yeah, it was one of those cheap things like you get at discount stores. You go in, buy it, activate it, and then call in for more minutes every month."

"You mean Dorie had a disposable phone?" Anne asked. "Are you sure?"

"It rang once at a conference. We were having a drink and someone called her. I noticed it wasn't her razor thin phone. I asked her about it when she hung up. She was pissed because it was a wrong number. Told me it was for personal use."

"Would the police have that, too?" Rose questioned.

"Having a second phone doesn't make sense," Nancy said. "Unless, Dorie didn't mix business and her personal life."

"Two phones are expensive, and we all know how Dorie hated spending money," Jen mused, and then jumped to her feet. "I'll be right back."

Anne glanced at her watch. "Let's get on with this. It's getting late."

They worked in silence until Jen returned.

"Found it!" she crowed holding up the small phone.

"Good job. Where was it?" Rose asked.

"In the linen closet."

"The linen closet? Why would anyone hide something in the linen closet?" Nancy wondered.

"My aunt did it all the time," Jen said. "She tucked her nice jewelry behind the towels. Claimed a thief would never think to look there for valuables."

"You know, in a weird way, that makes sense," Candace said, slamming another file drawer. "This is crazy. We aren't going to find anything."

"We just found a phone, didn't we?" Anne reminded her. "Put it in your pocket, Jen, and help Nancy with the credenza."

"I don't have one," she replied, patting her leggings.

"Here give it to me," Nancy said, and shoved the phone into her jeans then opened the door of the credenza. "There's not much in here. Whoa, what's this?"

She extracted a manila envelope and pulled out its contents.

"What is it?" Rose asked.

"It's the first three chapters of a book titled *Dead as a Doornail* and a synopsis. What a silly cliché for a title. No name or anything. Just a bunch of red edits, including a title change to *Death Becomes Him*."

"We'll take it and check it out later," Anne said.

"Wait a minute. That's the title of her new book.

She mentioned it when she called," Rose told them.

"Here's a folder marked 'Sandra, Jane, and Lydia Critiques'. Should we take it?" Candace queried.

"Yes. There might be full names or e-mail addresses somewhere," Nancy said.

"Those are her other critique partners. The online ones I think. I can't find anything on the bookshelves or in the bookcase, except one of your books, Nancy," Anne told them.

"One of mine?" she asked in a sharp tone. "Are you sure? Dorie didn't like historicals."

"See for yourself. It's between one by an author named Maude Lofton and a book by someone called Cassandra Moore."

"Imagine that," Nancy murmured with a catch in her voice.

"Let's clean up. I don't want anyone to know we've been in here," Anne said.

Rose's cell ringing caused them all to jump.

"Hello…Yes, Jack, we're still discussing the memorial service…I have no idea…Well, make him a bottle. Everything is on the kitchen counter. I'll be home as soon as I can…Jack, just change his diaper, feed him, and put him back down. He'll go to sleep…I said, I'll be there when I get there. Just go to bed." She hung up.

"Four kids and Jack doesn't know what to do with a crying baby?" Jen asked.

"Yeah, well, he's more into creating than maintaining," she muttered. "Anne's right. Let's get this mess cleaned up. The sooner I get home, the less grousing I'll have to listen to."

Anne shoved the last of the papers into the desk

drawer when all two hundred watts of overhead light flashed on, the sudden glare blinding her.

Chapter Four

"On your feet, ladies, and raise your hands," an authoritative male voice called out.

"Oh, my God," Candace muttered.

"Damn," Anne said.

"Oh, shit!" was Nancy's contribution.

"I don't believe this!" Jen exclaimed.

"Jack is gonna kill me!" Rose wailed.

Anne rose to her feet as everybody, including herself, grabbed for the ceiling. It didn't take a genius to understand the police had arrived.

"Uh, Officer, I can explain," she began.

"I'm sure you can, ma'am. Everybody turn around—slowly—and face me."

Five robots cautiously pivoted.

Anne stared at two cops, both with guns drawn, and swallowed. What had gone wrong?

"Okay, you," he said pointing to Jen as he backed out of the doorway. "Come into the hall. Put your hands and face against the wall."

Jen did as she was told, followed by Nancy, Anne, Rose, and Candace.

"Good job. Now spread your legs so I can search you."

"Wait a minute. Isn't there supposed to be a female officer present?" Jen questioned.

"Lady, this isn't a strip search. I'm only looking for

weapons."

"Yeah, but I've watched *Cops* and they always have a female officer search the women detainees."

"Jen, shut up and do as you're told," Nancy bit out.

The first officer ran his hands lightly over Jen's body. "You're clean," he said before moving on to Nancy and patting her pockets. "What's this?"

"Uh, my cell phone," Nancy answered.

"And this?" he asked, taking the manila envelope from her hand.

"That's…that's mine. It's a partial manuscript. Ms. Powell critiqued it, and I wanted it back."

Anne closed her eyes and broke out in a light sweat. Not only had they been caught in Dorie's house, but Nancy was compounding the problem by lying.

The policeman dropped it between Nancy's feet and patted Anne down. Her cell phone hit the carpet, too, as did Rose's. He pulled the file folder from Candace's fingers.

"And this?"

"It's a critique of a couple of my stories."

"Critiques are very important to us," Jen added.

Anne willed God to render Jen mute.

"Let me have your names." When they complied, the second officer said, "You can lower your hands. We'll go downstairs and wait for Detective Collins."

The five women hurried down the staircase and into the darkened living room. One of the officers turned on the lights.

"Have a seat," he said.

Anne and the others obeyed.

"Anybody care to tell us why you are in the house of a murder victim?" The officer tossed the envelope, file folder, and collected cell phones onto the coffee table.

Everybody's eyes swiveled to Anne. "Well, you see, Dorie had our critiques. We would have gotten them back at the meeting, but we didn't since she was dead and decided to do it tonight."

Anne wanted to die. She didn't even believe that lame excuse and turned her gaze onto her friends. *Come on, somebody back me up here.*

Jen stared at the ceiling, Rose sniffed trying not to cry, Candace fastened her gaze on a painting on the wall, and Nancy gave her a look that clearly stated, "Couldn't you have come up with something better than that?" The cops had the same expression on their faces.

*Thanks loads.* Anne decided to shut up. She couldn't explain in any way that made sense. Then, Detective Gil Collins walked in the front door. He took one look at the five of them and closed his eyes.

"Thank you, gentlemen. Take a look around and see what kind of damage they've done." They left the room, and he turned an exasperated gaze on them. "Okay, let me have it. What are you doing here?"

Anne licked her lips, giving him the same story she had a few minutes earlier, only a bit more coherently.

"You broke into a house for that? All you had to do was call and ask me. I would have released the stories to you. Now, suppose you start over and tell me the truth."

She read the determination in his eyes and realized the plan she'd constructed had a million holes in it. She decided to come, at least partially, clean.

"We thought maybe we could find something to help with the case. We understand the publishing business and from your comments the other day, it was obvious you don't. We thought…that is, we hoped…" she let the sentence die and sat back in her chair feeling like a fool.

"So, you decided to play detective."

"More or less."

"Did you find anything?"

Anne shook her head. "We can't find her address book. I guess you must have it."

"You guess right," he told her.

One of the policemen came in from the kitchen carrying the plunger and glass cutter.

"Found these on the patio table. A key was in the back door lock." He put them on the coffee table with the rest of the confiscated items.

"Which TV show did you get this idea from?" Collins asked, shaking his head.

"I can't remember. It might have been a *Magnum, P. I.* or maybe an old *Rockford Files*," Anne said. Heat flooded her face.

"Well, for the record, it probably wouldn't have worked."

"See, aren't you glad I found the key now?" Jen said with a nod and a smile.

Collins shifted his gaze to Jen's blackened face. "And who are you supposed to be? Rambo?" When Jen opened her mouth to answer, he held up his hand. "Wait a minute, forget I asked. I don't want to know."

"What are you doing here?" Candace asked.

"Where do I start? A neighbor saw two cars parked down the street and several people tiptoeing down the sidewalk to Ms. Powell's driveway. Then, he saw the same figures lurking on the front porch. About the same time, the neighbor in back saw someone scrounging around the patio with a flashlight. And may I suggest that the next time you decide to do a little breaking and entering, you remember to close the curtains before you turn on the flashlights. The same neighbor out back said the place looked like it was inhabited by a bunch of fireflies." He paused and shook his head. "Ladies, a brass band would have been more subtle."

"I told you this was a bad idea," Candace muttered.

Anne squirmed with embarrassment. So did the rest of her friends.

"Detective Collins, can we just take our things and go home?" Nancy asked. "We did something stupid, but that's all. We thought we could help."

"Right," Anne said. "It's been over forty-eight hours since the crime and you haven't made an arrest."

"I see you are a devotee of *The First 48*, too," Collins remarked. "Television and reality don't go hand in hand. I can see where you get it, though. You're writers and don't deal in reality either."

Anne bit her lip. That one stung.

"Can't you just let us go?" Rose asked quietly. "After all, we used the key to get in. That's not really breaking and entering."

"I won't explain the finer points of police terminology to you tonight. I'll take the envelope and file folder. You can have the rest."

Nancy snatched the cell phone and shoved it into her pocket. "And our critiques?"

"I'll look them over and let you know. How's the upstairs look?" he asked the other men when they descended the stairs.

"The office is a little messy, but nothing's been

damaged."

Collins sighed. "Ladies, promise me you won't do this again."

"We promise," Candace said.

Anne nodded. "Absolutely."

"Never again," Rose declared with a shudder.

Jen raised her hand. "Swear to God."

Detective Collins pressed the heel of his hand against his forehead. "Okay, you're free to go."

Nancy shot out of the room and headed for the front door with the others close behind. They all walked quickly past the police car with lights flashing and down the street to where they'd parked. Rose and Jen jumped into their car, firing the engine.

"Boy, I could use a drink," Candace muttered.

"Amen," Nancy echoed.

"Hey, Rose, Jen. Want to join us at Rafferty's for a drink?" Anne called out

Rose stuck her head out the window. "I've gotta get home. Jack has probably fed the baby a gallon of formula." She turned as Jen said something, and then yelled back, "Okay, just one though."

She pulled out, and Anne slid behind the wheel.

"Come on. Let's not linger," Nancy said. "Collins might decide to search our purses, and then I'd have to explain why I have two cell phones."

"Good point. Let's boogie."

Anne spotted Detective Collins and the officers on the front porch. She jammed the car into gear and hurriedly burned a little rubber in an effort to put as much distance as possible between herself and the law.

The drive to the restaurant didn't take long. Anne slipped into a chair at a large corner table. The rest of the group did likewise. Late on a Thursday night, Rafferty's was only a third full. Rose's phone rang again.

"Hello…Jack, I told you I would be home as soon as I could…I know it's late, but my friend was murdered and we are trying to plan a fitting memorial to a wonderful author. Did you get Graham fed?…Well, if the kids are all asleep, I suggest you go to bed, too. This shouldn't take much longer."

She hung up and made a face. Nobody commented.

A waiter arrived and placed cocktail napkins in front of each of them. "Welcome to Rafferty's, ladies. What can I get…" he broke off and stared at Jen before finishing slowly with a puzzled look, "…you to drink?"

"Jen, for God's sake, go wash your face," Nancy snapped. "You look like a terrorist."

"What?" She swiped at her cheek and gazed at the shoe polish blackening her fingertips. "Oops, I forgot. Sorry. I'll have a white wine," she told the waiter, sliding out of her seat and hurrying toward the restrooms.

The others followed Jen's drink choice with the exception of Candace who demanded, "Vodka, rocks, and not the cheap stuff. Make it Grey Goose." He nodded and left.

"I don't know about anyone else at this table, but I certainly feel like a fool," Anne said.

"It was the most humiliating experience of my life," Rose lamented. "What if we'd been arrested and Jack had to come bail me out—with the kids in tow?"

"I told you it was a bad idea," Candace said. "We should never have attempted anything like this. My heart damned near stopped when the lights were turned on."

"Oh, quit complaining. We were embarrassed and some cops had a good laugh—so what? We came away with this," Nancy said. She jerked Dorie's second cell phone from her pocket. "Thank God, I left mine in Anne's car."

"Thank God, they didn't search the car," Anne replied. She watched Nancy play with the phone and punch buttons. "Anything of interest?"

She'd had no idea Dorie kept a second phone and worried what information it held.

Nancy frowned. "That's weird. There aren't any names in her phone book, just numbers."

Anne's stomach clenched.

"Try the voicemail," Rose suggested.

Nancy pushed more buttons and listened. "It's never been activated."

"That's even stranger, especially if she used it for personal business," Candace said.

The waiter brought their drinks. As if on cue, they all picked up their glasses and sipped. Once again Candace was the exception. She drained hers and rattled the ice, silently ordering another.

He nodded and left just as Jen returned. The shoe polish had disappeared along with the stocking cap. It was stuffed into the waistband of her leggings. She slid back into her chair and fanned her face with her hand.

"Geez, I'm hot."

"Jen, it's July and you're wearing a long sleeved shirt," Rose told her.

"Don't get testy. I know why I'm hot. I was just making an observation." She punctuated the statement by dabbing her sweat-slicken forehead with a napkin.

"I have every right to be testy. We damned near got arrested. Weren't you embarrassed and scared?" Rose declared in a tight voice.

"A little, but it was kind of thrilling, too. In a way, I wish we had been arrested, although how I would have explained getting busted for breaking and entering had anything to do with a late night critique session, I'll never know. On the other hand, it might have helped with my new book plot."

Anne sighed. Only Jen would consider getting arrested as a positive career move.

"I don't think he was really listening, though. Being a commodities broker these days is demanding. When he's not on the phone, he's on the computer monitoring overseas markets. What are you doing?" Jen asked Nancy.

"Checking out Dorie's cell. She doesn't have voicemail and none of the numbers have any names to go with them."

"So, call a number and see who answers," Jen suggested, taking a long swallow of wine.

"And say what? 'Hello, I just stole Isadora Powell's cell phone and was wondering who you are.' I don't think so."

The waiter brought Candace's second drink. She took another swig before saying, "Tell whoever answers that you found the phone and could they tell you who it belongs to. Then ask their name so the owner can thank them."

"Would someone really give their name to a stranger on a cell phone?" Anne asked.

"People do all kinds of strange things, especially late at night," Rose replied. "Give it a shot. The worst that can happen is they'll hang up. The best is you'll get voicemail and a name. We can ask questions later."

Nancy shrugged and selected a number. They waited in silence. Then, Nancy hung up with a confused expression.

"Voicemail?" Jen asked.

"Yeah. I got the desk of Ian Collier at the Bank of the Bahamas in Nassau."

"Nassau? You're kidding," Candace said.

"Try another number," Rose urged.

Nancy hit another selection, listened, and hung up.

"The office of Roger Gates at First National Bank of Bermuda," she reported, repeating the process again. She listened for a moment. "That was the voicemail of someone named Alice Kartchman."

"Alice Kartchman? Are you sure?" Rose asked.

"You know her?"

"Alice Kartchman is Ruby Redd."

"The erotic romance writer? Why would Dorie have her number on what is supposed to be a personal phone?" Anne asked. "She hated the genre. Were they friends?"

"I doubt it," Rose replied. "Not in a million…"

"Excuse me, ladies, may I join you?" Detective Collins inquired.

Nancy jerked her head up and dropped the phone. Anne's breath stopped somewhere between her chest and throat.

He didn't wait for an invitation, but sidled around the table and slid into the empty chair between Nancy and Anne. The file folder and envelope hit the placemat in front of him.

"What…what are you doing here?" Anne asked,

eyeing Nancy who scooped up Dorie's cell and jammed it in her purse.

"Came to see you."

"Why?"

"I spent twenty minutes in the car trying to make sense of what was written on these stories. I finally gave up. By the way, who are the women listed on the folder?"

"Uh, those are members of Dorie's other critique group", Candace answered. "Do you need our help with something?"

"I need a literary interpreter."

"How did you know we were here?" Jen asked.

"You announced it loud and clear in the street."

Anne reached for the envelope and opened it, sliding out the papers inside. She gazed at them for a moment before saying, "This is a partial manuscript. From the edit marks, I'd have to say a first draft."

"Give me a crash course on writing," Detective Collins said. The waiter approached. "Iced tea." He turned his attention back to Anne.

Candace rattled the ice in her glass again. "Make it a double."

"Everyone writes differently. Some authors' rough drafts are stream of consciousness. They write whatever pops into their heads and edit later. Dorie was like that. I prefer to edit my writing next day. Still others edit as they go."

"And these?" He handed the file folder to Nancy.

"Critique comments," she told him, opening the folder and selecting the top few pages. "This one belongs to Dorie. The bubbles in the right margins are the reader's comments. See? Here it says, 'Awkward dialogue. Re-word.' I'd say the red slash through it means Dorie disagreed with the assessment."

"Thought you said these were yours." The waiter brought the iced tea and Candace's third drink. She gulped half of it.

Nancy licked her lips, and then shrugged. "No, they're Dorie's."

"Why did you want them?" he asked.

"We thought we could find out the names of her other critique partners," Rose answered.

"How many does she have?"

"It depends," Jen offered. "Some writers belong to several critique groups. We had the idea to talk to them and help solve the case."

Detective Collins sighed and gulped his tea. "That sounds like you suspect she was murdered by a friend."

"The thought did cross our minds," Candace replied, draining the last of her drink.

"I get the feeling some of you didn't like Ms. Powell."

Anne glanced at the others as silence reigned.

"Let's just say Isadora Powell had her moments and leave it at that," Nancy said.

"Let's not. Whoever killed her knew her routine." He pulled his notebook from his jacket pocket. "You ladies knew her routine. Who else would know it?"

"We didn't know her routine," Candace corrected, her words slurred. "We simply knew how and when she liked to do things."

"Sounds like a routine to me."

"What Candace means is we know she preferred working at night and didn't like to be disturbed if she worked during the day. We have no idea if she adhered to that philosophy day in and day out," Nancy explained.

"None of us is that organized, except Anne," Rose said. "If anyone can stick to a schedule, she can. Right, Anne?"

Anne looked up from the partial manuscript she'd been reading. "Hm? Oh, I guess so. You know, this doesn't look right."

"What?" Rose asked.

"This partial. Dorie always used the title and her name in the header. I think this is a copy—something done hurriedly. There's no header and the format is all wrong."

"Maybe she was using it as a contest entry," Jen suggested. "She did that, you know. She'd use a fake name and enter contests for unpublished writers, especially those that had money as a prize."

"You're kidding!" Nancy exclaimed. "She was taking an awful chance. What if she won and an editor or agent requested a full?"

"She'd ignore the request. All contest stuff was sent to a post office box."

"And you know this how?" Detective Collins asked.

"I saw her there once. I was mailing in a contest entry when she walked in and pulled an envelope out of a box. Naturally, I had to say hi, and I saw the return address was from some chapter in the Midwest. The words 'contest entry' were in the lower left hand corner. I know it was an unpublished contest because I entered it, too, and got my scores in the mail the day before." She paused to take a breath. "I placed second in my category and was very proud. At any rate, the addressee was Danielle Harris, so I asked who that was and Dorie told me to shut up and not to mention it to anyone. I later checked the chapter's website and saw the winner in romantic suspense was Danielle Harris. She was awarded a hundred dollars."

Anne marveled at how Jen could talk non-stop for so long without taking a breath. It was like a gift.

"I don't believe it," Rose said with a gasp.

"Believe it," Jen said. "When it came to money, Dorie would do damned near anything."

"So, if Ms. Powell was not a very nice person, why did you all associate with her?" he asked.

"Because in spite of her shortcomings, she was a hell of a writer," Anne told him.

Detective Collins snapped his notebook shut and finished his iced tea.

"Thank you, ladies. What I'm about to say is strictly between us. I can't have you interfering with my investigation, but if you happen to find out something pertinent, I expect a call. Pick a person to be my contact. I can be reached at the number on the cards I gave you the other day. No more breaking and entering and no meeting with strangers to ask questions. All you do is pass the information along to me. Is that clear?"

"You mean we can help?" Jen said, a grin creeping across her face.

"I mean, you may ask questions of people who knew Ms. Powell in the literary world. They might open up to you rather than a cop, but I expect you to tell me what's said. Now, who's going to be my contact?"

"I vote for Anne or Nancy," Rose said. "They're both organized. Jen and I have kids at home, and Candace…" She turned to look at Candace who was having trouble staying awake.

"She's not driving, is she?" he asked.

"No, I'll see she gets home, and I'll be glad to call, if that's all right with Nancy," Anne said.

"Fine with me."

Detective Collins rose. "Goodnight, ladies. And don't do anything too stupid."

"What do you think he meant by that?" Jen asked watching him walk out of the bar.

"I think it's self-explanatory," Rose told her. She glanced at the semi-conscious Candace. "I think it's time to go home. Can you handle her?"

"We'll get her home," Nancy said. She yanked the cell from her pocket and scrolled down. "Damn, Dorie had a butt load of numbers." Nancy shook her head, then stopped scrolling abruptly. "Rose is right. It's late and I have a deadline. I'll check these out tomorrow."

"I'll settle up. You guys can pay me back later. Help Nancy get Candace to the car," Anne said, wondering what had caused Nancy to suddenly stop scrolling. The possibilities made her stomach hurt.

She shoved the partial back into the envelope with trembling fingers and gathered the file folder with the critiques in it, then settled with the waiter. By the time she got to the car, Rose and Jen were gone while Candace dozed in the back seat. Anne added talking to Candace about the booze on her mental to do list. She slid behind the wheel and twisted the key.

She gazed at her friend in the rearview mirror. "You going to be all right?"

Candace's eyelids fluttered. "Yeah," she muttered. "It's been a hell of a night."

"Amen," Nancy exclaimed as they drove away.

The drive to Candace's house was silent even though Anne had a thousand questions swirling in her mind. Fear kept her quiet. She'd often wondered about Nancy with her frequent sharp tongue and reluctance to talk about herself. Tonight had shown a whole new side to her friend.

*Does she have secrets, too?*

They helped Candace to the door where she waved them away. "I'm fine. I'll talk to you later."

She entered her house and slammed the door.

Nancy shrugged. "She's a big girl.

"I worry about her."

"None of our business. Take me home. I'm exhausted and still have that deadline staring me in the face."

Later that night, Anne lay in bed staring at the ceiling in the dark. Sleep refused to come, so she made plans. First thing tomorrow, she'd call Kenneth and ask if the kids could stay another week or two. She didn't want them around a murder investigation. After the funeral, she and Nancy could get together and call some of the numbers on Dorie's phone. Then she'd ask Candace out to dinner. Anne remembered the anguish when she and Kenneth had split. She should have been more sensitive to her friend's needs.

Inevitably, her thoughts turned to tonight's fiasco. Thank God, Detective Collins had let them go. And his decision to allow them to help, even in a small way, made her feel useful. She just hoped she could find what she needed without having to tell him about it.

She turned on her side, pounded the pillow into shape, and glanced at the bedside clock. Geez, two o'clock and still wide awake.

Was Jen right about Dorie entering unpublished contests under assumed names? That sounded like Dorie—a cheat and a liar. Dorie didn't deserve half of what she received from the literary world.

The partial they'd found bothered her. The pages had been filled with red slashes and scribbled words, but everything about it was wrong. Maybe she tried a different approach to bring her career back on track. It must have worked. Yet it was odd her critique partners hadn't seen this particular story. On the other hand, she might have cut them out of the loop running it by one of her other groups. Anne made a mental note to check. *Or she did it on her own.*

Still, something was definitely out of whack.

\*\*\*\*

The next morning, Anne called her friends to see how they had fared from the night before.

"Jack was sound asleep and snoring like a trooper," Rose said over the high-pitched squalls of her youngest. "He didn't even ask questions this morning. I hope Nancy can make some headway with the phone. You know, I can't understand why Dorie would have Alice Karchman's number."

"Were they friends?" Anne asked.

"Not by a long shot. Dorie often insulted erotic romance writers by calling what they wrote porn. Rumor is she and Alice got into a screaming match one night at a conference over it. From what I heard, it was one of the few times Dorie had ever been bested. She walked out of the bar swearing revenge."

Anne digested this bit of gossip before answering, "Did she get it?"

"Let's just say that shortly afterward, rumors

surfaced regarding Alice's sexual orientation."

"Maybe a phone call to tell Alice her arch-enemy is dead is in order."

"Do you suppose Alice could have had the ultimate revenge after all?" A child's sharp scream sounded in the distance. "Oh, hell. I've got to go."

Rose hung up leaving Anne wondering if the suspect list was growing. *The more the merrier.*

With a shrug, she dialed Jen.

"Carl barely looked up from the computer when I got in, so I didn't have to explain anything. Did you get Candace home all right?"

"More or less."

"Eric is such a rat, dumping her like that. Poor Candace. She's floundering with a nasty divorce and lousy writing. I don't mean to be catty, but what a combination. Maybe we can help her more with the writing part. Has Nancy found anything on the phone?"

"Don't know. I haven't called her yet."

"Well, it's obvious, even to me that the only reason someone has banking contacts in the Bahamas is because they're hiding money. I'll bet Dorie's got piles of dough stashed in overseas accounts."

Anne's stomach dropped. *Oh, crap. Just what I needed to hear.*

Jen continued. "You know, Dorie didn't appear to curb her lifestyle any over the lean years with no books out. She must have had another source of income. Any idea what it could have been?"

Anne took a deep breath and let it out slowly. "None at all. She was always a penny pincher. Maybe she lived off of her savings."

"Maybe...Oops, my other line is ringing. I'll see

you at the funeral tomorrow."

Anne hung up and bit her lip. Dorie's second phone was going to cause big problems.

She tried Candace next, but got no answer. Rather than leave a message, she called Nancy instead, asking about the phone first.

"No, I haven't had a chance to look at it," Nancy replied. "I'm in deadline hell."

"Making any progress?"

"Some."

"Um, I meant to ask last night. What do you think the bank business is all about?"

Silence greeted her question before Nancy finally answered. "I have no idea. Knowing Dorie, she was probably dodging the IRS. Look, Anne, I don't have time to chat. We'll talk after the funeral tomorrow."

Nancy's abrupt cut off worried Anne. She had the distinct impression her friend was lying.

****

Candace sat on the sofa in the family room, a glass in one hand, the vodka bottle in the other. Ignoring the ringing phone, she slopped some in the glass and drank. The room refused to come into focus.

*So what if I'm drunk? Who the hell cares? Eric? Fat fucking chance. My friends?*

Anne had had a look on her face that said Candace's drinking habits would be a topic of conversation at a later date.

*Fuck her, too.*

She drained the glass and poured another.

Damn, she'd known going to Dorie's would stir up trouble, but had anyone listened? No-o-o-o. Anne had to play detective. At least Nancy had the cell phone, which with any luck would yield a suspect. Who cared about a bunch of critiques and an unidentified partial? There was nothing suspicious in those. The partial would probably prove to be a first draft of her book—the one to come out posthumously.

Candace slammed the vodka down in one gulp. The room spun. She didn't care. Everything she'd ever worked for was gone, shredded into pulp. She resented the fact that even dead, Isadora Powell would reap the benefits of good fortune, because the book would be a bestseller and make tons of money. Years of taking all Dorie's verbal abuse in the hope of one kind word bubbled to the surface.

"You bitch! I'm glad you're dead! Do you hear me in hell, Dorie? Listen over the roar of the flames. I'm glad you're dead!"

She swilled the remaining inch of liquor from the bottle, and then hurled it against the wall where it shattered into a thousand pieces.

Chapter Five

The remaining five members of the critique group stood by the coffin of Isadora Powell. Anne was flanked by Nancy to her left and Jennifer on her right, followed by Rose and Candace. The room smelled of flowers and incense. Voices whispered. Organ music, piped in from discreetly placed speakers, set a somber mood.

Anne sneaked a peek at Candace who resembled an unmade bed. Her clothes looked as if she'd grabbed them out of the wash hamper. The sleek, multi-shaded blonde hair could have used a brush, not to mention a touch-up at the roots. The long bangs fell into Candace's eyes requiring frequent hand gestures to sweep the unruly strands aside. Even though the room was not brightly lit, she wore sunglasses. The woman was a walking wreck.

She turned her gaze from her friend and re-focused on Dorie. Her severely styled jet-black hair—it had always reminded her of a Roaring Twenties flapper—contrasted sharply with the white skin of the dead. The crimson lipstick—the only color Dorie ever wore—made her look like a vampire who'd just feasted.

A rosary was draped through her hands, surprising Anne. She'd not realized Dorie was Catholic, but then one of the rules of the group was never discuss religion or politics. She cynically assumed it had been years since Dorie dared go to confession. If she had, she'd have been on her knees doing penance and saying Hail Marys for the rest of her natural life.

"It's fake, you know," Jen whispered loudly.

"What's fake?" Nancy answered in a low voice.

"Her hair. I found the box in her bathroom linen closet. *Midnight Raven* by WonderColor. I once asked her who did her hair and she was furious. Told me it was natural, but I knew she lied. Nobody has hair that black, unless they're Oriental or maybe African-American."

The first dart of pain signaling the onset of a headache flashed behind Anne's eyes. "Jen, be quiet."

Jen ignored her. "You know, I never realized how exotic Dorie looked. She has incredibly wide cheekbones and her eyes slant ever so slightly. It's a shame her nose is kind of smashed in, and her chin's rather prominent. If I squint, she looks a little bit like a monkey."

"Jennifer, for Pete's sake, have some respect," Rose said, hissing.

"Well, it's the truth," Jen protested.

Candace swiped her hand across her face, pushing the errant bangs aside, and then wiped her perspiring forehead with a tissue.

"Candace, take your sunglasses off. They look ridiculous," Nancy said.

"I'm having trouble with my eyes today. The light hurts." She brushed the back of her hand across her lips. "I don't feel so hot."

Anne cast a questioning glance at Rose who shrugged, and then at Candace clutching the coffin railing to steady her swaying body. Her friend was either drunk or hung over to beat hell.

"Let's sit down," Anne said. "With any luck, the service will be short, and we can have lunch. I've got a plan."

"Of course, you do. You always have a plan. I just hope it's better than the last one," Nancy replied in a low tone.

Anne drew a deep breath. She didn't need Nancy's sharp comments today. They filed into the third row and took their seats. Next to her, Nancy sighed as though bored, while further down Rose fiddled with her skirt, pulling the fabric over her knees. Candace slouched. Jen stared off into space.

Anne spared a glance around the room. The service was due to begin in fifteen minutes and so far, only the five of them, a man and a woman in the front, Detective Collins, and a couple of sobbing women in the back row comprised the mourners.

The woman in the front bore a strong resemblance to Dorie. Anne deduced she must be a relative, probably a sister, and that the man was her husband. Neither looked particularly grief-stricken.

She dismissed Detective Collins' appearance. He was a cop working the case. He had to be here.

Since the two crying women hugged Dorie's last book to their chests, she pegged them as fans.

"Not a very big turnout," she murmured.

"Not a lot of flowers either, although the one from our chapter is lovely," Rose said. "Who ordered them?"

Anne answered. "I called Gayle Milano. She said she'd send a display and notify WAA of Dorie's death. I think ours is the big one against the wall."

"I'm surprised her editor or agent isn't here. I

assume someone let them know," Rose commented.

"Her agent is my agent, so I called Pam yesterday. She said she'd inform her editor, Claire Chappelle," Jennifer told them.

With ten minutes left to go, four more people walked in, paid their respects, and spoke with the man and woman before taking seats. Anne had no idea who they were. Neighbors, perhaps? Finally, three members of the Southeast Florida chapter of WWA arrived. She recognized two of them as Dorie's other critique partners. The women nodded as they took seats several rows back.

Candace sprawled on the chair, fanning herself with her hand and wiping her sweaty brow.

"I'll be right back," she said, rising and heading out the door.

Five minutes later, she returned to resume her seat, leaving Anne to wonder if Candace had some liquid relief in her purse. She wouldn't have minded a belt herself. Her head felt like it was clamped in a vice.

The funeral director and a priest entered from a side door. Anne tried to keep her mind on the service, but her attention wandered. She'd had a lousy night's sleep and Dorie's cell phone preyed on her mind. How many numbers would match with people she knew? And was one of them the killer?

Out of the corner of her eye, she saw Candace pat her neck with the tissue. What was going on with her anyway? Up until discovering Dorie's body, she'd been tense, but focused on her writing and trying to get on with her life. Had Eric decided to marry the bimbo he'd left Candace for? Or were the alimony checks late? What would happen if the money dried up?

Anne knew Candace hadn't worked outside the home in over thirty years, and her computer skills were limited to word processing. She'd end up as a greeter or stocking shelves at the local discount store for minimum wage and little medical coverage. No wonder she was hitting the bottle.

Anne sensed something else wrong with Candace, but at the moment, needed to concentrate on other things. Like that damned cell phone. If the police discovered Nancy had it, she knew the consequences would be a bit more severe than a stern warning. They had withheld evidence. She didn't think Detective Collins would appreciate it, even if he was allowing them to help with the investigation.

And the absence of Dorie's editor and her agent was strange. Both stood to gain financially from this last book. Common sense said one or the other should attend the funeral—out of respect if nothing else.

"Let us pray."

The words jolted Anne out of her thoughts and back to the service. She bowed her head and tried to believe the words the priest intoned, but couldn't. No matter how hard she tried, Anne doubted Isadora Powell was anywhere near the vicinity of heaven.

After the service, she followed Nancy and the others, approaching the man and woman.

"Hello, my name is Anne Jamieson. I was Dorie's critique partner. I'm so sorry for your loss."

The woman smiled. "Thank you. I'm Irina's sister, Natasha. This is my husband Jeffery Sessions."

"Irina?" Rose questioned.

"Yes. Isadora Powell was not her real name. She changed it when she got rich and famous."

"We had no idea," Nancy commented. "Dorie never talked much about her family."

Natasha shrugged. "Family wasn't important to Irina. The only reason we knew she'd died was because the police found my name in her address book under emergency contacts. I hadn't seen or talked to her in years."

"I'm so sorry. I take it she won't be buried here in San Sebastian," Anne said.

"No. The family plot is in Chicago."

The sobbing women pressed forward. Anne decided to move on. "Have a safe trip home, and please accept our deepest sympathy."

They left and paused on the front porch of the funeral home where Nancy immediately lit a cigarette. The other ladies from the chapter joined them. After the usual "such-a-tragedy" comments, they went their own way.

"I had no idea Dorie used a pseudonym," Jen said.

"Neither did I," Rose replied. "I wonder why."

"It's out of character. You'd think someone as egotistical as Dorie would want her real name splashed on the covers of her books," Candace added.

"I'll be back in a second," Jen said, dashing inside.

"Nancy, for God's sake, must you smoke? There's not a breath of air and the smell is obnoxious," Anne protested, waving her hand to disperse the wispy cloud.

"Sorry," Nancy replied, crushing out the offending item and giving Anne a look that clearly stated she thought her friend was a pain in the ass.

Anne massaged the back of her neck. The pain in her head had increased. *God, I hope I have some aspirin in my purse.*

"Thank you, Nancy. I have a headache and the smoke was bothering me." *And why the hell am I explaining?* Maybe she needed food. "Shall we do lunch?"

"How about Rafferty's again?" Rose suggested. "It's quick, and I have to get home. I took the day off work for the funeral."

"All right with me," Candace said.

Anne noticed her hands still shook, but not as badly as an hour ago.

"Candace, would you like to get together with Anne and me for dinner soon? We can give you pointers on how to survive a divorce," Nancy asked.

Anne shot her a surprised glance. It was so out of character for Nancy-the-loner to suggest such a thing. She turned her gaze to Candace. "That's a good idea. The first few months are always the toughest. You pick the day and the restaurant."

Candace's eyebrows rose. "Thanks. I may take you up on the offer. The past week has been shitty."

Jen bounced out of the door and rejoined them.

"Petrovsky," she announced with a grin.

"What?" they all chorused.

"Dorie's family name is Petrovsky. I thought it might come in useful to know that."

The sobbing women exited and headed for the parking lot. The neighbors had long since vanished.

"We're going to Rafferty's for lunch," Nancy told Jen.

"Works for me."

Detective Collins opened the door. "Ladies," he greeted.

"Detective Collins. How goes the investigation?"

Anne asked.

"Working on it. We're still gathering information from neighbors. The maid had done a good job. We found a few partial fingerprints on the stairwell banister and in the office, but not enough to make a positive ID."

"Male or female?" Jen asked.

"Uh, fingerprints are not gender specific, Ms. Swanson. How about you? Have you talked to other friends of Ms. Powell's?"

"Not yet. I thought it would be better to wait until after the funeral," Anne replied.

"Probably a wise idea." He smiled and nodded as he walked down the porch steps and toward his car.

"What you really meant was you thought there'd be more of Dorie's friends here," Nancy commented.

"Yeah, I had visions of a larger turnout from the chapter," Anne said with a shrug. "I guess a lot of people are up north or on vacation."

"That detective gives me the creeps. Like he knows a lot more than he's saying," Candace muttered. "Come on, let's get out of here."

"Good idea," Nancy said.

Anne walked to her car, wondering exactly how much Detective Collins knew.

\*\*\*\*

Rafferty's was crowded, but they found a table near the back and squeezed around it.

"I need to order and get out of here," Rose said. "The babysitter is costing me a fortune."

"Same here," Jen offered. "I've got the kids parked at a neighbor's, but don't want to impose."

When the waiter arrived, they all ordered white

wine and salads, except for Rose who opted for the half-pound burger with fries. Anne thought the salad would have been a wiser choice. Rose's navy blue suit was tight in all the wrong places.

"I have an idea," Nancy said. "I think we should split up the numbers on Dorie's cell and call them."

"We already know that two of them were to overseas banks and one to an erotic romance writer," Rose replied.

"I called a couple last night. Both belonged to former chapter members—Sarah Masterson and Careen Holcombe," Nancy informed them.

"What did they have to say?" Candace asked.

"Voicemail. I didn't leave any messages. I'll call later."

The waiter brought them all glasses of water. Anne rummaged in her purse, found the aspirin, and downed two.

"What are we supposed to say?" Jen questioned.

"Just inform them of Dorie's death. Ask their names and say you want to include them on the program for a memorial service," Anne replied.

"That sounds plausible," Nancy said. "If someone asks how you got the number, just say it was in her address book."

"I don't think Alice Kartchman will want her name on anything concerning Dorie," Rose supplied.

"Why not?" Candace asked.

Rose told the rest of the group about the alleged argument in the bar.

Jen whistled softly. "Whew! They actually had to be separated?"

"That's what I heard. It happened in the wee hours

of the morning in the hotel lounge, so not a whole lot of people were there."

"Apparently, there were enough to spread the word. Why don't you give her a call?" Nancy replied, pulling Dorie's cell from her purse.

The waiter arrived and distributed the wine glasses, while Nancy scrolled, giving each woman five numbers to call. She set the phone on the table.

"This is a good start," Anne said, scribbling the last number on her cocktail napkin. "I suggest we all meet at my place in two days and compare notes. Make it around dinnertime. We'll order in pizza."

"Jack'll have a fit having to stay with the kids two nights this week," Rose lamented.

"Just use the memorial excuse again," Anne said.

Personally, she thought Jack Bennett was an over-sexed asshole who needed to see four kids from his wife's point of view. Rose was too nice to him.

The sudden ringing of Dorie's cell phone had all of them freezing like statues. They stared at the chirping instrument like it was a live snake.

"Answer it," Jen urged.

Nancy fumbled and finally opened the phone.

Clearing her throat, she answered in a low tone, "Hello?"

Anne, her headache intensifying once again, leaned forward as Nancy spoke.

"Yes, this is Miss Petrovsky…Yes, Mr. Collier, what can I do for you…I, ah, misplaced my phone…Mr. Collier, could you please give me my account balance? I also seem to have misplaced my statement…No, of course not. I meant I've lost the paper I last jotted everything down on." Nancy looked at the rest of the group and shrugged, then wrote rapidly. "...and twenty-three cents," she quoted. "Thank you very much, Mr. Collier...No, you've been very helpful. Goodbye."

She closed the phone, slumped in her chair, and then stared at the napkin in front of her.

"Well?" Anne said in an impatient tone.

"Who was it?" Rose asked.

"You're not going to believe this. That was Ian Collier at the Bank of the Bahamas."

Anne sat back as a rush of heat enveloped her. She swallowed. "What...what did he want?"

"He was calling to confirm Dorie's deposit of two thousand dollars last Monday. He apparently tried to contact her several times this week, but she didn't answer and has no voicemail."

"Well, of course she didn't answer," Candace said. "She's dead."

"Why was he calling to confirm it?" Rose asked with a frown.

"According to Collier, Dorie didn't want statements sent to her."

"I'm surprised he gave you the information without some kind of password," Anne remarked. *Oh God, will this never end? What the hell am I going to do?*

Nancy drew in a shaky breath and expelled it. "So am I, but as of this morning Dorie's account balance is fourteen thousand, six hundred-fifty seven dollars and twenty three cents. He also informed me that the transfer of twenty thousand dollars last month to the Bank of the Caymans has cleared."

"Fourteen thousand dollars?" Rose said in a squeaky voice.

"Fourteen thousand, six hundred fifty-seven dollars and twenty-three cents to be exact," she repeated, reading from the napkin.

"And she moved twenty grand out last month?" Jen said with raised eyebrows.

"Where the hell was Dorie getting all this money and why was she hiding it?" Candace asked. She drained her wine glass and signaled for a refill.

"She was obviously hiding it from the IRS," Anne replied.

The food arrived and all conversation ceased for a few minutes.

"Maybe the two grand was her advance for the new book," Nancy suggested.

"Dorie would get ten times that amount for an advance," Rose said.

"Perhaps the twenty thousand was the advance," Jen offered. "The two grand could have been from royalties on previous books."

"But both of those would be checks," Rose stressed. "The IRS could track them and find the offshore accounts. They might not get any information, but they'd know Dorie was hiding something and audit her. I'll bet she's dealing in cash. But from where I haven't a clue."

Anne shoved lettuce in her mouth, saying nothing. She wished they'd all shut up and cease speculating. *Can this get any worse? Fourteen thousand dollars? Oh, my God!*

"She must have kept account numbers somewhere in her house. I wonder if the cops found them and know what they are," Candace mused.

Even slightly loaded, Candace had hit on

something. Of course, Dorie would have the account numbers somewhere in the house. *Probably hidden and filed under a code of some sort. I have to find them.*

"I'll call Detective Collins later and see if we can get back into the house—legally this time," Anne said.

"The sister probably inherited, but probate will take a while. If we say there are critiques or something we need, she might let us in," Nancy replied.

"I'd say it's worth a shot," Jen declared.

"I wonder if Dorie had a safety deposit box," Anne said between bites of lettuce.

"She may have, but only for stuff she wouldn't use too often," Rose said, cramming a French fry into her mouth.

"If I had offshore accounts and didn't want anything mailed to my house, I'd keep the numbers close for easy access. I can't wait to make my calls. What do I say if I get a bank? Should I tell them Dorie's dead?" Jen asked.

"God, no, don't do that. They'll freeze the accounts. Then someone will know we have access to information we shouldn't," Candace said. She gulped a large portion of wine and played with her salad.

"If you get a bank, just hang up or say you've called the wrong number," Nancy told her.

Rose looked at her watch and yelped, then shoved the last of her sandwich into her mouth, washing it down with the remaining wine.

"I've got to get home." She slapped a twenty-dollar bill from her purse onto the table. "That should take care of my share of the bill. If not, let me know. I'll try to call those numbers today. See you in a couple of days."

She swiped the napkin across her lips and hurried out.

Jen pushed her bowl away. "I should be going, too." She rooted through her purse until finding her wallet and extracted a couple of bills. "Here, this should cover it. This is going to be so much fun! I feel like Nancy Drew. I can't wait to begin calling. Have a good one."

Jen left and Anne shook her head. "It may have been a mistake to let Jen call anybody. Lord only knows what she'll tell people."

"Whatever it is, I'm sure they'll be confused," Nancy commented.

Casting her gaze on Candace, Anne cleared her throat. "Uh, Candace, can I talk to you for a second?"

"What about? Where's that waiter? I could use another drink."

"That's what I'd like to talk about."

Nancy's eyes widened and a stern expression crossed her face clearly indicating this was not the time or place to bring up Candace's drinking. Anne hesitated, realizing Nancy was right.

Candace snapped her head around to stare. Her eyes held a frosty expression. Anne had no choice but to continue.

"Candace, you got drunk the other night, and are well on your way again today. Look at you. Your clothes are wrinkled, your eyes bloodshot, and did you even bother to comb your hair this morning?" Anne said. She tried to keep the tone gentle, but failed.

"Well, excuse me for not quite handling stress the way you do. Shredded the phone book yet? How about a week's worth of newspapers? Or better yet, your latest manuscript because it wasn't good enough? Leave me alone," she snapped.

"Candace, we're just concerned…"

"Yeah, like you were concerned when Eric filed for divorce? Boy, I wallowed in the support rolling in from my friends. Thanks, guys. And how about all the concern when my ex showed up at the country club with the bimbo on his arm while I was having dinner *with my lawyer*?" She turned and glared at Nancy. "And every time I called you to just talk, I got the brush off after ten minutes."

Nancy bit her lip. "I'm sorry, Candace. You're right. I should have been more understanding."

"I've been in your shoes, too," Anne said. "At least Kenneth didn't have a girlfriend. He just hated being married to me. I think I could have taken a mistress better than knowing he didn't care any more. Let's talk over dinner one night like Nancy suggested."

Candace's expression softened. "Thanks. I'd appreciate an opportunity to just vent, maybe even smash a few ashtrays. I was pretty drunk the other night, but this whole week has been awful. I guess the murder of a friend pushed me over the top. I could deal with Eric and the bimbo, but Dorie…"

"Her death upset all of us," Nancy said. "And everyone deals with stress differently. Unfortunately, some solutions aren't healthy. All Anne does is shred paper."

Anne laughed. "I haven't gotten around to the phone book yet. At least I don't babble like Jen."

"She babbles when she's nervous. I sometimes wonder if she doesn't play the ditz on purpose. Pretending to be stupid has its advantages. People tend to forget she's around," Candace remarked, sipping from her water glass.

"Yet she was gushing on all eight cylinders when she and Rose pulled up at Dorie's," Anne answered in a thoughtful tone.

"She always knows the latest gossip, too," Nancy said. "She's also sharp as a tack. She may talk a mile a minute, but not everything she says is nonsense."

"How much do I owe?" Candace asked, eyeing the check. "I'm going to go home and try to start a new book. Maybe I'll base it on Dorie's murder and us being amateur sleuths."

"That's a great idea, and I'll get the check," Anne said with a smile. "Don't forget. My house on Sunday night."

"I won't."

Candace rose and walked out the door. A new work? Anne guessed a new bottle.

After paying, Anne and Nancy strolled out to their cars. Nancy hesitated when they reached Anne's Honda.

"Uh, Anne, there's something I have to tell you."

"What's that?" she replied unlocking her car door.

"I lied to the others. After leaving Rafferty's, I went home and took a look at the numbers in Dorie's phone."

Anne's stomach clenched and her head pounded.

"And?"

"I recognized one of the numbers." She lifted her gaze to stare across the street, breaking eye contact. Anne bit her lip, certain what was coming next.

"Oh?"

"It was yours." Nancy paused. "I deleted it."

For a moment, Anne said nothing as relief flooded through her. "I didn't kill Dorie. I swear it."

Nancy pulled her car keys from her purse. "Doesn't matter to me if you did. Dorie was trouble for a lot of people, especially her so-called friends."

Finally, Anne opened the car door and slid behind the wheel, staring straight ahead through the windshield. "You did the right thing. I won't say anything if you don't."

She plunged the car into gear and drove away. And how many other numbers did Nancy recognize and delete?

Chapter Six

Anne paced her kitchen, a glass of iced tea in her hand. She was antsy as hell. The fear factor had arisen with Nancy's revelations at lunch, and she no longer wanted to make those calls on her list. She should be in her office organizing another proposal for her agent, but in her present frame of mind, knew nothing intelligent would emerge.

She hated funerals and Dorie's was the most depressing she'd ever attended. The lunch hadn't been much better. She worried about Candace. The woman walked closer to the precipice with each passing day, and while the divorce and Dorie's death may have had something to do with it, Anne sensed another reason for the self-destruction. The comment about shredding a manuscript had caught her attention. Did another rejection letter send the poor woman off the deep end? Would that cause her to guzzle vodka?

*She should be used to rejection by now. I wish just once Candace could hit the jackpot with something positive. She's always so optimistic and works so hard for success.*

As concerned as she was for her friend, what worried Anne was Nancy's confession about the deletion of her number from Dorie's cell phone, plus the presence of former Southeast Florida members' numbers.

She hadn't heard about or from Sarah Masterson in ages, but remembered her as bright and bubbly, always ready to support the chapter. Careen Holcombe had done a gargantuan job as conference chair several years ago. Her sudden move across three time zones and the decision to quit writing stunned everyone.

The doorbell's sudden peeling startled her. Setting her glass on the counter, Anne hurried to answer. She opened the door to a smiling Detective Gil Collins.

"Detective Collins, what are you doing here?"

"Have you got a minute? I'd like to talk."

"Of course," she said, stepping back. "What about?"

"I thought maybe we could discuss the case."

*Does he know something?* The thought flashed through her mind as she led him into the living room—a living room that hadn't seen an adult male in three years. "Please, have a seat. Can I get you something to drink?"

He hesitated. "I wondered if you'd like to go out—have a drink and catch a bite to eat. I know it's only five-thirty, but I'm off duty. If I go home, I'll just watch TV."

Anne's heart sped up and her mouth went dry. Good heavens, the man was asking her out on a date. She didn't like to admit to anyone that she hadn't experienced one of those since the divorce.

"Strictly business," he hurried to say when she paused. "I'll have you home early."

She liked the way the tips of his ears turned red. It made him less of a cop and more of a man.

Dragging in a deep breath, she answered, "I don't have a curfew, Detective, and I'd love to discuss the case."

He smiled. "Call me Gil, and is there someplace special you'd like to go?"

"You choose. Surprise me. And it's Anne."

Anne grabbed her purse. A date—an honest to God date—and she didn't care if it was strictly business.

****

Gil chose wisely. *Caruso's* was the best Italian restaurant in San Sebastian—the kind of place a man took a woman on a date that wasn't strictly business. Her ex-husband, Kenneth, had brought her here on their tenth wedding anniversary.

She pushed that memory from her mind and concentrated on the man sitting across from her. Anne ordered white wine and Gil surprised her by requesting Chianti Classico. She'd taken him for a beer or bourbon type of guy.

An awkward silence fell after the waiter left. Gil fiddled with his silverware and napkin, first placing it on his lap, then refolding it next to his forks.

Anne gazed at the décor. Faux stone walls in Tuscan colors with borders depicting grape harvests, and the discreet lighting hadn't changed since her last visit. Soft music played in the background. A light scent of garlic wafted from the kitchen area whenever the doors opened and waiters brought forth steaming plates. The odor wasn't overwhelming, but enough to remind her she was hungry.

Her gaze settled back on Gil. Someone had to break the uncomfortable quiet. She took the initiative.

"So, tell me, did you always want to be a policeman?"

"More or less. Don't know where it came from. As

a kid I watched old reruns of *Adam-12* and *Dragnet*. Maybe I was brainwashed," he said with a grin. "How about you? Did you always want to be a writer?"

"I kept lots of angst-filled diaries as a teenager, but it wasn't until I was in college that the bug bit." Their drinks arrived and she paused to take a sip of Pinot Grigio. "I had an English assignment to write a four-thousand-word short story. I had two weeks to turn it in. I finished in six hours."

"What was it about?" Gil asked sipping his wine.

"It was a fantasy about a little boy and his dragon. My professor gave me an 'A,' but said the next time to use a subject matter that wasn't from a Peter, Paul, and Mary song."

Gil laughed. His eyes crinkled and his mouth stretched wide across his face. He wasn't good-looking, but Anne liked him.

"What happened then?"

"I took a couple of creative writing classes, did well, and began submitting short stories to magazines. When I received my first check for a sale, I was hooked."

"Ms. Carlyle said you write about vampires and werewolves. How did you ever get interested in that?"

"While in college, I stumbled on a TV station that ran nothing but old movies and such. One of their programs was a soap opera called *Dark Shadows*. The hero was a vampire. It fascinated me." She leaned forward. "The hero's name was Barnabus Collins. Any relation?"

He laughed again. "I don't think so, but if I have a sudden urge to bite someone's neck, I'll let you know."

She took another sip of wine. "Actually, I'm

writing something new. The readers' tastes are always changing, so it pays to look in different directions. I have an idea about a modern day detective who happens to be a good vampire."

"A good vampire?"

Anne laughed. "He only drinks animal blood, but never kills to get it. I'm inventing a secret vampire support group."

Gil's look of amazement amused her.

The waiter arrived and took their food order—Veal Marsala for Gil and Chicken Scaloppine for her. They also ordered more wine.

"If you don't mind me asking, how long have you been divorced?" He stared at his wine glass while swirling the liquid.

"Three years."

"Any children?"

"Two—a boy, fifteen, and a girl, twelve." Anne wasn't sure she wanted to talk about Kenneth. The divorce was still painful. "How about you? Ever taken that walk down the aisle?"

"Twice. The first one lasted ten years. The second about ten minutes."

"Ouch. That must have hurt."

"A silly mistake on both our parts. The separation was amicable six months later."

"Any kids?" she asked.

"Two girls. Caroline's twenty and a sophomore at Florida State. She's wants to be a lawyer. Barbara is eighteen and on her way to Gainesville and the University of Florida in September—career choice still undecided."

Their salads arrived and as Anne spread her napkin

on her lap, she commented, "You know, we haven't discussed the case yet."

"I did promise strictly business, didn't I? I'm sorry." He dug into his salad.

"I'm not, but I do have a request." Anne wanted to heave a deep breath, but didn't. Instead, she stabbed a piece of lettuce with her fork. *Keep it casual. Don't let on how important this is.* "Would it be possible for us to get into the house—Dorie's office specifically? She had other things we'd like to get back."

"What other things?"

"More critiques. We didn't have time to get them all the other night. Plus, we may find the names of her other critique partners. I assume someone owns the house now."

"Apparently, Miss Powell didn't leave a will, which means next of kin will inherit most of the estate once probate and the state are through. I don't see any problem with you getting in." He paused and smiled. "Legally, this time. I'll call the sister tomorrow."

"Thanks." She crunched a bite of lettuce. "Is there anything new with the investigation?"

"Some. We're still waiting on the results of the hard drive search. We have the phone records from both her land line and cell along with the messages on her answering machine and voicemail."

"Anything of a threatening nature?"

"'Fraid not. Not one 'I'm gonna kill you' to be found."

Gil must have been hungry for he finished his salad and pushed the bowl away before raising his glass to sip the deep red wine.

"I am curious about several things, however," he

said.

"Like what?"

"Her answering machine has a message from you asking her to pick up, it was urgent."

Anne stopped eating and sipped, forcing the wine down a suddenly constricted throat, hoping her heart would cease pounding. She'd wondered how long it would take to get to this.

"Yes, I remember that," she answered more calmly than she felt. "I wanted to remind her about the last chapter I sent her for critique. I needed it."

"What was so urgent about it?"

"Not necessarily urgent, just needed." She waved her fork in the air. "I said it in case she was ignoring the phone."

"Did you mention it when she called you at four that afternoon, too?"

Anne shook her head and put her down fork to hide the slight tremor of her fingers, then shoved the bowl away.

"She interrupted me at work, and I kind of brushed her off. She was calling to remind me about the meeting the next day."

"She also called Ms. Carlyle at five o'clock and Ms. Swanson a little after six."

"Probably for the same reason."

"Yet she didn't call Ms. Bennett or Ms. Warren. Kind of strange to call only three out of the five people she was expecting."

Privately, she agreed and once again wondered about the phone in Nancy's possession. *Nancy deleted my number. Who else's?*

Anne took a deep breath and shrugged. "Maybe she

got distracted and forgot. Happens to me all the time."

"Her cell phone records show she received a call from Pam Graham at one o'clock that afternoon."

"Pam Graham is her agent in New York."

"New York? The relay shows the call was placed from Orlando."

Anne looked up in surprise. "Orlando? That's odd. Pam has a reputation of never leaving New York unless it's a dire emergency."

"They spoke for twenty minutes. I've been trying to contact her all afternoon. She isn't answering her cell phone, and all her assistant will say is she's out of town," Gil told her.

"Her assistant? How did you get the number?"

"Found the name in Ms. Powell's address book along with the office and cell numbers."

The waiter whisked their salad bowls away and replaced them with entrees. Gil's probing had lessened her appetite, but she dug into the tender chicken anyway. For once the enticing aroma didn't stimulate her appetite. She noticed her companion had no problem consuming his veal.

After several minutes, Gil resumed the conversation.

"There were also two calls from a man named Paul Proctor—one at two-forty-five and a second at two-forty-nine. He left a message to call him on the last. Any idea who he is?"

"Paul Proctor—never heard of him." At least, she could finally answer something with complete truth.

"No boyfriends?"

"Not to my knowledge. Dorie never spoke about her private life. She was all business and didn't really socialize with the rest of us. Did she call this guy back?"

"No."

Once again, Anne thought of the phone in Nancy's possession.

"Maybe it was a wrong number."

"Yeah, maybe. We called it and the guy denied knowing her, but he sounded nervous."

Anne chewed and thought, not tasting the food. How odd. Two out-of-towners had called Dorie within hours of each other—one her agent who hated leaving New York, and a nervous stranger who left a message. Dorie's answering machine and voicemail both clearly stated her name for the caller. She wondered if Gil had caught it. She lifted her gaze and stared as he finished his meal. *Of course, he did. He's too sharp not to have noticed something like that.*

The conversation on the drive home was mostly about their kids. Gil admitted not seeing his daughters as much as he'd like—they lived in Tampa with his ex and her husband—but he couldn't keep the paternal pride from his voice. Anne bet he'd be a great father, given the chance on a daily basis.

"Thanks for a lovely meal," she said when he walked her to the door.

Her heart skittered against her ribs and her knees shook ever so slightly. Was he going to kiss her goodnight? How should she respond? Keep her lips closed or open? How about her eyes? No, she always closed her eyes. What if he pulled her into an embrace? Should she clasp her arms around his neck or his waist?

The decision was taken from her when Gil leaned down and gently brushed his lips against her cheek.

Even that casual gesture made her nerves jump.

"Thank *you*. I enjoyed the conversation. Maybe we can do it again soon."

*He wants to see me again.* She wet her lips and tried to control the tiny tremors developing in her stomach.

"Yes, I think I'd like that," she responded, her voice barely above a whisper.

He grinned and twisted one of her curls around his finger before releasing it.

"I always did have a preference for redheads. Goodnight, Anne." He turned and walked away.

"Goodnight, Gil."

Anne opened the front door and switched on the living room lights. Out front she heard his car start and drive off. She sat in a chair and tried to calm the little flutters in her stomach.

*Talk about a strange turn of events.*

\*\*\*\*

Anne opened the door and stepped aside to let Jennifer in. As usual, she was the last to arrive.

"Am I late?"

"Not for you," she replied.

"I don't consider twenty minutes all that bad."

"Come on in. The pizzas and the wine are in the living room."

Jen poured Chianti into a glass and slid a slice of pepperoni pizza onto a paper plate. Anne resumed her seat on the floor next to the coffee table and cast an eye on Candace's wine glass. She was on her second serving, but handling it well. Tonight, she'd combed her hair and made an attempt at applying make-up.

"Can we get started? I'm in the middle of chapter

fourteen with two weeks left on deadline. I need to get home and back to work," Nancy said.

"Yeah, Jack's not real thrilled with being stuck taking care of the kids again tonight," Rose told them, helping herself to a third slice.

"I guess I can start by telling you what Gil said when I saw him the other night," Anne began.

"Gil?" Nancy asked.

"Detective Collins," she said.

"The other night?" Candace said with raised eyebrows.

Anne realized too late, she should have chosen her words more carefully. Knowing this bunch, they may never get around to discussing Dorie's murder.

"I'm more interested in the Gil part," Rose commented, grinning.

Anne ignored the warming in her cheeks.

"My interest lies in the other night," Jen replied with a laugh. "Did you sleep with him?"

Rose gasped. "Jennifer! Of course she didn't." Her gaze swiveled to Anne. "Did you?"

The warmth spread over her entire face and crept down her neck. Damn, she hated being fair-skinned.

"No, I did not sleep with him. He dropped by after the funeral to discuss the case and since it was dinnertime, he asked me out. Honestly, it was no big deal."

"Then why are you blushing?" Rose teased.

She didn't have a comeback for that one.

"Did you have a good time?" Candace asked. "He's not married, is he?"

"As a matter of fact, I did. He's a nice guy. I like him and no, he's not married. He's divorced," Anne said trying not to sound defensive.

"How tall are you?" Jen inquired.

"Five-six, why?"

"Don't wear heels the next time. You'll tower over him. He's on the skinny side, too, and his ears stick out, but I did notice his eyes. They're kind of a cross between blue and green," she replied.

"Oh, I don't think his ears stick out all that badly," Rose countered. "But he could use some meat on his bones. A good home cooked meal might be nice."

"Excuse me," Nancy said sharply. "But could we get back to Dorie's murder and discuss Anne's love life, or lack thereof, some other time? I think I said I *am* on deadline."

"Whew, you're testy tonight," Candace drawled.

"In the last week, I've had the grand total of three hours sleep a night. I'm running on fumes at the moment, so let's get this show on the road. Anne, what did Detective Collins—Gil—have to say."

For once Anne blessed Nancy's sharp tongue. She plunged into giving them the information from Gil before anybody could continue the former subject.

"And by the way, he said he'd ask the sister about us retrieving our things from the house. He called this morning and said she had no objections. We can go tomorrow morning," she ended.

"I don't get it. Pam calls Dorie and talks for twenty minutes, but doesn't call me? And what's she doing in Orlando in July? She's a winter person. She hates the heat more than Dorie did," Jen said, frowning and pouring another glass of wine.

"I think this Paul Proctor sounds interesting," Candace murmured.

"Probably a wrong number," Rose said.

"Yeah, but if it's a wrong number, why leave a message when the voicemail says, 'Hi, this is Dorie' or whatever? You just hang up," Jen replied.

"Maybe he just didn't listen," Nancy suggested, reaching for more pizza. "I called Sarah Masterson in Minneapolis. She was shocked to hear about Dorie's death and said she hadn't talked to her since she moved from San Sebastian. For someone who liked to chat as much as Sarah did, she was remarkably brief in her comments. Cut me off after five minutes.

"Careen Holcombe was even briefer. Said Isadora Powell was a nasty, unhappy woman, who probably deserved to be murdered. She said to tell you all hello and she's very happy on the farm raising her kids and vegetables."

"Sarah didn't like Dorie all that much either," Jen said. "I saw Dorie corner her at a chapter meeting once. Sarah looked angry and scared. She didn't come to many meetings after that and moved the following year."

"I'm surprised at Careen," Candace mused. "She was a nice lady with lots of problems. I know her mother was in the last stages of a terminal illness during the conference. She passed away a month later. Careen was burned out for a long time. If I remember correctly, Dorie criticized damned near everything about that conference."

"Remember how we used to call Sarah, 'the contest queen'?" Jen asked with a chuckle.

"She never met a contest she could resist entering. She entered right up until the day she signed her contract," Rose said. "What about the rest of your numbers? Anything interesting?"

Nancy shook her head. "No, they were authors or involved in the publishing world in some way. They all expressed sympathy, but that was it. Rose, what about you?"

Rose wiped her hands on a napkin and pulled a notebook from the depths of her purse, spilling half the contents on the floor. Anne poured another glass of wine, and retrieved two pacifiers, a plastic baggie with cookie crumbs inside, and a condom still wrapped in its foil pouch, then handed the items to her friend.

"A present for Jack?" she asked. *God knows the guy could use one.*

Rose's cheeks colored. "My son, Jason, found it. I shoved it in my purse and forgot about it."

Nancy rolled her eyes while Jen giggled and Candace refilled her wine glass.

Rose flipped the notebook open. "I called Alice Kartchman—Ruby Redd—and gave her the news about Dorie. She said, and I quote, 'Ding, dong, the bitch is dead,' end quote. She also said she hoped it was a painful, gory end. I told her I didn't know about the painful, but could testify to the gory."

"No love lost there," Anne commented.

"I asked why her number was in Dorie's address book and she said that every few months she got crank calls. She thanked me. Now she knew for sure who'd been calling. She only suspected before."

"Except it wasn't an address book, but a cell phone," Nancy said. "Would Dorie stoop to crank calls?"

"If Dorie had revenge on her mind, she'd make sure the recipient knew who was sticking it to them.

She wouldn't wait until you answered, and then hang up," Candace replied.

Rose flipped a page on the notepad. "This one was a little odd. I got the private office number of Oliver Harris."

"Who's Oliver Harris?" Jen asked.

"New York Times bestselling author, Gloria DeMarco's husband," she answered. "He conveyed his sympathies and said he'd pass the information along to his wife. He said they were good friends."

"Well, that's a load of shit," Nancy declared. "Gloria DeMarco is a huge snob. I watched her cut Dorie down at the Writers Association of America national conference one year. Wouldn't give her the time of day. Infuriated Dorie. Why would the husband's private office number be in the cell?"

"That's about it," Rose went on. "The other three were authors, one from the Ft. Myers area. I met her once at a conference, but the rest were strangers. All were sorry to hear about Dorie, but had no answers as to why their names and numbers would be in her address book."

"Jen, what about you? Find anything interesting?" Nancy asked.

Anne sighed as Jennifer dumped her hobo bag out on the sofa and pawed through numerous cosmetics, pens, notepads, loose change, and scraps of paper before finding what she sought.

"Well, four of mine were really dull—just three authors and an editor no longer in the business. None of them admitted to knowing Dorie very well, and when I brought up the address book thing, a couple hemmed and hawed for a few sentences before giving lame explanations. They were obviously lying." She took a deep breath. "However, the last number I called was the home phone of her editor, Claire Chappelle."

"Now, why would that number be in a disposable cell phone?" Anne wondered. "If she had the private number, why not keep it in her regular phone? Something doesn't make sense."

"I know. It struck me as weird, too. I mean most of the people we called barely knew Dorie, so why have their numbers at all?"

"What did she say?" Rose asked.

"Nothing. She didn't answer. I called around two in the afternoon and got a machine. I didn't leave a message. I was going to call back later, but forgot."

"It's probably a good thing you didn't talk to her," Candace said. "I don't think Claire would appreciate knowing her private phone number was in anybody else's hands."

Nancy glanced at her watch and frowned. "Candace, did you get a hold of your people?"

She nodded and drained her glass. "It's like everybody else. I had three published authors, one of whom swore she'd never even met Isadora Powell, and I reached the desk of Roberto Gonzalez at the Bank of the Caymans. I told him I dialed the wrong number."

"So, we were right," Anne said. "Anything else?"

"Yeah. You know, it's funny you should have called Claire Chappelle's private home number, Jen, because I caught Pam Graham's."

"You're kidding! Pam's? Geez, I don't even have that. Of course, she and Dorie have been together for years," Jen replied.

"Well, I called around nine-thirty at night and she

answered. When I found out who I was talking to, I almost had a cow. She wasn't pleased and told me to remove the number from Dorie's address book. Then she hung up with no offers of sympathy."

Something Gil had told her the other night came to Anne's mind. A tiny dart of fear stabbed her in the chest.

"Nancy, do you have the phone with you?"

"Yes."

"Does it show incoming and outgoing calls?"

Nancy pulled the cell from her purse and punched various options.

"Here they are. What do you need?"

"Let's start with incoming. Who called her recently?"

Nancy worked a few buttons and announced, "I'd say most of the incoming are the banks. The last one was the guy who called the day of the funeral."

"How far back do they go?"

"Three months. I guess they're automatically deleted after so much time or so many numbers."

Anne breathed easier. "Try outgoing."

Nancy punched a couple of buttons. "She had several about two weeks before she died and one on the day of her death."

"Call it and see who answers."

Nancy hit redial and waited.

"Hello, this is Nancy Smith. Who's this…Mr. Proctor, you don't know me, but I'm a friend of Isadora Powell's."

Anne heaved a sigh. Her instincts had been right. Dorie called this guy back on the second cell.

"I found your name in her address book and I'm

sorry to have to inform you that...Uh, well, maybe not her address book. Some of her friends made a list of numbers...I see. Yes, I understand. I'm sorry to have bother—" She hung up and frowned. "Whew! Are my ears ever singed!"

"What happened?" Candace asked.

"He said he'd never heard of Isadora Powell, couldn't possibly be in her address book, and to never call him again. Girls, he was furious."

"Paul Proctor, the name on Dorie's answering machine," Candace said. "Wonder why he's so mad."

"Because he's lying," Jen said. "What about the other numbers she called?"

Nancy gazed at the cell for a few seconds. "Nothing special."

"Let me see," Rose asked.

Nancy handed her the phone. They waited while Rose scrolled through the outgoing and incoming numbers several times, a frown on her face.

"There's a pattern," she finally reported.

"What kind of pattern?" Jen questioned.

"All of the outgoing calls are made between the sixth and the fifteenth of the month. The numbers appear to be random." She fiddled with the buttons. "The incoming calls are recorded between the twenty-fifth and the fifth of the month, and the numbers are constant."

"So, what have we got here?" Candace asked, stripping the cold toppings from a slice of pizza and popping them into her mouth.

Anne broke out in a cold sweat and glanced around the group. She made eye contact with Nancy who quickly looked away. Damn, she should have taken this up with Nancy privately.

"I have no idea," Nancy said, rising abruptly. "It's late and I have to get home." She took the cell out of Rose's hand and dropped it into her purse. "What time are we meeting at Dorie's tomorrow?"

Nobody answered. Instead, Candace asked, "What the hell is going on?"

"Match the numbers. The incoming calls are from banks, like the other day, but I have no idea where this is taking us," Rose replied still frowning.

Jen shoved the items she'd emptied from her purse back in and rose. "I'd say it's plain as the nose on your face. Offshore bank accounts, no paper trail, dealing in cash, and a bunch of secret phone numbers to people in the publishing business. Ladies, let's face it. Isadora Powell was into blackmail."

Chapter Seven

Anne's breath stopped somewhere in her throat and her legs wobbled. She was halfway up from her seat on the floor, but sat down heavily again. She didn't dare look at Nancy. She couldn't.

Damn. Who'd have thought Jennifer would be the one to put it all together? Rose sat frozen gripping another slice of pizza, her eyes wide open and staring. Candace drained her wine glass and quickly poured another, the expression on her face thoughtful. Nancy shot a scared glance at Anne.

"Blackmail!" Rose said, finally coming to life. "No, it can't be."

"It makes sense," Candace replied. "Look at the evidence. But why on earth would she be blackmailing Sarah Masterson and Careen Holcombe?"

"I don't know," Nancy said retaking her seat. "But you can be sure neither of them is going to admit to anything and tell us."

"But is everyone not a bank listed in the cell being blackmailed? Nancy, how many numbers were there?" Jen asked, also sitting down again.

"I didn't count—around thirty, I'd guess."

"I think we may be jumping the gun on this," Anne said in a shaky voice. "Blackmail is tough to pull off, especially with thirty potential victims."

"I don't know. If anybody could do it, it would be

Dorie," Rose replied, chewing a bite of pizza. "Look at the outgoing calls. They all took place between the sixth and the fifteenth, right? But the numbers are random."

"Yeah, right," Jen said slowly. "She was calling to remind some of her victims their payments were late."

"I wonder how much she squeezed out of people," Candace murmured. "And why."

Anne closed her eyes and shuddered. The why was so easy. She opened them again and stared at Nancy who kept her gaze centered on the floor and bit her lip. *Nancy? Oh my God. Nancy?*

"Dorie hadn't signed a contract in four years," Candace replied. "She had to pay bills."

"But her books are still in print," Rose protested. "I see them all the time in the bookstores."

"True, but we have no idea how she spent her money," Anne said. "Or if this is even possible. Maybe Ruby Redd is right and Dorie kept this phone for harassment purposes."

"Why would she harass or blackmail her editor and agent? Or Sarah and Careen?" Jen insisted, and then paused. "You gotta hand it to Dorie. The bitch had one hell of a retirement plan."

Nancy rose, a determined look on her face. "We *have* to get into Dorie's office. Screw critiques. We need to look for names and any kind of financial papers she had on file. When we find them, we should burn them. Then call everyone on the list and tell them their secrets are safe—forever." She fluffed the hair from her neck. "I'll delete the numbers and toss the phone."

"Good idea," Anne said. She also rose, willing her legs to stop trembling. "The cell will go inactive when the next round of minutes aren't bought, but why take a chance? Get rid of everything. Besides, sooner or later, Gil or some other detective will discover there's a second phone."

"And it won't take a genius to figure out who has it," Nancy added.

Rose, Jen, and Candace stood, preparing to leave.

*Oh, thank God. Everybody go—go now! I need to be alone. I have to think.*

"I agree," Jen said, a look of fear on her face. "Get rid of it."

"Makes the most sense," Rose concurred in a tight voice.

"Maybe we should turn it over to the police," Candace said. "It gives them thirty new suspects. Just delete Sarah and Careen's numbers."

They looked at each other in silence before Anne spoke.

"No. Delete and destroy."

The women nodded and left. Anne closed the door behind her guests and leaned her forehead on the raised panels. Damn, what else could go wrong? Thank God, Kenneth had agreed to keep the kids another two weeks. She couldn't handle male teenage angst or pre-teen female resentment at the moment. She was surprised she could handle anything. What was that quote? Something about a tangled web and deception. Well, Anne was caught like a fly in the web with the spider sidling ever closer.

Why, oh why, hadn't she privately asked Nancy about the last number called? And who'd have thought Jennifer would hit the nail on the head, calling it blackmail?

She pushed herself away from the door and walked into the living room where she gathered the empty glasses and took them to the kitchen.

*God, we are…I am…in so much trouble.*

Anne filled the sink with water and detergent. The familiar motions and gentle swishing of the soapy water helped calm her frayed nerves.

Gil would find out about the second phone. She knew it. Then there would be hell to pay. Was it possible to reclaim deleted numbers from phones? Did that work like computer hard drives? She had no idea and cursed technology if it were true.

And what could Dorie have possibly had on Sarah or Careen? Sarah sold her first book four years ago, just before the last conference—the one Careen chaired.

She set the rinsed glasses on the drain board, emptied the sink, and wiped her hands on a towel, trying to remember that last conference. The chapter had been awash in a sea of red ink. Careen had been devastated, but the outgoing chapter president refused to place blame. If memory served, Sarah, as vice-president and in charge of workshops, had also come under fire from some members for making poor choices. In many ways, the Southeast Florida chapter was like a dysfunctional family—sniping and petty, but circling the wagons when the situation arose.

Anne picked up the pizza boxes and paper plates from the coffee table, shoving them into a trash bag, then hauled the bag out to the garbage can. She shuddered. The image of Dorie's neighbor doing the same the other night popped into her mind. They'd been lucky. The next time their luck might not hold, especially hers. Gil had told her the police were still interviewing neighbors.

She wondered if any of them would remember seeing her knocking on Dorie's door the night of the murder.

*Oh, my God. What am I going to do?*

Anne leaned against the back door and sobbed.

****

Candace ordered her fourth vodka on the rocks from the bartender. She let her gaze wander around Sam's Bar and Grill. It wasn't quite a dive, but came close, yet she didn't feel out of place as the only woman among approximately fifteen patrons. The décor was heavy on NASCAR and the muted TV's were tuned into a baseball game and SportsCenter on ESPN.

A man at the end of the bar sidled over as the bartender arrived with her drink.

"How about I pay for that, little lady?"

"No, thanks. I pay my own way," she replied taking a generous gulp. Cheap vodka scorched her throat.

The man slid onto the stool next to her. "Well, now, you're a woman I can like." He edged closer. "You play pool?" he asked, thrusting his chin in the direction of the back of the room.

"No, and I don't talk to strange men, so beat it."

"I don't mean no harm." He moved closer, his thigh lightly brushing hers.

Candace sighed, slipped a hand inside her purse, and then briefly flashed her thirty-eight caliber snub-nosed revolver.

"I do. Now go crawl back under your rock and leave me alone."

The guy retreated and returned to the end of the

bar. Out of the corner of her eye she saw him speak to the bartender. She drained the glass, rattling the ice.

"Can you drive?" the bartender asked before refilling her glass.

"Yeah, yeah, I'm fine."

"Well, make this your last, lady. I don't like guns in my place."

"Whatever."

He poured the vodka and left. She played with the glass. Could she drive? Probably not. Several belts of Grey Goose before going to Anne's, the wine there, plus the drinks here, had given her more than a buzz.

*So, the great Isadora Powell had stooped to blackmail. That doesn't surprise me. The miserable bitch loved ruining lives. She got off on making people squirm and suffer. And when her victims were at their lowest, she'd hit 'em again—hard and in the gut.*

She took a swallow and chuckled. *Blackmail. If only others had known and used it to their advantage, turning the tables.* She laughed again. *I wonder how Dorie would have reacted to being blackmailed.*

The guy at the end of the bar shot her a cautious look. *Let him look. Who cares if he thinks I'm nuts? Maybe I am. Insanity is better than reality.*

She drained her glass and slapped a twenty on the bar. "Here, keep the change."

Candace slid off her stool. The room tilted. Not good. She made her way carefully to the door and bounced off the doorjamb. *I'm drunker than I thought.* A quick glance over her shoulder showed the bartender at the other end of the bar. He hadn't seen her inebriated exit.

Outside, she paused to suck in several deep gulps

of humid, July air, and then staggered to her car.

*You can do this, Candace. Home is only two miles away. Just take it easy.*

She jammed the car into gear and hit the accelerator, pulling a left out of the parking lot. The BMW jumped the concrete median strip. Shit, she'd forgotten the curb-sized barrier was there.

The blaring of several horns startled her. She tried to focus her eyes on the rearview mirror and the intersection behind her. God Almighty! Had she run a red light?

Candace eased her foot off the gas pedal and tried to keep the car between the lines. The auto swerved from side to side. She slowed further. Her heart pounded. The buzzing in her ears wiped out all other sounds. Images in front of her blurred, and the urge to sleep made her want to close her eyes.

She screeched to a halt at the next red light, turned right, and heaved a sigh of relief. She was in a residential area now with less traffic. With any luck, she'd be home in five minutes.

A man walking a small dog stepped off the curb in front of her. Candace hit the brakes and screamed, twisting the steering wheel viciously to the left.

"Jesus Christ, lady! You drunk or just stupid?"

She trembled and lurched away. That was Hanover Street—a four way stop.

*Oh, God, please let me get home without running over or killing someone.*

She took her time, stopping at every intersection whether there was a stop sign or not. The speedometer read a mere ten miles per hour

Finally, Candace turned onto her street and sobbed

with relief. She pressed the garage door opener, swung into the driveway, and misjudging the distance drove onto the edge of the lawn. She jerked the car back on course, entered the garage, but before she could find the brake, the BMW whacked Eric's workbench with a resounding thud.

She gripped the steering wheel and cried. What the hell was wrong with her? Maybe she *was* crazy. All it would have taken was one cop to see her erratic drive home. One cop and she'd have been hauled off to jail.

*And I'm a card carrying member of MADD. Imagine being slapped in jail for DUI.*

Candace hiccupped and laughed hysterically.

****

Anne slipped out of bed, pulled on a pair of shorts, and headed downstairs. Three o'clock in the damned morning and she hadn't slept a wink. The word *blackmail* kept repeating itself over and over in her head, the sound louder with each repetition.

She flipped on the kitchen light and grabbed a half-empty bottle of Pinot Grigio from the fridge, then poured a glass. Opening the back door, Anne walked onto the patio and settled into a lounge chair. The hot, humid air wrapped around her like a suffocating blanket. There was no hint of a breeze. She ignored the discomfort, preferring it to tossing and turning.

How deep had Dorie fished in blackmail waters? Was everyone, other than the banks, listed in the phone a donor? How much *had* she squeezed out of her so-called friends? How much a month were they forking over to buy the bitch's silence?

*Nancy's right. We need to concentrate on Dorie's personal stuff, not critiques. God only knows what she's got hiding around the place.* Even a whiff of what they suspected getting back to the police would have them all on the hot seat.

She remembered Nancy's expression tonight when Jen had uttered that bombshell of a word. Fear, not surprise, had been present. *Her number was in the phone, too. Had to be. What on earth could Dorie have had on Nancy?*

Even the others had more than surprised faces. Rose, especially looked stunned. But Rose's lifestyle was much too hectic to raise the eyebrows of a blackmailing critique partner. Although knowing Dorie, she could have found something on everyone.

And Jen, even though she had first brought the subject matter up, had left with fear in her eyes. What did she know—or suspect? If her number was in the phone, why mention blackmail at all? On the other hand, Jen often spoke before thinking. *Is she hiding something, too?*

Of them all, Candace had remained the most stoic. Thoughtful, perhaps, but not scared. No sudden guilty indrawn breaths. Or maybe she just wanted to get home. She'd had her fair share of wine, but Anne figured the vodka bottle had been abused the minute she returned. She shook her head. Candace had a problem, but right now Anne had a bigger one.

In spite of the heat, she shivered. How had she gotten herself into this? One weak moment. That's all it had taken. One lousy moment and she'd put her entire life in someone else's hands. Someone who had no scruples about profiting from the mistake.

Well, the bitch was dead, and Anne couldn't be happier.

She finished her wine and stared into the darkness of the night. Tomorrow. Tomorrow she'd talk to Nancy about the numbers Dorie had listed—and about what her friend was hiding.

*I wonder if we're all hiding something.*

## Chapter Eight

"Who has the key?" Rose asked.

"Gil said he'd meet us here with one. The sister granted us access on the condition that we didn't take the family silver," Anne replied in a dry tone.

She stood on Isadora Powell's front porch along with the rest of the group, except for Jen who was no doubt lost again, but would show up eventually.

"I can understand that. With no will, she stands to inherit a five-hundred-thousand-dollar-house, including all that's in it," Candace murmured.

Anne glanced at her friend. She didn't look too hung over, thank God. Maybe she hadn't hit the vodka last night after all.

"Technically, all those offshore accounts belong to her, too," Rose said.

"*Technically*, the money in them belongs to the people Dorie blackmailed," Nancy commented, moving downwind and lighting a cigarette. "But there's no way in hell we can access the accounts and return it."

"We can't very well tell the sister about them either," Candace said. "Anne's detective will want to know how we knew. Which reminds me, did you get rid of the phone yet?"

Nancy nodded and blew out a stream of smoke. "I drove out west until I found an isolated spot, deleted all the numbers, and tossed it into a canal."

Anne breathed easier. *Thank God. At least we don't have to worry about that anymore.*

And Gil Collins wasn't *her* detective. Geez, one little date and her friends had her marching down the aisle.

She glanced impatiently down the street. No sign of either Jen or Gil. Anne strode down the walkway for a better view.

"Good Lord, Candace, what happened to your car? The bumper's been mashed in."

"Some idiot nailed me in the mall parking lot. Didn't even leave a note. Pissed me off. And I just got it out of the shop last week for that crunch in the rear bumper when I backed into a light pole."

"Did you call the police?" Rose asked. "That's hit and run."

Candace snorted. "Hell, no. And tell them what? This is why I pay a fortune for uninsured motorist coverage."

A black car pulled up behind Candace's and stopped. A nice-looking young man in street clothes got out and approached.

"Good morning. I take it you are the ladies Gil asked me to meet. He's tied up with a case this morning," he said. "My name is Officer Watkins. Which one of you is Mrs. Jamieson?"

"That would be me," Anne said.

"Detective Collins asked me to allow you access."

Anne was both glad and disappointed about Gil's absence. If they found anything, she didn't want to explain in front of the others. On the other hand, she missed seeing him.

While he spoke, Officer Watkins extracted the key

from his pocket and walked to the front door. They all turned at the sound of screeching tires.

Jennifer had arrived. She parked behind the officer's car, her bumper two inches off his and blocking the driveway, then exited, and bounced up the walk.

"Hi. Sorry, I'm late."

"Where did you go this time?" Nancy asked.

"I didn't get lost—honest. I'm simply running late."

"And you must be Mrs. Swanson," the policeman said.

"How did you know?" Jen asked with a smile.

"I would imagine he's been forewarned," Anne said, and then laughed when Jennifer stuck out her tongue.

Officer Watkins opened the door and they all entered. Anne sniffed. The place smelled of dust and having been locked up for a week. It was also dark. Someone had closed the drapes. She walked over and pulled the cord allowing the morning sun to shine in. Dust particles, disturbed by the action, danced in the air.

"There, that's better," she said.

"Before you begin, I have to remind you that your search is limited to the office, and I'll need to document whatever you take with you," he told them.

"No problem," Nancy answered.

"Gil also asked me to give you this." He handed Anne several sheets of paper.

"What's this?"

"Copy of the address book."

"Thanks, I was wondering how we'd contact some

of the critique partners," she said, folding, and then stuffing them into her purse.

Dorie's office was just as they had left it a few nights ago. Only then the fingerprint dust residue hadn't been noticeable in the dark, and once the cops had arrived, they'd been too scared. Now, the gritty, black powder covered every surface.

"Yuck, what a mess," Jen exclaimed.

"Dorie would have a cow if she saw this," Candace said. "She liked everything clean and tidy."

"She was organized?" the officer asked.

"About most things," Anne replied. "She liked being able to get her hands on things and not search for them."

She wondered who in the group caught the irony of her statement. Jen had opened the desk drawers and was busy going through stacks of folders. Rose flipped through files in the cabinets. Candace and Nancy searched the credenza. Nancy looked up catching her eye with a knowing look.

Anne nodded, and then helped Jennifer with the desk. She didn't expect to find anything of value in the top middle drawer, but riffled through the unused notepads. Then something under the last pad caught her eye—a key. *Another house key? Has the same shape and size.*

Without stopping to think, she picked it up and cast a glance over her shoulder at the officer.

"Ah, here's something," Rose said from the file cabinets. "A folder full of critiques."

When the officer turned his head toward Rose, Anne slipped the key into her pocket.

"Good. Any names?" Anne asked.

"Sandra Abbott on this folder. Dorie may have kept separate folders for each partner."

"I know Sandra," Candace said. "She's my online critique partner, too. She worked with Dorie and another lady."

"Put anything we may need on top of the cabinet by the door," Anne suggested. "That way, Officer Watkins can make a list."

The policeman smiled and pulled a notebook from his pocket. Rose gave him the folder and returned to her task.

Candace yanked a folder from the back of the middle left desk drawer and flipped through it.

"Find anything?" Anne asked.

"No, not really."

It wasn't the words so much as the tone of voice Candace used that had Anne looking at her. Blocking the officer's view with her body, she pointed to a folder and mouthed the words "bank statements and correspondence".

Anne glanced at Nancy and Jen. Nancy sat on the floor looking through folders. Jen shot a look at the officer writing in his notebook, and nodded. If anybody could create a diversion, it was Jennifer.

"I'm thirsty. Would anybody like a glass of water?" Jen asked.

"I'd love one," Anne replied in a hearty voice.

"No, thanks," Nancy said. Jen nudged her with a foot. "Uh, on second thought, yeah, I am a little dry." She raised a questioning eyebrow.

Rose apparently noticed the by-play and said, "That's a good idea."

"Make it five," Candace chimed in.

"Officer, is it all right if I go down to the kitchen and get us something to drink?" Jen asked with a bright smile. "I promise not to touch anything. Can I get you something, too?"

He hesitated. The request would leave Officer Watkins with a dilemma—let Jen go downstairs by herself, or go with her and leave the rest of them unsupervised.

"I should keep my eyes on all of you. Not because I think you'll steal something, but because if something does show up missing, the police department may be liable."

"Oh, come on, Officer," Jen replied in a teasing tone. "I'm wearing shorts and a tank top. Where would I hide anything? I don't have that much cleavage."

Anne and the women laughed when his cheeks turned pink and he hastily answered, "Water would be fine."

"Six waters, coming up," Jen said cheerfully. Turning she disappeared through the door.

Anne continued to work and glanced at her watch every couple of seconds for the next two minutes.

Finally, Jen's voice called out. "Oh, officer, please, could you help. I can't carry all of them. Oh, nuts!"

The sound of water bottles hitting and bouncing down the steps and off the wall produced the desired effect. Officer Watkins immediately left the room to assist. Moving fast, Candace whipped the papers from the file, folded them in half, and shoved them into the bottom of her large satchel purse, then crammed the empty file into the back of the drawer.

Meanwhile, Jen's continuous chatter floated up the stairs.

"I am *so* clumsy. Thank you. Oh, there's one over by the front door. I must have short arms or something, because I have a problem carrying things. I always had to have a backpack when I was in school. Any more than two or three books ended up on the floor. And of course, all the kids teased me. Everyone thought I was a klutz. But I'm not. I don't count the time when I fell off the stage during my senior class play. I got all confused with the lights, and *of course*, I was nervous. Did you ever do any acting in high school? No, how silly, you probably played football or some other sport, didn't you?"

Jen and Officer Watkins re-entered the room. Anne bit her lip to keep from laughing at the look on the policeman's face. His eyes held that glazed look she'd often seen from people who'd been "Jenniferized." He also carried all six bottles of water with no problem.

"Oh, thank you so much," Jen said, taking them from his hands and distributing. She twisted the cap off and drank. "Ah, that hit the spot."

Nancy sighed and winked at Anne, then returned to the folders in her lap. Candace grinned before resuming her task. Anne abandoned the desk for the bookshelves.

"You know, this really is an eclectic collection. For someone who hated erotic romance, she has two of Ruby Redd's books. And I only see three historicals, including yours, Nancy. I've never heard of the other two authors."

"She hated erotica, and didn't care for anything historical," Nancy said with a catch in her voice. "Called them boring."

"I wouldn't call any of your work boring," Rose answered. "I enjoy reading them. Your heroines are

119

always women who defy conventions of the day and do gutsy things. Kind of like Jo in *Little Women*."

"Or any of Jane Austen's heroines," Candace added. "They tried to follow the rules of society, but also managed to let their opinions be known."

"Thank you for speaking of me in the same sentence with Louisa May Alcott and Jane Austen," Nancy said with a laugh. "Maybe in a hundred years, I'll be a literary icon and have my books considered classics."

"I still can't understand why Dorie published under a pseudonym," Rose said.

"Because Irina Petrovsky on the cover just doesn't sound as glamorous," Anne told her. "Her editor probably suggested the change. It's done all the time."

"Look at Annalee Collier. Her real name is Anna Maria Sarduccinelli. She was told it was too ethnic and hard to pronounce," Candace replied.

"Dorie selected her own name," Jen said, her head bent over a file drawer.

"How do you know that?" Rose asked.

"I looked it up."

"Looked what up?" Candace queried with a puzzled expression.

"The name Isadora. It's a combination of the Egyptian goddess, Isis, and the Greek 'doron', which means gift. In other words, 'gift of the gods'. And Powell is spelled very much like the word 'power'. Who else but Dorie would come up with such a name?"

Everybody ceased working and stared at Jen.

"Good Lord, you actually looked it up?" Anne said.

"Sure. Names can be very important, especially to

an author. It has to be easy for the public to remember. Isadora Powell flows and has strength. I even researched 'Irina.' It's also of Greek origin and means 'peace'—not a word I'd ever connect with Dorie. I have no idea what Petrovsky means," Jen replied with a smile. "It's probably Russian for 'bitch'."

"You know, for friends, you guys don't sound as though you liked her very much," Officer Watkins commented.

Anne stared as he wrote in his notebook. She'd forgotten he was in the room.

"Dorie wasn't always the nicest person. She could often be very sharp with her criticism and had no problem speaking her mind," she told him. "But we all understood that was Dorie and accepted it." It was as diplomatic as she could get.

"Do you like all of your friends all the time?" Candace asked, placing a folder on the cabinet for the policeman to record.

"No, but I'm not sure a bunch of guys would call a deceased friend a bastard. It must be a woman thing," he said.

"I'll ignore the obvious sexist remark and just say that women think and speak differently than men," Rose stated.

Anne gave up on the bookshelves even though it was the perfect place to hide secret papers. Searching through all the books would have looked odd. They were supposed to be looking for critiques and names of partners.

She glanced at her watch. They'd been in Dorie's office a little over an hour and had a respectable pile of folders, plus what Candace had hidden. She was about to suggest leaving when Nancy caught her eye.

The look on her face said she'd found something. She held several sheets of paper in her hand. Nancy shot a quick glance at the policeman, and then back to her.

Anne understood the problem. Candace's purse was full and the rest of their handbags were sitting out of the way on top of the file cabinets—right next to where Officer Watkins stood. She had no idea what Nancy had discovered, but knew it had to leave the house.

Nancy stood and picked up a previously discarded folder. She set it on the credenza and turned her back to the officer. Anne watched as she opened the folder and slipped the new papers on the bottom.

"Here's another critique," Nancy said, presenting it to the man.

Anne held her breath while he opened the folder to note the name inside. She didn't know what had been added, but the chances were Watkins wouldn't know either. Nancy gambled and it paid off. He handed the folder back with a smile.

"Well, I think we've found about all we're going to find," Anne said in a false, upbeat tone. "Thank you so much for letting us in."

"Hey, no problem. Gil said you might be able to lend a hand with the investigation. It saves us some legwork."

They trouped downstairs and out onto the porch where the policeman locked the door and pocketed the key.

"Have a good day, ladies," he said walking to his car.

"You, too," Anne replied, waving as he drove away. "What did you find?" she asked Nancy when the car was out of sight.

"A whole bunch of papers with initials, numbers, and dates on them. What about you, Candace?" she questioned.

"Bank statements and personal correspondence. I didn't get a chance to look at the statements, but the correspondence looked interesting." She withdrew the papers from her purse and flipped through them. "Whew, annotated rejection letters. Not very nice and all in the last three years."

"I suggest we split up the papers, like we did the phone numbers, and research them," Anne said.

"Works for me. Candace, since she's your critique partner, too, why don't you take Sandra Abbott?" Rose said. "I can take a couple of others."

"Dorie was in a bunch of critique groups. I'll take a few," Anne told her. Rose handed over one of the folders, and then distributed more to the others, while she removed the papers given to her by the officer. "I'll check this for any matching numbers from the Southeast Florida roster. Nancy, could you call Claire Chappelle? She might divulge information to you about Dorie's latest book. Jen, you take Pam Graham since she's your agent, too."

"Gotcha. I'll pretend I'm hurt because she didn't call me when she was in Orlando."

"Don't get too cutesy-pooh with things," Rose warned and looked at her watch. "Oh, geez, I've gotta go. I'm making up some of the time I lost from the funeral at work this afternoon. Anne, why don't you invite Detective Collins over for a nice home cooked meal and see what you can pry out of him?"

Jen snickered and Candace grinned. Nancy rolled her eyes. Warmth rose from Anne's neck to her cheeks.

"Yeah, I'd kinda like to see what she can pry out of him, too," Jen said.

"Jennifer, Rose is referring to information," she replied stiffly. Honestly, sometimes her friends drove her nuts.

"Oh, of course," Candace chimed in. "What else?"

Anne's face burned hotter.

"I think we've embarrassed Anne enough," Nancy said. "On the other hand, you are the one he prefers, so I guess it's up to you to deal with him."

"Very well, I'll call. Now, if you'll excuse me, I have a proposal to write." She turned on her heel and stalked to her car.

\*\*\*\*

Anne picked up the phone, stared at it, and then set it back in the holder on the counter. Instead of calling Gil Collins, she poured another glass of iced tea and grabbed a napkin from the drawer. She had no idea what to say. A lot of years had passed since she'd called a man, especially one she found attractive.

"Oh, grow up," she muttered. "You're an adult and don't need some high school excuse to call a male."

She added a couple of gingersnaps to the napkin and nibbled. Okay, she was nervous. She could admit that.

*It's not like I'm asking him to a sleepover*. The direction her mind took startled her. *Now where did* that *come from?*

Oh, good grief, she had to get a grip. Maybe she should write down what to say. No, that was a dumb idea. She'd sound stiff. Anne hated that word. Ken had used it in one of their arguments just before the divorce. He'd called her a stiff, uncompromising robot. It still hurt.

She finished the cookies and gulped the last of the tea, then rose and grabbed the phone again.

*Just do it.*

Anne punched in the first five numbers, paused, and disconnected. According to the business card lying in front of her, this was his work number. He'd scribbled his private number on the back. Maybe she should use that one.

Inhaling a deep breath, she dialed before her nerve failed.

"Hello, this is Gil. I can't answer the phone right now. Leave your name, number, and a brief message and I'll get back to you as soon as I can. Thanks."

Anne let out a huge sigh of relief—voicemail, thank God. The start message beep had Anne tongue-tied for a moment.

"Uh, yes, uh, Gil, this is Anne Jamieson and I'm just calling to thank you for getting us into Dorie's house today. Officer Watkins was very nice and helpful. Oh, and please thank Dorie's sister for allowing us to take our critiques. And, ah, oh, thank you for the address book. Maybe we can get together later this week to discuss…" The ending beep cut her off.

*Damn, I hate voicemail. I babble worse than Jen.*

She hung up and tossed the phone onto the counter with a clatter. Now what? She sat at the kitchen table and pulled the papers with the phone numbers from her purse. A quick scan revealed Anne had never heard of most of the people listed.

Shrugging, she picked up her cell and dialed the number next to the name "Aristotle's".

"Aristotle's Day Spa and Salon, may I help you?"

"Ah, yes, I'm a friend of Isadora Powell's and she recommended you a few months ago," Anne began.

"Oh, yes, we were so sorry to hear about her death. She was in for the usual massage and herbal wrap two days before she died. So tragic," the woman on the other end said.

"Yes, it is. Ms. Powell often sang your salon's praises."

"Well, wasn't that sweet of her? She recommended us to a lot of her friends. Our masseuse, Inga, cried when that nice Mrs. Holcombe moved."

Anne digested this news silently. Careen splurged on massages at a trendy day spa? The woman often complained about her lack of funds.

"Now, when would you like to come in and what would you like us to do?"

Anne thought quickly. Maybe a chat with Inga was in the cards. People like Careen often talked about personal things to hairstylists and masseuses without realizing there was no expectation of confidentiality.

"As soon as I can. Could I book an appointment with Inga? Dorie said she was the best and I can use a facial, too."

"Let's see, Inga's booked solid tomorrow, but she can take you at three-thirty on Wednesday. And let me check Denise…yes, she's free to work on your face at four-thirty. Is that convenient?"

"Yes, that's fine."

"And your name, ma'am?"

"Anne Jamieson."

"Excellent, Ms. Jamieson. Have a good day, and we'll see you on Wednesday."

"Thank you. Oh, did Miss Powell also get her nails done at Aristotle's? They always looked so nice."

"Oh, yes. We did her from top to bottom, so to speak," the woman laughed.

Anne forced a laugh, too. "Well, thank you and I'll see you in a couple of days."

She hung up and drummed her fingers on the table. Careen and Dorie frequenting the same spa? Coincidence or coercion? Did Dorie bribe the masseuse for information? The bitch couldn't have been blackmailing everybody in San Sebastian.

On an impulse, Anne called Rose's cell.

"How would you like a trip to the hair salon?" she asked when Rose answered.

"What?"

"Dorie was a regular at Aristotle's over on Ocean Drive. So was Careen. There must be a connection. I think Dorie was buying information. I've made an appointment on Wednesday for a massage."

"I can't afford a hundred and fifty dollars for a haircut," Rose said. "Jack'll kill me."

"Then get a manicure."

"I can't afford that either."

"My treat. Look, I can't talk to everybody. Please, just call the salon and tell them you're a friend of mine and want to come in at the same time on Wednesday."

"Oh, all right. Look, can we talk later? My desk is piled to the ceiling with insurance claims."

Anne said goodbye and hung up, then called Jen.

"Jen, want to help me with something?"

"Sure, what?"

She told Jen about Aristotle's. "Ask for Dorie's stylist and see what you can find out."

"Wow, like a real detective? Undercover? Sounds like fun. Count me in. I could use a trim and a few new highlights. When do we do this?"

Anne told her. "And don't be late."

"I won't get lost, I promise. Personal gratification is involved."

She hung up and sighed, hoping Jen would shut up long enough to let the stylist get a word in edgewise. Candace might have been a better choice, but Anne didn't trust the vodka factor. And Nancy had bluntly said she wasn't available for anything for the next two days.

The kitchen phone rang, startling her. Very few calls came through on it anymore. Everybody had cells, so Anne assumed the caller was a telemarketer and ignored it. The answering machine picked up.

"Hello, you've reached 555-1234. Please leave a message and I'll get back to you as soon as possible. Thank you."

"Hello, Anne. This is Gil returning your call. I'm not…"

She scrambled to reach the phone before he hung up. She'd forgotten she'd called him.

"Gil? It's me."

"Hi. Just returning your call."

Anne ran a hand through her curls and swallowed.

"Ah, yes. I just wanted to thank you for getting us into Dorie's house and office this morning. If you see her sister, please thank her, too."

"Glad I could help. Did you find anything useful?"

"Some critiques and names. We split them up.

Thanks for the copy of the address book, too."

Silence stretched between them. *Say something, dummy! Invite him to dinner.*

"Uh, Gil, I was wondering…"

"Would you like…"

They spoke simultaneously, and then laughed.

"Sorry. Ladies first."

"I was wondering if you'd be interested in a home cooked meal. The kids are still at their father's and we wouldn't be interrupted." Anne immediately wanted to smack herself in the head. Now why had she said that? It sounded like a come on.

"I haven't had good home cooking in years. Name the day and the time."

"Are you free tonight—say seven-thirty?"

"I'll be there. I'll bring the wine. What are we having?"

Anne said the first thing that popped into her mind. "Steaks, baked potatoes, and salad. Okay?"

"I'm hungry already. See you at seven-thirty."

They hung up and she stared at the phone in consternation. Why steaks? She didn't have any. Now, she had to go to the grocery. And, my God, the house was a mess. Should she change the sheets on her bed?

*Why, you idiot? You're not going to sleep with him. Get a grip.*

Anne slammed the phone back into the holder and swept the clutter from the counter top into a drawer. Anticipation hummed along her nerves. Another date with Gil. She'd use the dining room, of course, and the good china. Would candlelight be too much? Probably. After all, both of them sought information from each other.

*Or are we drifting toward something more personal?*

She rummaged through the sideboard, extracting a damask tablecloth and silver candlesticks. Even if she didn't light them, they would look good. And a centerpiece—she needed a centerpiece. Maybe she could find something simple, but elegant at the grocery. How about her grandmother's crystal? Definitely—Gil was bringing wine. Sterling instead of stainless? Why not?

Anne dashed around the house like a woman possessed—or one who was getting her feet wet with dating again.

Just in case, she changed the sheets.

Chapter Nine

Anne adjusted a flower in the centerpiece and paced to the mirror above the sideboard. Staring at her reflection, she fluffed her hair. She needed to remind herself this was business.

*Yeah, right. That's why I changed the sheets and splurged on New York strips.*

The doorbell rang. Anne inhaled several deep breaths, then walked on less than steady legs into the foyer and opened the door to Gil, cradling a bottle of red wine in his arms.

"Hi. Am I late?"

Anne waved him in. "Not at all." She accepted the wine, peering at the label. "This is excellent. I had you pegged as a beer and bourbon kind of guy. Come on in. Have a seat." She led him into the living room.

He laughed. "I can be, but you don't seem like a beer and bourbon woman. Shall I open it?"

"By all means. Corkscrew's in the kitchen."

Her nerves hummed with a pleasant vibration as he followed her. She found the corkscrew and handed it to him, then watched as he popped the cork with ease.

"Have a seat." She motioned toward the breakfast bar with a plate of cheese and crackers sitting on it. "Are your hungry?"

"A bit. I skipped lunch."

"In that case, let me get dinner started."

"No hurry. I can hang on a while longer."

Anne laughed. "Can't have a policeman fainting from hunger on my kitchen floor."

He laughed with her. The action crinkled the corners of his eyes. She liked hearing a man's laughter in the house again.

"So, how was your day?" he asked, taking a seat and munching on a chunk of cheddar.

She couldn't help thinking. Kenneth used to do the same thing, only minus the wine. He drank scotch. But she'd accepted that part of her life was over. Maybe this *was* a new beginning. *About time*.

She also nibbled on a morsel of cheese before answering. "Rather dull. As I said when you called, we got some information, but to tell you the truth, I don't think it'll turn up anything new. Critiquers don't often socialize, especially online partners."

"Explain to me this critique thing again. You sit around and criticize each other's work?"

Anne pulled the steaks from the fridge along with the previously tossed salad and homemade Italian dressing.

"More or less. We try to be constructive, but occasionally, you just have to say, 'hey, this sucks' or words to that effect." She slapped the steaks onto a plate and fired up the indoor grill.

"Bet that can lead to hard feelings."

"Sometimes. It's never easy to hear you have an ugly baby."

He laughed again. "I guess I never thought of it in those terms. And Isadora Powell was your critique partner?"

Anne washed the potatoes, pierced the skins with a

paring knife, and placed them in the microwave.

"Yes. One of several."

"Was she critical of other's work?"

She poured the dressing over the salad. "Dorie didn't mince words. If she thought you weren't giving her your best work, she let you know. And if it was your best work, but still bad, her comments hurt."

"Must have made people angry."

"Dorie was a highly critical person, especially with romantic suspense. I often wondered if she feared other people's success. When her claws came out, she could be nasty."

"Was she ever nasty to you? Where are the wine glasses?" Gil asked.

To avoid answering his pointed question, Anne walked into the dining room and retrieved them from the hutch. He was interrogating her and she didn't like it. She held one of the glasses up to the light. Damn. Water spots. How long had it been since she'd used them? *Too long.*

Back in the kitchen, she washed and dried the spots away before setting them on the countertop. Gil poured. The soft gurgling always raised her expectations of a good meal. He smiled and raised his glass in salute before sipping.

She answered his salute and tasted an excellent Cabernet Sauvignon. "Hmm, delicious. The grill's almost ready. How do you like your steak cooked?"

"Medium rare works for me. Shall I set the salad out?" At her nod, he set his glass down and carried the bowl into the dining room, then returned. "You still haven't answered my question. Was Isadora Powell ever highly critical of your work?"

"Am I being interrogated?"

"Just a little."

"All right, but turnabout's fair play. I expect to hear about the investigation from you, too."

"Fair enough." He sipped his wine and raised his eyebrows.

She answered the question. "Not usually. I'm published and know the finer details of writing a good book. She saved her barbs for unpublished writers. Nancy's also published, so our group wasn't too contentious. Dorie critiqued with another group of Southeast Florida members with less stellar results. She went through a lot of partners."

Anne slid the steaks onto the grill and listened to the sizzle. She loved that sound.

"I gather none of you liked the deceased very much."

"When Dorie moved to San Sebastian ten or twelve years ago, she was nice. A few months later, after signing her first contract, she changed. Pressure to do better than the previous book is high. Making the New York Times bestseller list with your first endeavor is hard to top."

She only lied a little. Dorie had never been nice. Less abrasive was a better phrase. And she did that to worm her way into the inner circle of published authors from the chapter.

The microwave dinged, and using an oven mitt, she set the baked potatoes on a plate with individual cups of sour cream, butter, and fresh-chopped chives.

"Is there anything I can do to help?" Gil asked.

"You can take the wine and the potatoes into the dining room. I'll turn the steaks and join you in less than five minutes."

He did as she asked while Anne flipped the steaks. The raw meat hitting the hot grill rendered another angry hissing. The smell made her mouth water. It had been a long time since she'd cooked *good* steak.

*And why haven't I? What's wrong with treating myself to a good meal once in a while? Why settle for meatloaf when I can afford steak every couple of weeks? When did I become so boring?*

Two minutes later, she forked the meat onto the platter and presented it with a flourish. "Your food, sir."

He helped himself to the nearest steak and grinned. "I like this restaurant. Prompt service, fantastic food, and a beautiful waitress."

Familiar warmth spread from Anne's neck to her cheeks. "You don't know about the food yet," she admonished.

He cut off a piece of meat and slid it into his mouth. She held her breath.

"Yes, I do, and I was right. This is wonderful."

Anne relaxed. For several minutes, both of them concentrated on eating. She savored the steak; glad to see she hadn't lost her touch.

"So, how goes your end of the investigation?" she asked. "Come up with anything new?"

"It's slow, but progressing."

Anne waited patiently for him to continue, and when he didn't said, "And?"

He put down his silverware and sipped his wine, then said, "We finally tracked down the maid. She said Ms. Powell called the day before the murder requesting a thorough cleaning. The maid had a key, and standing instructions to enter and leave through the back door.

You called it. Her orders were to clean the downstairs only. She saw the closed office door and didn't go up. The maid cleaned, grabbed her check off the kitchen counter, and left, relocking the door."

"So, she didn't see or hear anything. Of course, Dorie had been dead for several hours. What about the neighbors?"

"The neighbors directly across the street left for Chicago early in the morning, so we haven't talked to them yet. The neighbor to the north said she saw a man leaving Ms. Powell's around six in the evening."

"A man?" Anne stopped eating and stared.

"He said the man acted angry. Slammed his car door and revved the engine before putting the pedal to the metal."

Anne ate a bite of salad. A man? Well, Dorie's blackmail web might not be restricted to authors and women. At least none of the neighbors had seen *her* at the front door that night.

"That all?" she asked.

Gil shrugged. "The neighbor in back saw nothing. Didn't even know there'd been a murder until his wife noticed all the cops. The couple to the south said she had a lot of cars in and out of the driveway, but didn't pay any attention. And some guy walking his dog up the street says a dark-colored car was parked near the corner the night of the murder. The only reason he remembered was because the windows were cracked open a few inches for a dog inside. The dog barked as he passed."

"Car could have belonged to anybody."

"I agree." Gil finished his wine and poured them each another glass, then resumed eating. "We've got her bank records. She lived off royalties and some sound investments. Nothing suspicious there."

*Of course not. All the real money was offshore.*

"She also had a post office box," he said.

Anne recalled Jen's comments about Dorie entering contests illegally. "Lots of writers have boxes so their fans can write. I do. So does Nancy. I haven't had any problems with weirdoes, but I know of several well-known authors who've been stalked."

Gil swirled the contents of his glass. "Did you know Isadora Powell was not her real name?"

"Yes. We found out at the funeral. Her sister told us." She finished the last of her steak and pushed her plate away. "Surprised us."

"Surprised her sister when we notified her, too. She had no idea Irina and Isadora were the same person. We're checking for the financials of Irina Petrovsky. According to the sister, she may have used both names, which I find suspicious. What was she hiding?"

A light sweat broke out on Anne's forehead. She mopped it unobtrusively with her napkin. The second cell phone was probably listed under her real name. Gil would uncover that morsel of information soon. Damn, they should have thought of this.

"Probably money from the IRS," she answered. "Dorie hated parting with a dime."

Gil grinned. "I can understand that. We're going through background on her now. Her sister also clued us in on Ms. Powell's ex-husband."

Anne choked on her wine and set the glass on the table. She coughed for several seconds to clear her throat.

"Ex-husband! Dorie never mentioned anything

about an ex-husband."

"Got divorced before moving here. Can you guess the ex-husband's name?"

Confused by the question, it took Anne a few seconds to make any connection. Then a bulb lit.

"The guy on the answering machine? Paul Something-or-other?"

"Proctor, and bingo."

"But he said he'd never heard of Isadora Powell."

"He hadn't. According to him, he only knew her as Irina Petrovsky."

"Wait a minute," she said. "You said a neighbor saw a man leaving her house."

"We called the number he left on the answering machine. He says he was nowhere near San Sebastian, but in St. Louis. The cell tower, however, says Melbourne, Florida. We're trying to get his cell records to see if he's telling the truth. He hasn't been seen at his home in over a week. And there's no Paul Proctor registered at any hotel in this area. We're still looking for him. I'd like to have a little chat."

Anne rose to clear the table. Gil helped carry the dishes into the kitchen and offered to assist in any clean up.

She refused. "I'll only be a minute. Make yourself at home."

Alone, she filled the dishwasher and placed the silver in the sink. She reentered the living room to find Gil gazing at the pictures on a bookshelf.

"Are these your kids?" he asked, holding a photo in an ornate frame.

"Yes. That's Ken, Jr., and Lisa. It was taken about five years ago when we were on a ski vacation in

Montana."

"I've never skied. Do you like it?"

"Not really, but my husband loved it. He was originally from New England and never did get used to a lack of winter in Florida."

Gil replaced the picture and picked up another. "I take it this is your ex." He gazed at the likeness. "He's a handsome man."

"Yes, he is."

She'd forgotten about that photo. It had been taken a few months before Kenneth had walked out. The only reason she'd kept the damned thing was because Lisa had pitched a fit when she'd tried to remove it.

Gil replaced the frame and glanced at his watch. "I hate to eat and run, but I have a full schedule the next couple of days. I'll be out of town."

"But it's only nine-thirty."

"I know, and I apologize." He turned from the bookcase and clasped her shoulders lightly, then brushed his lips across hers. "Maybe next time. Thank you for a terrific dinner. I'll be in touch."

He headed for the front door. Anne trailed behind at a loss for words.

"Goodnight, and thanks for coming," she called out as he walked to his car.

He turned, waved, and smiled, then slid behind the wheel and left.

She closed the door and didn't know whether to curse or cry. Anne spent the next half an hour scrubbing down the indoor grill.

*I'm an idiot. I should have dumped that stupid picture in a drawer. I'm so used to the damned thing being there, I didn't see it.*

She pushed the Mr. Tuffie pad up and down the grill with hard strokes. Rule number one of dating after a divorce—keep all photographic references of the ex-husband out of sight.

*Now Gil probably thinks I'm unable to let go of Kenneth.*

Anne slowed her motions and rinsed the grill, then wiped it dry before replacing it. She walked into the dining room and swept the crumbs from the tablecloth. Her anger transferred to Gil.

Men. Here she went to all the trouble of setting a lovely table and he'd never once mentioned the centerpiece or the china or the damned candlesticks.

Anne stomped upstairs, brushed her teeth, and climbed into bed. She pulled the crisp, clean sheet up to her chin and sighed. *Damn all men anyway.*

\*\*\*\*

Candace opened her eyes, rolled over, and fell off the sofa. Coming to full consciousness wedged between the sofa and the coffee table, she crawled away on her hands and knees, finally staggering to her feet. An empty vodka bottle and glass lay on the floor.

What time was it? A slightly unfocused glance at the clock on the DVR receiver answered the question—two-forty. The sunlight streaming through the window told her it was afternoon. She ran a shaky hand through her tangled hair and plopped her fanny on the couch where she gave in to misery and cried.

The last thing Candace clearly remembered was rifling through Dorie's office yesterday morning. The first thing she'd done upon arriving home had been to grab the vodka bottle. Candace remembered little from the night before—another sleazy bar, rebuffing another man by flashing her gun, but that was all.

She dried her tears with her hands and rose. Only then did she notice her clothing—a black, spandex miniskirt and a low-cut, form-fitting red top. Her red high-heeled sandals lay next to the sofa. No wonder she was fighting off strange men in bars.

*I look like a hooker. I have to stop this.*

Now seemed like a good time to start. Candace gathered her courage and as many liquor bottles from the bar as she could carry, then marched into the kitchen. Setting them on the counter, she turned and immediately stepped into a puddle of liquid. The smell and color told her it was urine.

Oh, my God! Bruno. Where was Bruno?

"Bruno, here, boy. Come to Mama."

The little multi-colored Shih-Tzu trotted into the room, then stopped and hung his head at the sight of his owner standing in his mess.

Candace rushed to him and scooped him into her arms.

"It's all right, baby. It's not your fault. I'm a bad mama."

She buried her face in his shaggy coat and tried not to cry again. Poor dog. He depended on her for everything and she'd let him down. When had she last fed him? She didn't remember.

Kissing the top of his head, she put him back on the floor and filled his dishes with food and fresh water. While he ate, she cleaned up the puddle, and then resumed her trek with bottles from the bar.

With determination, she poured every last drop of alcohol in the house down the kitchen sink.

*And no more bars. I'll stay home and drink soda or*

*water. I'll read, watch old movies, anything to keep my mind occupied.*

A hot shower and change of clothing made her feel better. God knows when she last ate, so Candace popped a frozen dinner into the microwave and made a salad. It was early, but she needed food.

She removed the steaming Chicken Francaise from the oven when the doorbell rang. She opened up and stared at a policeman.

"Yes, officer?"

"Ah, yes, ma'am, my name is Officer Shelton and I wondered if I could come in and speak to you for a moment."

Her heart thudded in slow, heavy beats and she sucked in a short, hard breath. This was it. What she feared. "Of…of course, is something wrong? Has something happened to one of my children?"

"No, nothing like that, ma'am. Are you Candace Warren?"

"Yes. Please, have a seat." She gestured toward the living room where he sat in a chair and she on the sofa. "What's this all about?"

"Last night there was a disturbance at The Corner Bar. It's located over on Palmdale. Are you familiar with it?"

Damn, was that the place she'd been last night? And what about the night before? No, that bar had been really sleazy, and on the way home, she'd almost hit that guy walking his dog. Or was that another night. God, the nights blended together, overlapping and confusing her.

"No, can't say that I am. Why?"

"A female patron got drunk and when a male

customer tried to pick her up, she pulled a gun on him."

"Good heavens! What's this got to do with me?"

"The woman paid with a credit card a few minutes earlier, but left it behind. She split after the gun incident. The name on the card was Candace Warren. The bartender chased after the lady, but she was pulling out of the parking lot. He described the car as light in color, but that was all. We checked DMV and got this address."

Oh, shit! She didn't remember—at least not entirely. This wasn't about a forgotten credit card, but the gun.

"My credit card?" Candace rose and ruffled through her purse sitting on the hall table. "Oh, no! It's gone. I was running errands most of yesterday morning. Let's see, where was I last? Oh, that super discount store over on State Road 116, what's its name…Lotta Stuff. I must have left it there. I guess someone picked it up."

"Are you sure you weren't at The Corner Bar last night?" the officer said.

Candace's stomach clenched and sweat popped out on her forehead. She returned to her seat, trying to quell her trembling extremities.

She tried, but failed to look him in the eye. "No, I was right here all night. I can't prove it, of course. I was alone."

The officer heaved a sigh, and then rose. Candace rose with him, escorting him to the door.

"If I were you, ma'am, I'd call the credit card company and get that card canceled."

"Yes, I'll do that right away. Luckily, it's not one I use too often."

He paused and gave her a hard stare. "Mrs. Warren, we both know you didn't leave your credit card at a discount store. Consider this a warning. Don't flash guns or drive drunk again." He opened the door and left.

She closed the door behind the policeman and sagged against it. That was close. The cop didn't believe her for a minute, but had gotten his point across. She'd been warned.

Candace returned to her cooling dinner and pushed the plate away. She wanted a drink. Her gaze slid to the empty bottles still on the counter. The car keys were on the hall table next to her purse. Roscoe's wasn't that far away. It was a nice bar, not a dive.

She jumped to her feet and yanked a can of soda from the fridge, popped the top, then took a long deep swallow. Candace resumed her seat, pulled the food back in front of her, and ate.

Tonight she'd keep busy phoning critique partners and talking about Dorie. And she'd make it up to Bruno by taking him for a walk.

She kept her word. She made the calls, jotted notes, and walked Bruno's legs off. The exercise helped, but she couldn't control the tremors in her hands and knees.

Upstairs, Candace pawed through her jewelry box until finding the little gold cross with the broken chain. She crawled into bed with it clutched in her hand, the sharp edges digging into her flesh the way they had at Dorie's that day. She shook from head to foot.

*God, give me strength. I can't hold on much longer.*

Candace clasped Bruno and sobbed into his coat.

****

Anne met Jen and Rose on the corner near Aristotle's Salon and Spa. For once Jen was on time.

"Okay, I'm getting the massage and the facial. Rose you're having a manicure, and, Jen, you're doing your hair. Rose, keep the conversation general, but find out as much as you can about Dorie and who she recommended. Jen, do the same, but for Pete's sake don't talk the hairstylist's ear off."

"I won't. I promise."

"Let's go in separately and leave the same way. We'll go home, make notes, and finish any calls, then meet at my place tomorrow morning at ten sharp. Okay?"

"All right, but I've got to tell you, this whole affair is making me sick. I eat junk food all day, and then throw up. I'm not sure how much more of this I can handle." Rose clutched her stomach and breathed in deeply.

"Well, don't throw up here," Anne said. "How are you coming on your calls?"

"I have a couple of names left to go on my list. I'll do them tonight after the kids are in bed."

"Jen?"

"Almost finished. I can't get a hold of one of the ladies. Must be on vacation."

"It's almost three-thirty. Are we ready?"

At the nods of the other two, Anne headed for the spa. She pushed open the ornately carved front door, entering the world of aromatic luxuries.

"Hello, my name is Jamieson and I have a three-thirty appointment with Inga," she told the receptionist.

"Oh, yes, Ms. Jamieson. Inga's waiting." The woman rose from her desk and led her through a door.

"I think you're going to enjoy this experience. As soon as Inga's finished, Denise will do wonders for your face. Not that you need much. You have lovely skin."

Anne entered a dimly lit room and was greeted by a tall blonde woman in a smock.

"Hello, I am Inga." She spoke with a thick accent. "You go in that room. Take off clothes. There is robe. Put it on and join me. I will work magic."

Anne stripped, donned the robe, and walked back into the room. Slipping the robe off, she lay on the table face down. Inga smoothed an aromatic cream on her back.

Magic was the right word. From the first touch, Anne's bunched muscles relaxed.

"Ignore hurt. Is good for you."

Anne gasped when Inga hit a nerve. The tingling pain lasted a second, and was then replaced by soothing numbness.

"Oh, my God, that feels wonderful," she said groaning.

"You will leave a new woman."

"I understand that Careen Holcombe was a client of yours," Anne said after a few more kneaded muscles cried out.

"Such nice lady. I am sorry she move."

"Yes, she was the head of our last writer's conference. That can be very tense. No wonder she came here."

Inga didn't respond. Her hands moved from Anne's shoulders to upper back. If it weren't for the questioning, Anne could fall asleep.

"Ah-h-h-h!" Anne said with a gasp. Well, almost fall asleep.

"Oh, that was very tight. Perhaps you need to do yoga. I have friend who gives lessons. You want her card?"

"Uh, yeah, sure. I understand Isadora Powell was also a client."

Inga's hands stilled for a second, then resumed their motion. "Yes, I do her, too."

"She recommended Aristotle's to a lot of people."

Inga didn't answer, but continued massaging.

"I'll bet Miss Powell was a handful." Anne tried to keep her tone light.

"Some clients are more demanding than others."

"And Miss Powell? I'll bet she didn't tip worth a damn."

Inga gave one last knead to the small of her back and grasped her upper thigh. "You're tensing up again." The thick Swedish accent had thinned.

*She's no more Swedish than I am.* Did she and Dorie have an arrangement? Did the masseuse worm information from her clients, and then pass it on? For money, perhaps?

*No, that doesn't sound right. Dorie wouldn't pay for information. And why pick on Careen?*

Anne remembered from casual conversation that Careen had gone through the deaths of both parents within a short time frame. That coupled with conference duties had almost driven the poor woman to an asylum.

And yet, her name and number had been in Dorie's secret cell phone. *What the hell could Dorie have had on Careen?*

Then a forgotten scene popped into her mind. She'd arrived early for a chapter meeting one day and seen Careen crying on Sarah Masterson's shoulder.

"Don't worry," the chapter president had said. "We'll work something out."

Embarrassed at being an unintentional witness to an emotional moment, Anne had backed out of the room. A month later, Careen announced she was moving to Oregon.

*Sarah! Sarah knows! That's why her name was in the phone, too.*

But what the hell had Careen done to warrant blackmail? And how had Dorie discovered it? *Dorie and her damned research. She always discovered secrets.* Anne tensed with the realization.

"Relax. It will hurt less," Inga warned.

"Oh, sorry. I was thinking about Miss Powell. Her death was certainly a shock."

Inga worked her way to Anne's feet. "Yes. Very shocking."

Anne remained silent. It was obvious the masseuse would divulge nothing. Or had no information to impart. Further questioning was useless, so she concentrated on the fabulous foot rub.

"You're finished," Inga said giving her foot one last rub.

Anne sat up. "Damn, you're good. I feel fantastic."

The door opened and the receptionist poked her head in. "Oh, good, you're done. Denise is ready whenever you are."

"Thank you very much, Inga. I'll put your tip on the credit card."

The heavy accent returned. "Very welcome. You feel good now, *ja*? Come back and see me. We make you weekly client."

Anne dressed, and walked into the main salon. Rose was gone, but Jen sat in the stylist's chair chatting and probably channeling Mars through the foil in her hair.

A short, dark-haired woman approached. "Hello, I'm Denise. Are you Mrs. Jamieson?"

"Yes."

"If you'll just follow me, we'll have your skin glowing in no time."

Anne obeyed, inhaled a deep breath, and relaxed as the technician's fingers applied a light film of oil to her skin followed by a cool aromatic paste. The light tingle spreading across her skin felt refreshing. She forgot about her troubles to enjoy the moment.

Finished, Anne thanked Denise and walked to the reception desk.

"Was everything to your satisfaction, Mrs. Jamieson?" the receptionist asked.

She handed the lady her credit card. "And beyond. Your people do good work."

"Yes, they do. Please tell your friends about us. If they make an appointment, you get fifty dollars off your next visit."

"Oh, really?" She took a shot in the dark. "I'll bet Miss Powell practically lived here free of charge."

The receptionist laughed, ran the card through the machine, and handed it back. "She was what I'd call a semi-regular. She came in only after one of her friends."

So, Dorie was making money off of Aristotle's, too. Anne signed the receipt. "I enjoyed the massage and facial. Please tell Inga and Denise their tips have been added."

"Of course. Thank you so much for coming in. Have a good evening."

Before leaving, she glanced toward the hairstylist's chair. Jen was gone, but her voice floated over the partition separating the lobby from the shampoo area.

"And she was such a close friend. I'm going to miss her. Do you think the police…"

Anne turned, pushed open the doors and left. She had to talk to Sarah and find out what had happened.

*The suspect list is getting longer, and my name's still on it. Damn, how do I get out of this?*

She had no idea.

Chapter Ten

Anne opened the front door admitting Rose, the last of the group to arrive.

"Sorry I'm late. The sitter didn't get there until nine-forty-five, and then I got caught up in traffic."

"Don't worry. Go on into the dining room. There's coffee on the sideboard along with some sweet rolls."

Rose placed her hand over her stomach and headed for the dining area. "I'd better not. I've gained weight, and my stomach's been acting up ever since this whole mess began. But the coffee sounds good. Hi, everyone."

Nancy and Candace answered her greeting, but Jen shoved the last of a cinnamon bun into her mouth and waved.

"I was just bringing Nancy and Candace up to date on our trip to Aristotle's yesterday."

"Sounds like you didn't make much headway with the masseuse," Nancy said.

"True, but Rose left before me and Jen after. You guys have anything to report?"

Jen shook her head. "I told him Dorie was my best friend in the world, but he didn't really have much to say. At those prices, no wonder Dorie colored her own hair. But the guy is good. These highlights look great." She ruffled her hand through the multi-blonded strands.

Anne wasn't surprised at Jen's information. If the stylist had said anything important, Jen would have called. Same with Rose. Her attention was diverted by Candace who picked up her coffee cup with shaking hands. She looked like hell, but at least her eyes were clear for the first time in a long while.

"Candace, did you discover anything?"

"I called the critique partners on my list. All three are Southeast Florida chapter members and said they were about to drop Dorie from the group. Her critiques had been insulting and hateful the last few months. These women are published authors and resented it, but not enough to kill. May Howard told me Dorie argued with every line edit and comment they made about her work, too."

"What about those bank statements?" Anne asked.

"I haven't had a chance to look at them yet, but they're in Dorie's handwriting, so I'm guessing they're notations from the offshore accounts."

Rose covered her mouth with her hand. "Excuse me for a moment," she mumbled, and then left the room.

"Anne, what about you?" Nancy said.

"I called a couple of gals Dorie critiqued with online. One lives in Ft. Lauderdale and the other in Tampa. Both told me Dorie dumped them about eight months ago. Said she was too busy to critique anymore."

"That was probably the time she wrote this last book," Jen commented.

"I wonder who critiqued it," Nancy mused.

"I never thought of that," Anne said. "I know it wasn't me. And none of the women I talked to said anything about it either."

"You mean she sent it in uncritiqued?" Candace

asked. "That's ballsy."

"I'll say. Dorie was damned good, but she needed several pairs of eyes going over things," Anne replied.

"Did you talk to Gil?" Nancy asked.

"I invited Gil to a home-cooked dinner Monday night."

"And?" three voices chorused.

Rose returned with a sick look on her face.

"Are you all right?" Anne asked.

"No, I'm not. This whole business has me sick all the time."

"Anne was just going to tell us about her dinner with Detective Collins," Candace explained.

Anne launched into the evening with Gil and the information he gave her.

"An ex-husband! No way!" Jen said with a laugh.

"And Paul Proctor claimed never to have heard of Isadora Powell when I called him," Nancy exclaimed.

"Gil's looking for him."

"Maybe he killed Dorie," Candace said.

"Why wait all these years? I'm more concerned about the Irina Petrovsky angle. After all, it's her real name," Rose said. "Do you think the cell we found is under that name?"

"I'd stake my next royalty check on it," Anne replied.

"Doesn't make any difference," Nancy said. "It's gone and no one can prove we took it."

"I'm curious about the post office box," Jen told them. "I wonder if she rented it under the name Danielle Harris, like on the contest entries."

"Who knows? Postal employees look at the box number, not the name," Anne answered. "And Gil's still talking to neighbors."

"Sounds like grounds for another date to me," Rose said.

"What did you have for dinner?" Jen asked barely suppressing a grin.

"Steaks."

"Whew! She broke the budget for this one."

"Anything dirty go on?" Candace said.

"Of course not! He ate, we exchanged information, and then he left. He was gone by nine-thirty. Honestly, you people. It was strictly business."

"Yeah, sure," Jen replied. "I can see it now. The dining room dimly lit, candlelight sparkling off crystal and sterling silver, good wine, and Anne wearing a low cut blouse."

"That is not true!" Heat flooded Anne's face. She hoped the others didn't notice confirming that part of Jen's description had hit home.

"Give Anne a break," Nancy said. "Jen, what about you? Find out anything?"

"I didn't get much from the critique partners. Dorie's behavior was somewhere between nasty and didn't give a shit. Bertie Saunders said her group was about ready to tell her to take a hike—they didn't need a pubbed author's opinion that bad."

"Did you get a hold of Pam Graham?" Anne probed.

Jen nodded. "Last night. I wasn't very subtle. I asked why she hadn't contacted me when she was in Orlando, that I'd have loved to have had lunch, talk about my book, yadda, yadda. At first, she denied being here, but then wanted to know how I knew she was in Orlando. I said the cops told me."

"Bet that shook her up," Candace said, blotting a band of perspiration from under her bangs, and then raising the coffee cup to her lips again. The hand trembled more than a few minutes ago.

Anne eyed her before asking, "Are you all right?"

"I'm fine. Just burning up. Must be a hot flash," she said with a chuckle that sounded forced.

Jennifer continued. "Pam asked how the cops knew she'd been in Florida. I told her they tracked Dorie's phone calls. Pam backpedaled like crazy. Said she had personal business in the area. Claimed to have called Dorie about her new book, and then caught an early afternoon flight back to New York."

"But I wonder if she did," Anne said, shooting Candace a quick glance. Pale, shaking, and with dark shadows under her eyes, the woman looked sicker as the minutes passed.

"Well, I'm sure Detective Collins will check the flights," Rose said. "Can't imagine why her agent would want her dead. She stands to make a bundle. Nancy, what about you?"

"Pretty much the same as far as the critique groups go. Most of them were fed up with Dorie. I must have left a dozen messages for Claire Chappelle, her editor at Orion Publishing. She finally called last night. I more or less told her the truth—that we were helping the police with the business end of things. She was tight-lipped. Only said that publication might be delayed due to legal issues."

"Legal issues?" Anne asked.

"I guess she referred to the murder and who inherits. She didn't elaborate, and when I asked, she stated she couldn't talk about it. It was a polite way of saying mind your own business."

"Once again, why would her editor want to kill Dorie? The potential profits from a posthumously published book from a murdered bestselling author are staggering," Rose said.

"What about the papers you found?" Jen asked Nancy.

"Three or four letters followed by three numbers. I have no clue what they are, but I'll have another look tonight if I have time. I finished chapter sixteen of my work in progress late last night. I'm winding down and need to get it done. I have an August tenth deadline. Besides, we don't know if what I found is important."

Anne had a hunch the papers were damned important. "That leaves you, Rose. What did you find out?"

"Nothing from the manicurist, but you ain't gonna like what I found out from my phone calls." She took a deep breath. "Dorie kept a journal."

"A journal?" Candace said.

"What kind of a journal?" Nancy asked in a tight voice.

"Damn!" Jen exclaimed.

Anne closed her eyes. *And just when we thought it was safe to go back into the water.*

"Who told you this?" she asked.

"Susan Barnes. She's one of Dorie's online critique partners from Jacksonville."

"And she knows this for sure?"

Rose nodded. "They were at a conference a few months ago. It was late and Susan went into the bar for a nightcap. Saw Dorie and asked what she was doing. Dorie said just keeping a diary for research."

"Research?" Candace asked with raised eyebrows.

"Probably jotting down conversations she overheard from future victims," Nancy said.

"You know what this means," Anne said, tugging a curl.

"The meticulous bitch had a back up," Candace replied.

"So, all those blackmail victims' names might be recorded elsewhere? Well, damn. Now, what do we do?" Jen wondered.

"We have to get back into Dorie's office and look for it," Nancy told her.

"But we were just there. We didn't see a journal," Rose protested.

"We weren't looking for one," Candace said.

"That's right, we searched for papers. I looked at the bookshelves and thought it would be a great place to hide something, but never examined anything," Anne stated, her stomach clenching with anxiety. "Any idea what it's supposed to look like?"

"Susan said it was one of those hardcover journal type books. You know—the ones sold in bookstores— pretty covers with lined pages inside," Rose answered.

"Well, this certainly complicates things," Jen said. "Maybe the police found it."

"No, I don't think so," Anne said. "It's still there— somewhere."

Anne sighed and visualized Dorie's office bookshelves. One set occupied the wall from floor to ceiling between the door and her desk, a distance of at least twelve feet. A shorter bookcase containing books on craft, grammar, and research sat next to the window. She recalled no books in or on the credenza. If this journal existed, Dorie would have kept it close at hand—and probably hidden.

"Nancy's right," Jen said. "We have to go back and get it. What if the sister finds it and decides to take up where Dorie left off? For all we know, bitchiness and greed are family traits."

"Oh, no, not again," Candace said. "I say we forget it. The police have already searched the place. They either found it or they didn't. It can hardly matter now."

"I agree," Rose answered. "I don't think the sister or the police will buy the critique story again."

"Can't hurt to try," Nancy insisted.

"Count me out," Candace demanded.

"Me, too," Rose said. "Jack is asking too many questions. The memorial service thing is wearing thin. Especially since we have no intention of holding one."

"How would we get in?" Jen asked.

Anne's hands clenched on her coffee cup. *I have a key.*

It wouldn't take but a few minutes to enter Dorie's house, search, and then get out. And she *had* to find that journal. God only knew what it contained.

*If I find it, I'll destroy it just like Nancy did the phone. I won't even read the damned thing.* She darted a glance at her friends. Would Dorie put any of her blackmail schemes down on paper? Anne shivered. She couldn't take the chance. She had to know.

"And I still say it's worth a shot."

Nancy's voice still insisting on action brought Anne out of her thoughts. "Let's just ask the police to let us in. Tell them we're missing a very important critique and need to find it."

"And another cop will record what's taken. A

journal is not a critique," Anne stated.

Frowning, Candace set the cup down with unsteady fingers. "I still say this is silly. You have my cell and home numbers. Call if you need bail money."

Under no circumstances could Anne risk any of the group finding that diary before she did.

"Rose is right. The police either have it or they don't. We can't do anything about it. And even if the sister finds it, she probably won't get the significance of what it says," she said.

Silence greeted her words. Jen caught her lower lip between her teeth while Nancy averted her eyes to stare at the floor.

"I don't think Dorie would be dumb enough to put something incriminating like blackmail in a journal," Jen finally conceded.

"That's my point," Anne said quickly, surprised Jen had echoed her thoughts of a moment ago.

Rose pushed back her dining room chair, stood, and gathered her purse. "Are we finished? If I don't get home soon, I'm going to finance my babysitter's next car payment."

"I think we're done," Anne replied.

Candace also stood. "I'll check into those bank statements tonight." She slapped her sunglasses on and left with Rose.

Jen said her goodbyes and also departed.

Anne stared out the open door. "Candace is coming apart at the seams."

"I know. I just hope the police don't get a hold of her. She'll spill her guts about what we know," Nancy answered. "I'm worried. She's got to stop drinking."

"I think she has. She's showing every symptom of

withdrawal." Anne turned to look her in the eye. "So, tell me the truth, what do you think those letters and numbers you have mean?"

"I think we found Dorie's hit list—her victims and how much they paid."

Anne gazed at Nancy seeing the same fear in her eyes that clawed in her own gut.

****

Anne cast a quick glance up and down the street before approaching Dorie's front door. So far, so good. She'd picked five-thirty as the time to arrive. People were just home from work and inside preparing dinner or relaxing. Her logic proved correct. No one had paid any attention to her as she walked down the street from her car parked around the corner.

Heaving a sigh, she inserted the key. The door opened. Anne sensed trouble the instant her sandals hit the tile. A creepy chill skittered up her spine and the hair on her arms rose. It was the same feeling she'd experienced the day they'd found Dorie's body.

She paused in the living room entryway and inhaled a sharp gasp. Her heart rate accelerated.

Someone had searched the room. Sofa and chair cushions were askew and pillows tossed carelessly onto the carpet. End table drawers and the drawer of the secretary in the corner stood half closed. An antique clock rested on its side next to the bookcase along the far wall. The books lay on the floor, intermingled with every CD and DVD from the entertainment center. A quick glance through an archway to the dining room revealed the sideboard had been given the same treatment.

*I have to get out of here.* She whirled to run, then

stopped and turned to look again.

The clock read two-fifteen. Whoever trashed the place had probably done it very early this morning or just a few hours ago and was long gone. She quaked inside and took several deep breaths to bring her nerves under control.

*It must have been thieves who read about Dorie's death in the paper.*

She should call 911, but how would she explain her presence? *No, get upstairs, find the damned journal, and get out.* Ignoring her nerves, she climbed the stairs.

Dorie's office was just as ransacked. The office door stood wide open. The floor was strewn with books, papers, and file folders.

Anne dashed down the hall. The bedroom looked the same. Clothing all over and the mattress half off the bed. *Whoever did this started downstairs and got frustrated as he or she went along.*

Anne stared in disbelief at the mess. What kind of valuables would a thief expect to find in an office? *Something like a journal or a diary? How about papers with initials and numbers on it? Try on bank statements for size.*

Anne shivered and her heart thumped in her chest. Maybe Dorie's killer had returned to search for something the group already had. It was not a pleasant thought. How discreet had any of them been about assisting the police? And God only knew what Candace had said between shots of vodka.

Shaking off her forbidding thoughts, she entered Dorie's office, pushed the door partially closed, and tackled the pile of books on the floor. Finding nothing like Rose had described, she jerked open desk and file cabinet drawers. Most were empty, the contents dumped next to the books.

*Nothing, absolutely nothing. Maybe the woman Rose talked to was wrong. Maybe there was no diary.* Anne didn't know whether to cry or cheer.

A sound from below had her freezing in place. Someone was at the front door. Then the door opened and closed. Footsteps paused in the foyer.

Anne's breath caught in her throat and her heart hammered in her ears. The killer! The killer had come back to search again. The footsteps advanced and she heard someone breathing as they climbed the steps. She was trapped in the office. The door was across from the head of the stairs.

Shaking with fear, she backed up until bumping into the credenza. A weapon! She needed a weapon. Not thinking clearly, she grabbed the first thing she saw—a book. She had no idea what to do except throw it. If her aim was decent she might be able to run past and down the stairs.

The door slowly swung open. She closed her eyes. Unable to stop trembling, Anne took a deep breath, and threw the book as hard as she could, then opened her eyes. The intruder raised an arm at the last moment. The book bounced onto the floor.

"Ow! God dammit!"

Anne gasped and clasped the edge of the credenza to keep from collapsing. "Nancy! What the hell are you doing here? You scared the crap out of me."

Nancy rubbed her arm and glared. "I might ask you the same question." Her gaze took in the mess on the floor. "Jesus, what did you do?"

"I didn't do anything. It was like this when I got

here."

"How'd you get in?"

Anne regained her composure and straightened. "I found a key in the desk the other day. How'd *you* get in?"

"Dorie was obsessive. I figured she must have had another key besides the one Jen found the night we got caught. I was right. Found it under a rock in the flowerbed next to the porch steps."

"Why are you here?"

Nancy stared. "Probably for the same reason as you—to find that journal. Did you?"

"No. But the room is such a mess, it's hard to know where to begin."

Nancy lifted a file folder with the tip of her sandaled foot. "I guess it would be easy to spot in spite of everything. How about her bedroom? She might have kept it there."

Considering she'd found nothing, Nancy's suggestion made sense. "Let's go check."

She led her friend down the hallway to Dorie's bedroom.

"Got this, too, huh? Somebody sure wanted something."

"I just hope it's nothing we already have."

"What a cheerful thought." Nancy moved toward the bed, knelt, and lifted the bedskirt. "Nothing under the bed." She found the nightstand drawer and turned it over. "Nightstand's clean. What about you? Find anything?"

Anne did the same with the dresser drawers. "Most of her clothes are on the floor and there's nothing taped anywhere. Let's try the closet."

The closet had been trashed with clothing jerked off hangers, and boxes opened and dumped on the floor. Nothing resembling the book they sought came to light.

"If the thief was looking for the diary, my guess is he or she found it," Nancy said. "Or maybe Dorie put it in a safety deposit box. The police must know about it by now. Did Gil say anything to you the other night?"

"No." Anne looked at her watch again. "Let's get out of here. Let the next person who comes in discover the mess."

They retraced their steps back to the office for a final glance. Had they forgotten to search somewhere? Nancy pawed through the books on the floor.

"Did you check behind the furniture?" she asked.

"Never thought of that," Anne admitted, turning her attention to the back of the desk and credenza. She finished as Nancy straightened.

"What about the file drawers? Did you check behind the metal divider at the back that holds everything upright?"

Anne shook her head. "Never thought of that either."

She hit paydirt on the second drawer. "Whoa, wait a minute. What's this?"

Her fingers grasped a cloth covered tome no bigger than an ordinary trade paperback book. She pulled it out.

"Look what I found." She leafed through the first few pages.

"Don't read it now," Nancy said. "Just cram it into your purse."

"Uh-oh, bad news. This begins ten years ago and

ends…" she flipped to the last page, "…eight years ago. Oh crap, that means there are more of them."

"Well, I sure haven't seen any," Nancy told her.

"Maybe she destroyed them after a period of time and just overlooked this one."

"Or maybe she transferred them to her computer," Nancy suggested.

"In which case, the police have them on the hard drive."

Heaven only knew what Dorie had written and possibly transferred. How long would it take a technician to decipher everything? And how long after that would Gil Collins come knocking on her door demanding answers?

"I doubt we're searching for eight- to ten-year-old material anyway," Anne replied. "The blackmail started after she began her slide."

"How do we know? This could be a hobby dating from way back," Nancy said.

Anne's gaze took in the mess in the dimming light as she jammed the diary into her purse. It wasn't the journal they'd sought, but would have to do. It occurred to her that they may have come to the end of their investigation.

"Come on, let's get out of here."

Anne led the way down stairs. A vase of dead flowers stood on the hall table. Combined with the stagnant water, they gave off a foul odor. The house smelled of death. With any luck, she'd never have to set foot inside Isadora Powell's home again. Tomorrow, she'd call Sarah Masterson.

"I'll read through the journal as soon as I can. Should we meet tomorrow at my house?" Anne asked.

"I can't. I need a day or two to finish my book."

"All right. Wednesday at ten work for you? We'll do brunch."

Nancy sighed as though wanting to argue. "No, I guess that'll do."

Anne jerked open the front door and stood face to face with Dorie's sister.

Chapter Eleven

"Oh!" Anne yelped in surprise.

She jumped backward, her foot treading on Nancy's in the process. To avoid falling, Anne twisted sideways and grasped the door.

"Ouch!" Nancy cried. She made a grab for her foot and, hopping one-legged, backed into the small foyer table.

Breaking china told Anne the vase with the dead flowers in it had bitten the big one.

She turned her attention back to Dorie's sister. The woman's expression was anything but pleasant.

"Why the hell are you people in my house?"

"Oh, hello. Nice to see you. Natasha, isn't it?" Anne replied, saying the first thing that popped into her head. Busted—again. Embarrassed heat flooded her face.

The sister pushed her way past Anne while Nancy bent to retrieve the pieces of broken vase before giving up and massaging her foot instead.

"Nice, my ass. I said what're you doing here? How did you get in?" She then stepped into the living room. "Jesus Christ!" The woman turned with a frightened expression.

"Wait a minute!" Anne said. "We didn't do it."

Apparently figuring the two of them were no threat, indignation replaced the anger. "Holy shit!

What's wrong with you women? I said you could take your papers. What were you looking for—jewelry, cash, the family silver? Look at my living room," Dorie's sister yelled.

"We didn't do it," Nancy said, placing the larger pieces of the vase on the hall table. "We found it this way, took one look, and turned around to leave when you came in."

The sister fumbled in her purse and retrieved a cell phone. "A likely story. What're you doing here?"

"I…I remembered that Dorie, my critique partner, had my latest proposal. I needed it," Anne answered, making it up as she went along.

Natasha flipped the phone open. "I don't believe you. All you had to do was ask."

"We were on our way to dinner and thought we'd drop by on the chance someone was here," Nancy told her in a calm voice, slipping her sandal back on her injured foot.

"And how did you get in?"

"The door was ajar," Anne replied, not daring to look at Nancy.

"I want you nutcases out of here," the sister stated, and then dialed three numbers.

*Oh, no!*

"Hello, nine-one-one? I want to report a break-in…fifteen-fifteen Winchester in San Sebastian. It's my murdered sister's house…The culprits are still here denying everything. And the place has been trashed…What? No, no, they're not armed, unless you count being stupid as armed…Oh, Natasha Sessions…Thanks." She hung up and glared at Anne, then Nancy. "Cops are coming."

Anne closed her eyes wanting to take off in the worst way, but what would be the use?

She opened her eyes again. "There was no need to do that. We didn't take anything."

"It's my house and you ain't invited inside."

"Seems to me it's Dorie's house until the will goes through probate," Nancy added with a frown.

"Yeah? Well, Irina's dead and I'm her only living relative, so that makes everything mine."

Nancy's upper lip lifted in a sneer. "And maybe she left everything to charity."

Natasha snorted. "My loving sister wouldn't leave a plugged nickel to charity unless she could get a dime in return."

Nancy's voice rose. "That still doesn't make it yours."

"I still have more right to be here than you. Now, haul you asses outside."

They filed out the front door. Anne and Nancy huddled on one end of the porch, while Dorie's sister strolled to the other. Nancy snatched a crumpled pack of cigarettes from her purse and lit up.

"It's the truth, Mrs. Sessions. We didn't do this," she said in a placating tone.

"You people are odd, you know that? I heard all about what happened last week when you broke in from one of the neighbors. The police got you then, too. I can't figure out why you're all not in the slammer. Just stay away from me," the woman said when Anne stepped forward.

Anne recognized the futility of carrying on a conversation or offering explanations and fell back, waving Nancy's cigarette smoke from in front of her face.

"Put that damned thing out," she demanded.

The irritation in her voice had little to do with the smoke and everything to do with yet another plan gone wrong.

"Stand upwind," Nancy retorted.

"You know I hate it."

"And you know I smoke. Live with it."

Nancy inhaled a deep drag, blew the smoke out, and crushed the cigarette under her foot.

"There! Are you happy now?"

"Yes!"

A police car turned the corner and pulled to a stop in front of the house. Two officers got out and moved toward them. Nancy promptly lit another cigarette.

"What's the problem?" the first man asked, while the second headed to the back yard, his gun drawn.

Natasha told them in a sharp tone. When she finished the cop turned to Anne.

"What are you doing here?"

Anne went into her explanation, ignoring the derisive snorts emanating from Dorie's sister.

The policeman turned back to Natasha. "Why are you here?"

Her eyebrows drew together in a scowl. "I gotta right to be here!"

"Maybe, maybe not. Why are you here?"

"Yeah, I'd like to hear that myself," Nancy commented blowing a stream of smoke in the woman's direction.

Natasha fluffed her hair, dropped her gaze to the caladiums surrounding the porch and shifted from foot to foot. "I was gonna take an inventory. Guess that's impossible now."

"So where's your pad of paper. I don't see it fitting in that tiny purse you're carrying," Nancy continued.

Anne bit her lip. *Shut the hell up, Nancy. You aren't helping. And for God's sake don't mention purses or their contents.*

The second policeman opened the front door and rejoined them. "The glass was broken in the back door. That's how the vandal got in."

"I knew it!" Natasha pointed a finger at Anne and Nancy. "I knew finding the door open was a bunch of shit. I locked it when I left the other day. Arrest them for breaking and entering. And search 'em. They probably robbed me blind."

"Oh, get a grip," Nancy snapped. "If we were going to do that, we'd have done it by now. Besides, Dorie didn't have any personal items we'd want."

"That's right," Anne insisted in a pleading tone. "I swear all we want are critiques and such. They're important to us. I know that doesn't make a lot of sense to someone not in the business, but good grief, we would never steal from the dead."

"Save your breath, Anne. This ignoramus isn't going to believe anything we say." Nancy glared at Natasha, flipped the half-smoked cigarette into the bushes, then pulled another from the pack, and lit up.

The sister glared back. "Ignoramus! Are you the one who showed up drunk at the funeral?"

Nancy's eyes widened. She sucked in a deep lungful of smoke, and then blew it in Natasha's face.

"I don't remember anyone being drunk," she said in a tight, angry voice.

"Then you must have a lousy memory. You

probably write lousy books, too!"

"How would you know? You probably can't read."

Anne had had enough. The rhetoric was building toward a knock-down, drag-out catfight. "Cut it out, you two."

"She started it," Nancy said.

"Like hell. I'm not the one in the wrong house."

"Ladies," the first policeman said in a stern tone. "I suggest everyone wait until the detective in charge gets here before you say anything else."

*Detective in charge? Gil? Oh, no! Please God, don't let him show up.*

Anne's silent prayer went unanswered when a few moments later, a familiar car pulled into the driveway. Gil Collins emerged and walked up the porch steps.

The expression on his face was a cross between exasperation and resignation.

He shook his head, stared at her, and murmured, "How come I'm not surprised to see you here?"

Anne wanted to sink through the floor. *How many times can I humiliate myself when he's around?*

He directed his attention to the policemen. "Okay, give it to me. What's happened?"

Anne exchanged a glance with Nancy, who shrugged, while the first cop gave his report. Explaining this was going to be hard. The critique lie was wearing thin, and Gil was getting suspicious.

Gil turned to Anne. "Tell me why you were in the house this time?"

Anne licked her lips, and gave him the usual excuse.

"And the door was open?" he asked.

"That's right."

"So, you just walked right in without a thought that this might be unusual."

Anne broke eye contact and shrugged. "We didn't really think about it. Not the smartest thing to do, I guess."

Gil gazed around the front yard and at the street. "And where is your car?"

She swallowed and cast a glance to Nancy who jumped into the conversation.

"We came in my car. It's parked across the street."

"Why not the driveway?"

"Because I didn't want to park in the sun."

"It's early evening. Why would you assume anyone was here when the driveway's empty?"

"How the hell should we know? Maybe they took a cab."

"Mrs. Carlyle, why are you really here—both of you?"

"Oh, for crissake!" Nancy's voice rose. "Why the hell would we trash the place? We walked in, saw the mess, turned to leave and call it in, when we ran into Twisted Sister here."

"Bullshit! I want them searched," Natasha demanded.

Gil sighed and from the look in his eyes, Anne deduced he was ready to kill all of them.

"Ladies, if you don't mind, would you open your purses?"

"Well, I do mind," Nancy said.

"Why? You got something in there other than regular cigarettes?" the sister said.

"Watch it, cow. You're skating on Florida ice!"

"Who are you calling a cow, you chain smoking,

scarecrow? I'll deck you!" Her hands fisted at her sides, and she took a step forward.

"Yeah? Well, bring it on, Beulah!" Nancy also advanced.

Gil quickly moved his body between Nancy and the sister.

"Knock it off—both of you! Everybody go to neutral corners." The two women glared at each other.

Anne breathed a sigh of relief when Nancy, taking a deep breath, backed down.

Dorie's sister stuck her nose in the air and strutted to the far side of the porch.

"All right, let's see those purses," Gil said, turning back to them.

"Don't you need a warrant or something for this?" Anne asked.

Gil heaved what Anne could only describe as an irritated sigh and glared at everyone.

"I wish you'd stop watching cop and crime shows on TV. I don't need a warrant. As long as I have probable cause, I can do anything. And finding you in a house where you had no business being *and* has been vandalized is probable cause. And why I'm justifying this, I have no idea. Now, open up."

Anne jerked her satchel bag open. Gil searched the neatly arranged contents before extracting the journal.

"What's this?"

Anne snatched it from his hand. "Really, *Detective Collins*, this is my diary," she said in an indignant tone.

"You carry your diary with you?"

"I'll never know when I might have something profound to record."

He riffled through the pages, and then frowned.

"This diary is full and the dates are old. Wanna try again?"

She wiped away a rivulet of sweat trickling down her cheek with shaking fingers. "I was in a hurry, and must have grabbed the wrong one." *Oh God, this can't be happening.*

"Uh-huh." He turned to the middle and read for a minute. "This talks about people that I assume are members of that group you belong to. It's not very nice."

Anne drew a deep breath, straightened, and held out her hand. "Southeast Florida Writers Association of America is the group. It's a diary. I vent in it. And sometimes I'm not very nice. May I please have it back?"

He returned the journal. "Your turn, Mrs. Carlyle."

Nancy paused for a moment, crushed out the cigarette, and then handed the purse over.

"What are these?" he asked, pulling out three books.

"Those are mine. They're for a friend who's having an auction. As you can see, I authored one. The other two are out of print and may fetch a nice bid."

Anne glanced over Gil's shoulder and made eye contact with Nancy. Her face was tight, but whether with residual anger from her argument with Dorie's sister or fear, she couldn't tell.

*Oh, crap. What the hell is Nancy thinking? She's going to land us in jail.*

Gil handed the purse back to Nancy with the books. "All right, you're free to go."

Anne made a beeline for the steps with Nancy right behind.

"What? You're letting them go?" Dorie's sister cried.

"Just a minute," he said, stopping them in their tracks. "Give me the key."

"Key?" Anne asked, feigning ignorance.

"The key. The front door was not ajar. The back door was. Whoever did this came and went that way. Now, give me the key or we can go to the jail and have you strip searched."

Anne fished in her pocket and handed it over, for once without a word.

Natasha pointed with a trembling finger. "Ah-ha! I knew it! Probably stole that, too."

"Thank you. I don't even want to hear how you got it. Now, go home, or out to dinner, or wherever. Don't come back here again." He looked at Anne with a stern expression. "I'll be in touch."

She nodded, turned, and hurried down the front walk.

"I don't know about you, but I need a drink," Nancy stated. Pausing next to her car, she gazed up and down the street. "Where did you park?"

Anne rubbed the back of her neck while twisting her head from side to side. She never wanted to repeat the past hour again in her life.

"Around the corner." She opened the door and slid inside Nancy's car. "Just drop me off. I could use a belt myself. Rafferty's?"

Nancy got in and started the engine. "Why not? They're getting to know us on a first name basis. Can you believe that bitch? She's just like Dorie. Did you hear it? *My* house. *My* living room. She sure has become possessive all of a sudden."

"Oh, who cares about the sister?"

A quick glance at Nancy showed a face still tight with anger. Strange—she'd never heard or seen Nancy combative. She was usually cool and verbal.

"She'd inherit anyway. Would you really have hit her?" Anne asked.

"You're damn right I would. I could have taken the scrawny heifer, too. Candace doesn't know how close she came to making good her promise on bailing us out."

Nancy eased the car into gear and pulled away. Turning the corner, she glided to a stop. Anne got out, saying, "Rafferty's in a few minutes."

Nancy nodded and drove off.

Behind the wheel, Anne's scalp prickled. She had the feeling there was something she should remember, but couldn't grab onto it. She rubbed her arms, and then shrugged. *Oh well, probably not important anyway.* She started the car and headed for the restaurant.

Anne pulled into the parking lot at Rafferty's and found a space near the entrance, then met Nancy at the door. Inside, the hostess seated them at a table along the far wall. When the waiter appeared, they ordered wine.

"I can't believe we were humiliated again," Anne said after he left.

"I'm getting used to it."

"Why did you swipe those books?"

"I don't want anything of mine in Dorie's or that sister's possession. I'd have snatched Ruby Redd's stuff, too, if I could have found it."

"But why the other two?"

"Because they're good books. I've read both of them. Dorie hated historicals. They might as well be in my bookcase. I appreciate them."

Anne reached across the table and laid her hand on Nancy's arm. "Your phone number was in Dorie's secret phone, too, wasn't it?"

Nancy bit her lower lip and nodded.

Anne drew in a ragged breath. Confirmed. She wasn't the only one. "I'm not going to ask any questions. It's over and done with. No one knows."

"Your detective will sooner or later. Dorie was sneaky and secretive about her financial matters, but not sneaky or secretive enough to avoid exposure from a police investigation."

"And the IRS wouldn't have come after her on a whim. I'll bet her tax returns were all in order."

"Probably better fiction than she wrote."

"And he's not my detective."

The waiter brought their drinks and took the food order, burgers and fries.

"You know," Anne said, sipping the chilled Chardonnay. "I don't think I've ever seen you angry. You usually slice and dice with sarcastic or pithy comments. For a moment there, I thought you and Sister Bitch were going to go three rounds. You're so reserved, sometimes aloof."

Nancy raised her glass of Pinot Noir to her lips and drank before answering. "It wasn't always that way. I married Gary Carlyle when I was twenty-two. He was fresh out of law school and I had a degree in business administration clutched in my hand. Can you believe this—I wanted to open a bookstore?"

"No kidding. Did you?"

"That takes money, which we didn't have, so I worked in one instead. On the job training, if you will."

"I'm more surprised at the business administration thing. I had you pegged as a history or English lit major," Anne said, taking another sip of wine. "So, you didn't have the money for your own business. Is that why you started writing?"

"I'd been doodling for several years. I started writing seriously in college. Sold my first book a few months after I was married. Gary was brilliant and moved up the corporate ladder fast. Of course, it didn't hurt that the law firm Carlyle, Willoughby, and Carlyle was family run."

"When did you get divorced?" Anne asked. "It seems to me you were footloose and fancy free when I met you—what, eleven years ago."

"Gary and I suffered through four very long years before the split. We argued constantly. He used reason and logic to shred my grievances. I'd get mad. I'd scream, throw things, and on a couple of occasions, I attacked him."

*Nancy? Calm, aloof Nancy? And all these years I thought she was cold, unemotional.*

"You're lucky you weren't arrested for domestic violence," Anne said.

"Gary finally had enough and left, saying if I didn't get my temper under control, I'd end up in jail. He was right. You should have seen my road rage. I got a therapist, and took anger management classes before moving here from Columbus, Ohio." She gulped half her wine. "I have my moments, like tonight, but they're few and far between. I usually punch a pillow."

"Wow. And I thought I had problems," Anne said.

She fiddled with the stem of her wine glass. She'd never talked much about her divorce to anyone in the group. She'd never wanted to, but now the urge to unload bubbled up.

"I thought Kenneth and I had the perfect marriage. He worked hard, brought home a damned good paycheck, and let me do whatever I wanted. The first cracks appeared about two years before the divorce."

She raised her glass with a shaky hand and sipped again.

"We never argued, but Kenneth withdrew emotionally. He talked less, and our sex life dwindled. He said he was tired, or he'd stay up late until he was sure I was asleep. I thought maybe it was mid-life crisis, or maybe another woman. I didn't want to know."

"So, you didn't talk to him?"

Anne shook her head. "It all came to a boil one day in the kitchen. The kids had left for school, and he and I were discussing the coming weekend. I was making a list of what had to be done when he jumped up and exploded."

"Exploded how?" Nancy inquired.

"He shouted. 'You and your goddamned lists. You have everything planned out to the last second. Can't you ever be spontaneous? It's like being married to a stopwatch. I've put up with fourteen years of this nonsense. I can't, and won't, take any more.'

"I was stunned, unable to think or say anything. Then he threw his napkin on the table. 'Anne, you're a great mother. I respect you for that, but I want out. I want a divorce. I don't love you anymore. I like you, but hate being married to you.'"

Anne's hand shook as she raised her glass and drained it. God, this was the first time in three years she'd told anyone about that humiliating day.

"I'm sorry, Anne," Nancy said, reaching over to give her hand a sympathetic squeeze.

Tears welled in her eyes and she blinked to clear them. Throughout the divorce, she'd held her head high and stayed in control, saving tears for the privacy of her bedroom. Now, she wanted to bawl in a restaurant.

"I have to admit, Kenneth was right. I'm organized to a fault. I can't help it. It's just the way I am."

"And it shows in your books. Anybody can tell your plots are well thought out."

"Thanks." Anne tapped her fingers on the rim of her glass. "It was hard that first year. Getting the finances straight was tough. I was often short of money, but we finally worked it out."

The food arrived. Anne used the next few minutes spreading mayo on the bun and dumping ketchup on her fries to rein in her emotions. Nancy's revelations had lifted a barrier that had always stood between them.

"Nancy, how about we ask Candace out to dinner tomorrow night? We said we'd give her tips on coping with divorce and now seems like a good time."

"Especially now," Nancy replied between bites of burger. "She's going downhill fast. Scum sucking Eric. Hope that bimbo dumps his ass for a younger or a richer man. Serve him right. Friday and Saturday nights are tough. Gary and I used to make Fridays our night out. I think every couple needs those." Nancy nibbled on a fry. "I guess we all have personal lives and problems the rest of us don't know or talk about. Look at Rose. All those kids and an insensitive husband who keeps knocking her up. If I were her, I'd castrate him."

Anne laughed, and then sobered as a vision of

Nancy with a knife flashed through her brain. "I know. Sometimes I feel sorry for her. He makes a decent living owning a sporting goods store, but it's never quite enough for Rose to do everything she'd like. The kids come first, which is the way it should be. All Jack wants to do is watch sports on TV and create little Bennetts."

"It's nice to know he's good at something," Nancy said dryly.

They finished the meal, paid, and afterward went their separate ways.

In spite of the early evening disaster, tonight had been enlightening, and Anne felt closer to a friend she'd known for years.

****

The doorbell rang while Anne was making coffee in the kitchen. In a good mood for the first time in weeks, she was determined to finish the proposal and send it off to her editor.

She hurried through the house, wondering who would be at her door at eleven-thirty at night. Her heart skipped a beat when she peeked through the peephole and saw Gil standing on the porch.

She didn't want to answer any more questions tonight, but opened the door anyway.

"May I come in?" he asked.

"Sure," she replied, stepping back and pulling the lapels of her robe closer together. "Look, I'm sorry about tonight, but…"

"I don't want to hear any more about that. I just dropped by to tell you that as of now, you and your friends are out of the sleuthing business. You got lucky tonight. As far as we can determine, nothing was stolen

182

and I talked Mrs. Sessions out of pressing charges. Plus, I think you're lying. You know a lot more than you're telling me."

The heat blossomed in her face. "Gil, we haven't made contact with everyone yet."

"I don't care. From now on, the police will take care of things." He ran a hand over his face. "I'm going home. I'm tired and cranky. Dinner tomorrow night?"

His invitation threw her off balance and she stammered, "I…I'd love to, but I already have plans."

"I see. Fine. I'll talk to you later."

Gil stalked out the door and Anne closed it gently behind him. They were off the case. She wasn't ready to accept that, and then stopped to think.

Maybe they *had* reached the end of the game. Further access to Dorie's was out of the question. The evidence they'd retrieved and the conclusions they'd drawn could only hurt innocent people, even if it pointed to the murderer.

Anne returned to the kitchen and poured a cup of coffee, then walked upstairs to her office. She stared at the computer screensaver watching virtual fish swim aimlessly in a virtual aquarium.

Dorie was dead and deserved to die. She was a blackmailer, a fraud, and made everyone around her miserable.

Anne sat upright and moved the mouse, sending the fake fish and the aquarium into cyberspace. She pulled up her latest proposal. Her fingers flew across the keyboard.

She didn't give a tinker's damn if Isadora Powell's killer was ever caught.

An unpleasant thought swept through her mind,

stilling her fingers. She stared at the screen remembering the chaos inside Dorie's.

*What if the smashed clock's reading of two-fifteen was in the afternoon? What if Nancy hadn't gone home after leaving here? What if she went there instead? What could she be looking for? Certainly not books.*

Could Nancy have ransacked the place and for whatever reason left, only to return later?

*Oh, that's silly. It doesn't make any sense.*

She shivered. Dorie's death had been a crime of passion with rage fueling the blows. And her friend had just confessed to not only having an anger management problem, but to being on Dorie's blackmail list.

Anne buried her face in her hands. *Oh God! Nancy?*

## Chapter Twelve

"Forty-eight hours, Bruno. That's how long I've been sober," Candace said to her shih-tzu. She cuddled the nuzzling dog, laughing when his tongue tickled her ear. "And I couldn't have done it without you. You're my bestest buddy in the whole wide world."

She chuckled at her nonsense and set the dog on the floor. Searching her closet for something to wear tonight, she hummed a commercial jingle and slid hangers along the rod to the beat. For the first time in weeks, she wanted to laugh and sing. Nancy had called late last night with the invitation. She was sober and looking forward to dinner with her and Anne.

*A girl's night out. I haven't had one of those in years. I'll get tips on coping with divorce and a great Italian meal at Caruso's.*

She found what she needed, a gauzy white skirt, and a turquoise, scoop-necked top. Candace held them up in front of the mirror and gazed at the reflection. Perfect. The skirt showed off her tanned legs, and the top deepened the blue of her eyes. Her silver sandals and sterling jewelry would finish the ensemble.

"Bruno, I am going to look like dynamite."

It was about time. For over a year, she'd looked, and felt, like hell. Today—tonight—would signal a new beginning. Maybe she'd ask Anne and Nancy if they knew any nice men. Dating sounded both intimidating and thrilling.

And her hair! Candace pushed the wayward bangs out of her eyes. She needed a trim and her roots touched up. She'd call the salon today and take the first appointment her hairdresser had available.

"Get ready, Bruno. With any luck, there could be a new man in our lives."

The dog wagged his wavy-haired tail and cocked his head as though understanding and giving approval.

Candace laughed and tossed the clothing on the bed, tweaked the blue bow in Bruno's topknot, then scooped him into her arms and danced around the room. Not even Dorie's death bothered her today. It had been almost two weeks and the police still hadn't made an arrest. Maybe they never would. That was fine with her. Nobody mourned the dead author, and in view of the bitch's activities over the last few years, she didn't care if the killer was ever brought to justice.

She pushed the unpleasant subject of Isadora Powell to the back of her mind and headed downstairs, Bruno still in her arms and her bare feet slapping on the tile of the hallway.

"How about some lunch, handsome? It's almost one o'clock. I could use a sandwich. You want a little taste of chicken, too? Does Mama's boy want chicky?"

She was halfway down the hall when the doorbell rang.

"Now, who can that be?" she murmured in Bruno's ear.

Opening the door, her gaze locked on to Detective Gil Collins.

The sunny day disappeared. Her heart plummeted to her toes and, for an instant Candace wondered if he was here about her drunken drive of a few nights earlier.

*Don't be silly. He's homicide, not traffic. Good God, did I kill someone and not remember?*

She suppressed the urge to laugh hysterically.

"Why, Detective Collins, how nice to see you," she lied. "Won't you come in?"

Gil entered the foyer. "Good afternoon, Ms. Warren. Who's this?" he asked, scratching behind the dog's ears.

"This is Bruno. Don't worry, he's very gentle. He barks at cats and other dogs, and only then from a safe distance. What can I do for you? I was just about to fix lunch. Would you like something?"

Candace couldn't believe she sounded so normal. Inside, her heart hammered, and lunch was the last thing she wanted now. Her stomach would reject anything that hit it. Thank God, Bruno hid her trembling hands.

"No, thank you. I was wondering if we could talk. I have a few questions to ask."

"Certainly."

Candace turned and walked into the living room, gesturing for him to be seated. He chose a chair. She sat on the edge of the sofa, wishing she wore something nicer than the faded cutoffs and oversized T-shirt.

"What's this all about?"

"We've been interviewing Ms. Powell's neighbors."

"Oh, yes, Anne told me. Are you making any progress?"

"Some. The neighbor across the street is still out of town, but due back soon." He paused and removed a notebook and pencil from his pocket. "We talked to a man who lives around the corner from the victim. He told us that on the night in question, he was walking his dog around ten o'clock when he passed a dark-colored car. He remembered it because a small dog inside barked as he came along side. It startled him. He didn't recognize either the car or the dog. In your initial statement to us the day you found the body, you mentioned having walked your dog the night of the murder at Sunshine Bark Park. Could you explain further?"

Candace's fingers clenched in Bruno's hair and she swallowed the lump forming in her throat. For a moment, she'd thought he was going to nail her for almost hitting that man and his dog. Couldn't be the same guy, could it? Confusion and a blurry memory didn't help.

She licked her lips. "Of course. I often take Bruno over to the Sunshine Bark Park. On the night Dorie died, I did so about seven or seven-thirty, I think. I let him run for a while, and then headed home."

"You didn't make a detour passed the deceased's house?"

"No. I was going to see everybody the next day anyway. Did the neighbor get a license plate number?"

"No, he just said it was a dark-colored sedan with a dog inside. He's not good with makes and models. He said that by the time he returned home twenty minutes later, the car was gone."

"Couldn't have been me, Detective Collins. I drive a white BMW, and I was home watching TV at ten o'clock."

Her heart rate slowed when he wrote in his

notebook, and her hands released Bruno's fur. She stroked his head to calm her nerves.

"Would you mind showing me your car?"

"Of course not. It's in the garage." What the hell else was she going to say?

He followed her down the hall, through the kitchen, stepped into the garage, and eyed her BMW.

"You have a little front end damage," he commented, and then gazed at the leg of Eric's workbench. It was splintered and bent inwards.

"I know. I'm a lousy judge of distance, especially at night. I came home after dark a few nights ago and ran into the workbench. I've been meaning to call the insurance company, but keep forgetting."

Anne's detective smiled and re-entered the kitchen. "Thank you for your time, Ms. Warren. I hope I haven't kept you from anything."

"Oh, no, just the usual. I'm going out to dinner tonight with Anne and Nancy, but that's not until seven."

"I see. Well, thanks again."

Candace closed the door behind him and gently set Bruno on the floor. Would he check with the officer who'd come earlier in the week? A report must have been filed about the credit card and the gun or the cop wouldn't have shown up. She'd retrieved the credit card, but now wondered if someone had also copied a partial license plate number from the night of the dog incident. Perhaps the guy she almost hit.

She buried her face in her shaking hands. "Oh, God, Eric and the bimbo will have a field day if I'm arrested. Shit, what am I going to do?"

The euphoria of fifteen minutes ago had

evaporated. All the humiliation and anger of the past year crashed around her in mental shards. She shook from head to toe.

She needed a drink. There wasn't a drop of booze in the house. Candace ran to the kitchen and jerked open the refrigerator door. Not even an old bottle of wine or beer graced the shelves. She'd done an excellent job purging the joint.

Leaning against the counter, she clutched her hair and sobbed. The last two weeks flashed through her mind—Eric, the bimbo, Dorie, the blood, the bars—all of it in living color. *That is what I can remember.*

Candace wiped her cheeks and breathed deeply in the hope of regaining control.

"Oh, God, Bruno. What am I going to do? I can't handle this anymore. I just can't live like this! I'd rather be dead!"

With a choking cry, she clapped her hand over her mouth, but it didn't stop the sobs from emerging.

****

"Why isn't she answering?" Anne demanded and rang Candace's doorbell again. She shivered remembering those were almost the same words and actions she'd performed the day they'd found Dorie.

"We're a few minutes early," Nancy replied.

"Maybe she's in the bathroom."

"She's not Jen. Candace was looking forward to this when I called last night. She'd be ready."

Anne reached for the doorknob when the door suddenly opened. She stared at the barefoot woman in front of them wearing cut-offs, and a baggy shirt. Her hair was disheveled. She clutched a glass containing ice and a clear liquid in her hand. Candace blinked owlishly as though trying to focus her eyes.

"Oh, sorry. Forgot you were coming," she said, her words slurring.

"Hells bells," Nancy said, pushing her way inside. Anne followed and slammed the door. "What the hell happened?"

Candace drained the glass and hiccupped. Nancy leaped forward, wrenched it from her hand, then she and Anne each grabbed an elbow and marched her back to the den where they lowered their friend to the sofa.

"Candace, what happened? You were excited to go to dinner," Anne said.

Candace sat back, her eyes welling with tears. She sniffled and rubbed her nose. "I...I...huh? What was the question?"

"Oh, for Pete's sake. How long have you been drinking?" Nancy demanded.

Bruno came in, sat at his mistress's feet, and wagging his tail, whined piteously.

"What's wrong with him?" Anne asked.

"He probably has to go out. Candace, when did you last let Bruno out?"

"I dunno." She tried to rise. "I need another drink."

"I don't think so. Nancy, why don't you let Bruno out and start a pot of coffee? Take the vodka with you."

Nancy nodded and snatched the Grey Goose bottle from the bar. "Come on, Bruno. Wanna go out? Out?" She turned for the kitchen with the shih-tzu trotting close behind.

Anne made an exasperated sound as Candace fell against the back of the sofa and closed her eyes.

"Oh, no you don't," she said gritting her teeth. "You're not passing out. Come on—on your feet." She hauled her friend upright. "We're going to walk."

She steered a staggering Candace around the den for several minutes until the woman appeared more cognizant, and then eased her into a chair.

"Now, what happened to put you in such a state?"

Candace started crying again and babbled in a slurred, incoherent voice. Anne only caught every third word or so between the sobs, hiccups, and sniffles.

"Good God, she's in a bad state, isn't she?" Nancy said returning from the kitchen with a tray and three mugs of hot, aromatic coffee. She set it on the table in front of the sofa. "What's she saying?"

"I don't know. She keeps jabbering on about white cars, workbenches, questions, and men walking dogs. I can't make any sense out of it."

Nancy picked up a cup from the tray. "Here, Candace, drink this."

Waving a drunken hand at the offering nearly hitting it, she said in a petulant voice, "No. Don't wanna."

"I don't give a goddamn if you want it or not. You're going to drink it," Nancy replied.

Candace crossed her arms over her chest and clamped her lips shut.

"If you don't drink this coffee, Anne is going to hold your nose until you open your mouth, and then I'm going to pour it down your throat. Now, drink!"

"Stop treating me like a child," her inebriated friend said with a scowl.

"Stop acting like one," Anne snapped back.

Candace heaved a deep breath, took the cup, and sipped. Forty minutes, three cups of coffee, and two trips to the bathroom later, she looked less loaded and able to marginally function. She resumed her seat while Nancy and Anne sat on the sofa next to her.

"Now, what happened?" Anne asked.

Candace swiped a hand through her hair, shoving the errant bangs out of the way. "Well, I didn't go home the night we had pizza. I went to a bar and got really stinking drunk. On the way home I almost hit a guy walking his dog. I was so scared and shaking I could barely make it into the garage. That's how I damaged the bumper."

"So, you didn't get hit at the mall?" Anne said.

"I wasn't about to tell everyone I rammed into Eric's workbench," she replied in a defensive tone.

"Never mind. It isn't important except to your insurance company," Nancy said. "Go on."

"I don't know why, but I hit another bar the next night only this time I don't even remember driving home."

"Oh, Candace, you're lucky you didn't get stopped," Anne with a groan.

"The last thing I remember was this guy hitting on me and scaring him off with my gun."

"Gun! What gun?" Anne asked, horrified. Candace armed and drunk? She shuddered.

"You have a gun?" Nancy asked.

"Oh, yes."

Her matter of fact tone sent a chill down Anne's spine.

"What the hell for?" Nancy demanded.

"For protection, of course. After Eric moved out, I heard noises all the time, so I bought a little thirty-eight revolver and keep it in the nightstand. When I go out at night, I slip it into my car console or my purse. I figure if anyone tries to mess with me, I can scare them off."

"Oh, Jesus," Anne said, sitting back on the sofa and turning her eyes to the ceiling, visualizing a drunken Candace waving a gun under some poor schmuck's nose.

"Do you even know how to use the damned thing? Good Lord, Candace, what if you killed someone?" Nancy said.

"Of course I know how to use it. Used to go to the gun range all the time. Besides, it's not loaded."

"Well, thank God for small favors. Let's get back to your story. What set you off tonight?" Anne asked.

"The day after the last gun incident, a policeman came."

She spent the next several minutes telling them about the warning. Her story was still disjointed, but Anne managed to follow most of what she said.

"So, naturally when he came by this afternoon, I thought it was about my drinking and driving, but he asked questions about the night Dorie died."

"Why did the policeman come back and ask that?" Anne said in a perplexed tone.

"Not that cop. Your detective."

"Gil was here questioning you about the night Dorie was killed?" she asked. Gil hadn't mentioned he planned on doing that. Of course, given last night's discussion it didn't surprise her.

"What did he want to know?" Nancy said slowly.

"What color car I drove. Some man walking his dog passed a dark car with a dog inside parked near Dorie's."

"And you have a dog," Anne said. "Is that what upset you? I wouldn't worry. He just wanted verification, that's all."

"I...I got so upset and felt so guilty about what I did, I couldn't help myself. I went to the liquor store and..." She dissolved into tears again.

"Let's get you cleaned up," Anne said, helping Candace to her feet. "You need food in your stomach. When did you last eat?"

"Toast this morning, I think."

"Nancy, why don't you call some place with delivery and order? I'll deal with her."

"Not pizza," Candace said.

"I'll find something else," Nancy promised.

Anne assisted Candace up the stairs and helped her out of the grungy clothes and into the bathroom. While Candace showered, Anne turned down the bed and picked up the discarded clothing. She cast a glance at the bathroom door. Candace had been in there forever. Was she all right? Maybe she should check and make sure the woman hadn't drowned.

*Don't be an idiot. Who the hell drowns in a shower?*

The abrupt end of water running told her Candace was okay—at least for the moment. Finally, the bathroom door opened and Candace came out, wrapped in a towel. Anne handed her a pair of red satin pajamas she'd found under one of the pillows.

"Thanks," she mumbled and disappeared back inside, emerging a minute later tightening the belt of a white robe. Her face was pale and dark circles underlined her eyes, but she looked more in control.

Remembering the gun, Anne's gaze settled on the nightstand. "Uh, Candace, where is that gun now?"

She smiled. "In the nightstand drawer where it

belongs."

"Why don't you let me keep it for a while? I'd hate to have you picked up for carrying a concealed weapon. You aren't still hearing strange noises, are you?"

"No, and I am trying to stop drinking. I poured everything out and actually quit for a whole forty-eight hours."

"We noticed." She extracted the gun from the drawer, and then flipped the cylinder open. Empty, just like she'd said.

The doorbell rang. "I guess that must be dinner," Anne said, handling the gun with care.

"Before we go down, I want to thank you and Nancy for…helping."

"I'm glad we could finally be there for you."

"I didn't want to burden my friends with my personal problems, but when I reached out, nobody seemed to care."

Guilt hammered at Anne as she remembered the several times she'd cut Candace off when she'd called. "And I'm as guilty as the next person. Sometimes we get so caught up with our lives, we forget our friends may have problems. The next time you feel like talking, I'll listen."

"As long as you're not on deadline," Candace said with a smile.

She laughed. "As long as I'm not on deadline. Come on, let's go eat."

In the den, Anne shoved they gun into her purse. They joined Nancy in the kitchen. She had set the table and was doling out Chinese food from several white cardboard cartons.

Anne sniffed the garlicky aroma with appreciation,

then opened the refrigerator and hauled out three cokes.

"This looks good," Candace remarked sitting down and opening the coke can.

"Chicken or pork?" Nancy asked her.

"Chicken."

"Chopsticks or a fork?"

"Chopsticks."

"Anne?"

"Pork and a fork. I never mastered the art of eating with two sticks."

They ate silently for several minutes. Anne kept a close eye on Candace's consumption. So far, so good. She'd eaten close to half of what Nancy had ladled onto her plate.

"I'm scared," Candace said, laying her chopsticks aside and gulping soda from the can. "He suspects me. I know it. Why else would he ask me questions when I've already given him my statement?"

"He just has to make sure," Anne said in an attempt to reassure.

"He'll probably check our statements, too," Nancy replied. "We were all upset that day. He may want to know if time has improved our memories. One of us might remember something useful we forgot in the heat of the moment."

"You think?"

"Of course," Anne said, patting her friend's hand.

Candace cast a glance at the counter. "What did you do with the vodka?"

"It's in the trunk of my car," Nancy told her. "I just couldn't bring myself to pour Grey Goose down the drain. Consider it a contribution to my liquor cabinet."

"Are you still scared?" Anne asked eyeing

Candace's shaking hands.

"A little. I'll probably dream about prisons."

"Would you like me to stay tonight? If you can't sleep, we can talk. You can vilify Eric and the bimbo."

Candace reached across the table, squeezing her hand.

"Thanks, I'd love that."

****

"So, I guess I have to give up my membership. It's too humiliating seeing the two of them together and knowing all my friends pity me," Candace said.

She'd talked for over an hour after Nancy had left. Anne was glad she suggested doing this. Candace needed someone to listen.

"Maybe it's the perverse imp inside of me, but why give up your membership? Do you enjoy the country club? Do you play golf or tennis?" she asked.

"Yes, both. I miss it."

"Then pay the dues and go whenever you want. So what if Eric shows up with—what's her name?"

"Missy," Candace replied with a sneer.

"Missy—what a name. Go there and hold your head high, even if you have to dine alone. Let them be the ones bothered by *your* presence for a change. I bet you have more friends on your side than he does on his."

"You know, you may be right. Would you like to come with me tomorrow night?"

"I have to finish my proposal, but would love to come next week sometime. Why not ask Jen and Carl? They're members, aren't they?"

"Yeah, Jen would do it. She can be downright snotty at times," Candace said with a laugh, and then yawned. "Oh, dear, I think the booze…that is everything…is catching up with me. It's only eleven o'clock, but I'd better get to bed. You can have the spare room. It's all made up and next to the bath. I even have a clean pair of pajamas."

They rose from the sofa. "Thanks, but what if I told you I sleep raw?"

Anne followed a laughing Candace upstairs where her hostess showed her the bedroom and unearthed a new toothbrush. She then picked up Bruno, said goodnight, entered her room, and closed the door.

Eleven o'clock was much too early for Anne. She was accustomed to later hours. She brushed her teeth, washed her face, and returned to the room. It was nicely furnished, but had no books or a TV available. She wondered if it would be rude to look in other rooms for something to read. She didn't want to disturb Candace. The woman was reasonably sober, but probably sound asleep already.

Anne tiptoed down the hall to another room she knew to be the office and flipped on the light. File cabinets graced one wall while an old computer table filled in space next to the window. A bookcase stood in the corner, flanked by a cream-colored loveseat.

One of the file drawers caught her eye. It was partially open. Giving in to temptation, Anne peeked inside.

It contained hard copies of several old manuscripts. She closed the drawer and opened another. File folders were organized behind dividers. Anne pulled one labeled, "Contests," opened it, and then wished she hadn't.

The score sheets dated from the year before and the

points awarded hovered in the two-to-three range out of five possible. She remembered Candace talking about this contest at one of the group meetings. She'd told them the score was good—in the high eighties. The sixty-three at the top of the page said it all.

The next folder held rejection letters—lots of them. Anne winced at the blunt wording from one agent who wrote that under no circumstances was the writing good enough to be considered by her firm. Agents weren't usually so cruel. Anyone could write the next blockbuster, so why be insulting? A quick flip through the file showed that Candace had submitted to this particular agent over ten times in the last two years. The woman's patience had obviously snapped.

Anne returned the folder and closed the drawer, then walked to the bookcase and made a selection. On her way out, she noticed another folder on the loveseat, the papers inside askew as if someone had tossed it there and forgotten about it. Candace's handwriting graced the front of the manila portfolio—*Auto Insurance and Repairs.* Unable to stand the disorder of the file, she opened it to straighten the pages. The contents contained statements from her insurance company along with the repair bills on the BMW for the past year.

The latest was on top—a repair invoice from Skyway Body Shop for a brisk six hundred dollars to fix a battered rear bumper. A canceled check was attached.

She flipped through the rest of the pages. Skyway again, the BMW dealership twice, then another body shop appearance, and so on. She counted a total of eight. Also clipped together were several car rental receipts. They coincided with the Skyway bills. The dealership would have given her loaners for a couple of days.

Anne read on to the insurance papers. Candace's premiums had gone up with each accident.

*Poor Candace. She obviously hit things while under the influence. She must have spread the repairs around so nobody would notice how often she needed them. And it all began within a couple of months of Eric leaving her.* She fingered the checks clipped to the Skyway invoices. *And paid cash for some of the repairs. If she turned them all in to the insurance company, her policy would probably be canceled.*

She straightened the papers and returned the folder to where she'd found it. Her friend needed help—professional help—to deal with the drinking. *Tomorrow I'll see what kind of programs are available for people with substance abuse problems. Maybe I can get Candace to agree to go to meetings or whatever is involved.*

Back in her bedroom, she undressed, slid under the covers, and opened the book, but did not read.

Poor Candace. If there was an award for writing perseverance, her name had to be engraved on it. She tried, but never made the connection. Maybe she and Nancy could help her out with critiquing and mentoring.

Dammit. Suddenly, she wanted Candace to publish at least one book in her lifetime.

Chapter Thirteen

Anne stood next to Jen's sideboard and poured a cup of coffee. She needed the caffeine, not the cherry Danish, but took one anyway. She glanced out of the window and sighed. The rain slanted down in blowing sheets. A tropical wave hovered over San Sebastian and the forecast predicted rain and wind for the rest of today and perhaps tomorrow. The lyrics of an old pop song about rainy days and Mondays ran through her mind.

Candace joined her and also helped herself to the coffee. "Depressing weather, but then, its summer in Florida."

"How are you feeling?"

"Fine. I've kept busy, and decided to take charge of my life."

"Good for you."

Jen brought in a bowl of miniature chocolate bars and placed it on the table.

"Jen, thanks for hosting this," Rose said. "You saved me a baby sitting fee."

"Hey, no problem. My kids will get a kick out of looking after yours, especially Wendy. She's great with little ones. And there are enough games and toys in the playroom to open a store."

The five women gathered around the dining room table for a combined meeting of the support and critique groups.

"Help yourselves," she said, waving them in the general direction of the sideboard. "Are we ready to begin?"

"I am," Nancy said, taking a seat and a huge bite of banana nut muffin. "I am officially finished with my latest book. I edited into the wee hours of the morning and e-mailed it to my editor this morning. Am I ever glad that's over! It's not my best effort, and I'll have a mountain of revisions, but at least it's on the way."

Jen rose, reached into the bowl and extracted a fistful of candy bars, dropping them beside Nancy's plate.

"Congratulations. Having a deadline in the middle of all this mess with Dorie deserves a double helping. Who's next? Candace, would you like to tell us about your weekend?" Jen smiled and winked.

"Well, ladies, I have decided to quit drinking and begin living."

"Good for you," Rose said, smiling in encouragement.

"I'm proud of you," Nancy added.

"Me, too," Anne commented. "What did you do?"

"Saturday, I went to the country club for dinner with Jen and Carl. It was crowded, but we got a seat next to the dance floor, and guess what?"

"What?" Rose asked in an eager voice between bites of Danish.

"Eric and the bimbo put in an appearance. A week ago I would have left the room, but not any more. I held my ground. Eric looked surprised I was there, and Missy looked downright astonished. I had a wonderful meal," Candace finished with a smile and a sigh.

"You didn't tell them the best part," Jen said,

dropping two handfuls of chocolate in front of her friend. "Bert Cooper, the president of the club, asked if he could join us. He's recently divorced, too, and naturally we said yes. So, we were a foursome when Eric and Messy—er, Missy—strolled in. The only table available was back near the kitchen. Eric wasn't just surprised, he was flabbergasted. Miss Boob Job of the Century, glared, and I mean glared, especially when Bert asked Candace to dance. And tons of people stopped by our table to say hi and how glad they were to see Candace." Jen stopped and took a deep breath.

"Did Eric say anything to you?" Anne asked.

"Not a word," Candace replied.

"And very few people even acknowledged the terrible twosome," Jen said, her breath replenished. "Who's next? I want to unload this chocolate and get to the investigation."

"My weekend was the same as usual. Jack worked and watched sports on TV. The kids were a handful because of the rain, so I spent a lot of time trying to keep them from killing each other. I really hesitated to foist them on you today," Rose said.

Jen waved her hand. "Don't worry about it. This is something new and they'll be fine, at least for a couple of hours."

"I'm amazed at how you handle four young children," Nancy said. "You must have the patience of Job."

"I'm more amazed you aren't living on Xanax," Anne said with a laugh.

"I did manage to get another chapter done after the kids went to bed last night. That puts me up to eight and the plot is coming together. I think *Too Hot to Handle* may be a winner."

"Chapters are good and deserve a reward," Jen replied. She piled several chocolate bars in front of Rose. "Personally, I thought *Night Heat* was great. I read the proposal, remember. I can't figure out why it wasn't published."

"I'll send it out again," Rose said not making eye contact with any of them. She opened one of the candies and popped it into her mouth, then shoved in three more.

Anne eyed her friend. Candace found solace in the bottle, but Rose wallowed in food. If she didn't control her eating soon, she wouldn't fit into any of her clothing. Her tummy bulged in the jeans and her shirt stretched across her breasts. She looked dumpy.

"Anne? Your turn."

"My weekend was dull," Anne told them. "I finished my proposal, sent it off on Saturday, and then indulged myself with a trip to the mall. Unfortunately, when I came out, my car wouldn't start, so I had to have it towed."

"How did you get here?" Rose asked.

"I have to make do with a rental for a few days. Bad alternator or something like that. Sunday was spent with tea and reading all day. Kenneth still has the kids and doesn't seem to mind. He's taking them to Disney World next weekend, and then bringing them back. School starts soon and we need to do the dreaded back to school shopping."

"Here, have a bunch of chocolate," Jen said. "School shopping is right up there on my list of least favorite things to do. The kids always want what isn't on the approved list from the school and we end up arguing in the middle of the store."

"Do you have any news to report?" Nancy asked her.

"Not a whole lot. My work in progress is in chapter six, and for once I have a coherent synopsis, so I sent the first three chapters off to Pam Saturday. I also got suggestions from my editor for revisions. There weren't as many as I thought and I can deal with the changes." She set a single candy bar in front of her place at the table. "I win the prize for the most boring. Now, can we get down to why we're really here?" Jen stared pointedly at Anne.

"I went to Dorie's to find that journal."

"I had the feeling you might," Rose said. "Did you find it?"

Anne shifted in her chair and tossed a glance toward Nancy who avoided eye contact.

"Things got a little complicated," she replied.

"What happened?" Candace asked her eyes wide. "And how did you get in?"

Anne gave them the *Reader's Digest* version of the experience, omitting Nancy's presence.

"Who could have tossed the joint?" Rose wondered.

"Pick a suspect—any suspect," Nancy said.

"And Dorie's sister wanted you arrested?" Candace asked with raised eyebrows.

"I'll say. She carried on something fierce about *her* house and *her* possessions. I hope they find a will that cuts her out of everything," Anne answered.

"I can't believe you had the nerve to go upstairs and search," Rose muttered. "Suppose the burglar had still been there?" She shuddered.

"Well, they weren't," Anne said.

"Did you find the journal?" Jen asked.

"Yeah, but it doesn't say anything important. It's an old one. Mostly, all Dorie did was slam chapter members."

She cast another look at Nancy. The woman's silence regarding her involvement in the fiasco concerned Anne. Nancy apparently didn't want the others to know she'd shown up, too. Her stomach clenched. Nancy was hiding something.

Her gaze slid around the table. *Who else has secrets?*

Anne inhaled a deep breath before imparting the real news. "I called Sarah Masterson last night."

"What did she have to say?" Jen asked, pouring another cup of coffee and nibbling on a muffin.

"I lied like the old proverbial rug. Told her the cops suspect one of us committed the murder and that we'd found a diary suggesting both Sarah and Careen had been paying Dorie on a monthly basis."

"The cops *do* suspect one of us," Nancy said. "What was her reaction to the blackmail news?"

"I didn't actually use the word *blackmail*, but she understood. The first question out of her mouth was who else knew. I assured her I was the only person who'd read the diary."

"What did she say?" Candace asked as she selected another muffin.

Anne sighed. "It ain't pretty. Apparently, Careen kind of…manipulated the conference books."

"Manipulated? How?" Jen demanded.

"She used the chapter credit card for personal reasons, and faked a bunch of receipts to make it look like conference expenses."

"Careen embezzled?" Candace said with a frown. "She was so sweet and easy to talk to. I just can't picture it."

"The post-conference audit showed the discrepancies. If you'll remember, the treasurer's job was open. Marilee Williams had moved and Sarah was doing the books from February until May when Alice Patrick took over."

"That's right," Rose murmured. "Sarah had taken over as President in March, too. For a while, she held two board positions. Some members were upset about it."

"I remember. The president resigned and moved right after the conference. As Vice President Sarah filled in until elections in April," Candace remarked.

"So, only Sarah and Careen knew about it," Jen said.

"But why?" Nancy asked.

"Careen's mother was at the end stage of a terminal illness. The bills were staggering. Her father had passed away the year before, also with a lot of debt. According to Sarah, Careen was about to lose the house, and her marriage was unraveling fast. So, she took a cash advance, just enough to get some of the creditors off her back, and wrote it off as buffet items and travel expenses for editors and agents. Marilee wasn't detail oriented and never questioned her."

"But Careen knew there'd be a post-conference audit," Nancy said.

"Maybe she didn't think that far ahead," Jen replied.

Anne continued. "Sarah said when she confronted

Careen, the poor woman broke down, swearing it was an act of desperation, and that she would make restitution. She begged Sarah to let her pay off the debt quietly."

"And knowing Sarah, she would have agreed because she was a soft touch and exposing Careen would damage the chapter," Nancy mused.

"So, how did Dorie get a hold of the information?" Rose asked.

"God only knows," Anne replied. "We all focused on the bottom line of losing over four grand and must have missed the holes in the final report before the audit. It's the kind of thing only a treasurer or someone tight with numbers would notice."

"And Dorie, as we all know now, was very tight with numbers," Candace said, curling her lip. "I'll bet she pulled the information out of the audit company."

"I wouldn't put it past her," Jen answered. "Somehow, she found out, and tackled Careen and Sarah."

"That's how Sarah explained it. Said Dorie threatened to turn them in to the police unless they paid hush money. Sarah had just signed her first contract and Careen could have gone to jail. They paid. Not even moving spared them, although Sarah thinks Careen may have finally told Dorie to shove it up her ass."

"Why does she think that?" Nancy inquired.

"Sarah called Careen when she heard about the murder. Careen told her she hadn't had anything to do with Dorie in months."

"I'd love to know what Dorie's reaction to that was," Rose murmured.

"That's all I have," Anne said, glad her reporting

was over. She'd felt sorry for Sarah. The scene she'd witnessed must have been Careen confessing to theft. Sarah tried to help a friend and got caught up in Dorie's evil manipulations. "Candace, what about you? What were you checking on?"

"The bank statements. They're in Dorie's handwriting, which means they're probably from the Caribbean banks. It's just a list of dates starting from January three years ago. Each month she recorded the bank and the balance. I don't know if she transferred the information to her computer and kept this for back up or not."

"In that case, the police have it, too," Nancy said.

Anne wondered if Gil would have mentioned something to her if he'd known. "No, I doubt if Dorie put anything on her computer regarding the offshore accounts. If the IRS ever did come down on her that would be the first thing they'd check."

"At any rate, the last entry is two days before the murder. The 'BOB' listing has a question mark beside it."

"Bank of the Bahamas and Nancy took the call," Rose said. "What is the total from all the banks?"

"Well, the new one in the Caymans isn't listed anywhere, but we know she transferred twenty thousand bucks. Unless there are other new accounts, the total is—hold on to your hats, girls—three hundred fifteen thousand, four hundred sixty-three dollars and seventy-six cents."

"You've got to be kidding," Jen said with a gasp. "My God, how long was she blackmailing people and for how much?"

"That has to be wrong," Anne insisted.

"Hey, I was sober, and I can add. I checked it three times," Candace told her.

"For all we know, she sent other income down there. Maybe she got a divorce settlement," Nancy said.

"I think you may be right," Jen offered.

Anne stared into her coffee cup. "In the diary Dorie talked mostly about moving here and starting over. She was happy to be rid of her lawfully-wedded asshole as she called her ex, and was equally glad to dump the sister. Called her a bitch."

"Must run in the family," Nancy commented.

"Anything else in the diary?" Candace asked.

"Other than unflattering comments about chapter members, nothing that would interest us. It was mostly about her press tour, hitting the bestseller list, and her next book." Anne paused. "There was one strange comment. It was a vague reference about money. It said she figured they'd try to find her for the money, but it wouldn't do them any good. They'd never get it."

"You mean like the money she got from her books?" Nancy asked. "And who are 'they'?"

"She wrote it early in the journal when she talked about the husband and sister, before she was pubbed so, I don't think it has anything to do with advances or royalties."

"Maybe there was a settlement," Rose said.

"Why would the husband and the sister feel entitled to that? And why change her name so the family couldn't find her? Why hide from them?" Anne replied.

"The sister might tell us," Rose opined.

*After Nancy almost going ten rounds with her on the front porch? I don't think so.*

"I'd just as soon not deal with the sister," she replied.

"I guess we'll never know and can't see how it's important anyway," Candace said.

"Rose? What were you investigating—and I don't care what Gil Collins says, we *are* investigating," Jen said.

"You gave me the correspondence," Rose said, biting into another muffin, her fourth. "Where did these letters come from, by the way? I'm surprised Gil didn't get a hold of them."

"It was in a folder along with the bank statements," Candace answered. "The file was marked 'proposals'. I almost passed over it."

"So it was hidden?"

"More or less."

Rose dusted muffin crumbs from her fingertips. "I can understand why. It dates back about four years and consists mostly of rejection letters. She was under contract to three houses and they all rejected her work. Now, I found this very amusing—she also submitted under a pseudonym to Red Hot Publishing."

Candace laughed. "Isadora Powell, the well-known hater of erotic romance, submitted a manuscript to an erotic romance publisher? The fucking hypocrite!"

"I don't believe it," Jen snickered. "She must have come close to having a stroke when she got the rejection."

"What a pity she didn't. It would have saved someone the trouble of killing her," Nancy said, joining the laughter.

"She also had several comments written on some of them. Things like, 'jealous bitch', 'fat pig'—a response to Diana Coleridge's thanks-but-no-thanks over at Hillcrest Publishing, and 'you'll be sorry'. Dorie didn't take rejection with the same philosophy as the rest of us."

"This shows Dorie was getting desperate quite a while ago," Anne said. "She must have begun the blackmail to pay the bills just like we suspected." Anne thought for a moment remembering past critique sessions. "I told her she needed to freshen her approach. Her writing was stuck in a rut of the same old thing."

"Oh, I'll bet that went over big," Rose said.

"She ignored me. That was about four years ago. Not long after, she said she was taking a break from writing."

"Let's see, four years ago? That was right after her last book was published. The one she won her third Campbell for," Candace said with a frown. "I read it and for the life of me couldn't figure out how she won. It wasn't that good."

"Moving on," Anne said hurriedly. She didn't care about Campbells or any other award. "What else did you find?"

Rose finished her coffee before replying. "Things went on in that vein for a while until last summer. Then I came across a letter from Ideal Press saying that due to a change in editorial staff, the house was sorry, but they would not extend her contract."

"She got dumped?" Nancy said, her eyebrows raising.

"It gets worse," Rose told them. "Two months later, Premier Press did the same thing—dumped her."

Anne couldn't believe it. From the stunned silence around the table, apparently no one else could either.

Everyone stared at Rose with varying degrees of astonishment.

"I'm trying to remember her last year at this time," Candace said slowly. "I was so caught up with Eric and the divorce I didn't pay much attention to Dorie."

"I was at the September chapter meeting," Jen said. "If I'm not mistaken, that's when she got into it with Jane Hamilton."

"What happened? Nancy asked.

"I don't think I was at that meeting either," Anne replied.

"I missed a lot of meetings last summer. I hid in the closet and cried because Eric preferred a silicone stuffed twenty-two year old to me. What happened?" Candace asked.

"Well, I wasn't at their table, but you know Jane, she's not the most tactful of people," Jen said. "She asked Dorie when was she going to produce another book, and then had the stupidity to say she thought Dorie's last one wasn't up to snuff and could see why it only got two and a half stars in this one review."

"I sort of remember that," Rose said when Jen paused for breath. "Dorie said something back like, 'when you actually publish that bullshit you write, let me know what kind of review you get' or words to that effect."

"That sounds like Dorie," Nancy answered with a shrug. "I just don't remember her acting any differently."

"No, but she must have been a simmering pot ready to boil," Anne replied.

"There's more," Rose said. "Last February, her primary publisher, Orion Press, sent a letter saying that if she didn't submit publishable work by the end of this month, they would not renew either."

"But she did and saved her ass," Candace said in a hard tone.

"Yeah, but I found a copy of a query letter Dorie wrote to Fulbright Press in March. It was for *Dead as a Doornail*."

"That's the original name of the one she just sold," Nancy said.

"But why is *she* contacting the editor? That's her agent's job," Anne protested.

"I don't get it," Jen commented.

Nancy snapped her fingers. "Try this on. Orion is a major player. They're the biggest romance publishers in North America. Fulbright is fairly new on the scene. So she bypasses Orion and submits directly to Fulbright, who is only too happy to have an author of Isadora Powell's caliber on their list."

"Legal issues," Anne said. "Remember? Claire, her editor at Orion, wouldn't talk about it because of legal issues. Dorie was submitting something Claire Chappelle and Orion had first right of refusal on to Fulbright before her contract with Orion expired."

"But why?" Rose chimed in.

"Who knows? Maybe she was pissed and decided to cut them out of everything. Let the contract expire, and then announce a new signing with a new publisher," Jen said.

"Only, she signed with the new house before her present contract was up," Nancy said. "Whew, Dorie had balls."

"I have something else, too," Rose said. "It's a handwritten draft of a letter dated the day of the murder. It's to her agent. It says, in part," she picked up a sheet of paper and read, "'as per our conversation of earlier this morning, our *author-agent relationship is terminated.*'"

"She fired Pam?" Jen asked with a gasp. "Holy shit! Pam was sending in those manuscripts that were getting rejected. Dorie must have been pissed as hell and cut her out of this last one. That's why she made the submission herself."

"How like Dorie," Candace said with a sneer on her lips. "She kept her agent on a string in case the new book didn't sell, and then fired her when it did. In her mind, she was saving fifteen percent. What a cheap bitch."

"What a motive for both Claire and Pam. And Pam was in Orlando the day of the murder. It wouldn't be hard to rent a car, drive to San Sebastian, kill Dorie, drive back, and then hop a flight home to New York," Nancy said.

"She told me she was on an early afternoon flight," Jen reminded them.

"What she told us and what's the truth are two different things," Rose stated. "She's probably sweating bullets right now wondering if the cops are checking the airlines."

Anne lifted her coffee cup and drank the cold remains. Maybe it was a good idea they were off the case. They had a load of information and while it led to new suspects, it also led closer to the real character of Isadora Powell. How long before one of her victims came clean and confessed paying blackmail? That could open a new can of worms, and like a worm, she squirmed in her chair.

*No, that mustn't be allowed to happen. The word blackmail must never pass beyond the five of us.*

She was about to tell the others that when her cell phone rang. Apologizing to her friends, she answered.

Gil's voice came through loud and clear. "Anne, we have to talk."

Chapter Fourteen

Anne tried to steady her racing heart and control her ragged breathing. His voice didn't sound encouraging.

She cleared her throat. "Good morning, Gil. Talk about what? Let me guess, you heard we were having coffee and donuts and are angling for an invitation. Sorry to disappoint, but we only have muffins and Danish."

He didn't rise to her jest. "Anne, I don't have time for witty repartee."

"Well, what *do* you have time for, Detective Collins?"

She couldn't keep the tartness from her tone and tossed a quick glance at the dining room table. All conversation had ceased and four faces stared at her with varying expressions.

Nancy's was guarded, almost blank, and revealed nothing. Rose looked curious with yet another muffin a few inches from her mouth. Candace caught her lower lip between her teeth, tension and fear in her eyes. Anne wanted to put an arm around the woman and tell her everything would be all right, as though comforting a child. Even Jen's normally open and readable countenance was shuttered.

"I want to talk to all of you in my office this afternoon. Two o'clock. I'll also need Mrs. Swanson's and Mrs. Bennett's fingerprints."

"What for?"

"I'll tell you when you get here. There's been a development."

"Development? What kind of development?"

"You crossed the line by entering a house you had no business being in. It doesn't matter if you used a key or smashed in a window. The key didn't belong to you."

"I apologized. What more do you want?"

"The truth for a change. My office. This afternoon. Two o'clock. And don't be late."

He hung up without saying goodbye. Anne swallowed and slowly turned to face the others. This didn't sound good at all.

"Well, what did he want?" Nancy demanded.

She told them, her voice catching in her throat. "He is not a happy camper."

"But why me?" Rose wailed. "I wasn't there."

Jen didn't say anything, just licked her lips and looked away.

"I have no idea, but he obviously knows we're lying about things," Anne replied.

"Maybe they got something from Dorie's computer," Nancy suggested.

Could this get any worse? Who knew what Dorie had on her computer regarding blackmail and the Caribbean bank accounts? It was the safest place to keep such information. *After all, I'm sure she didn't consider the possibility of being murdered.*

How long would it take Gil to put two and two together and come up with the five of them? Anne shuddered, swallowing the lump of fear in her throat.

Were Jen, Rose, and Candace also harboring secrets?

Rose raised her cup to her mouth with a shaking hand. "I'm not sure how much more of this I can take. All I do is worry and feel sick. I can't even write. I reread what I'd written a few nights ago. It sucked. This Dorie thing has to end. I need to get back to critiquing."

"Maybe it has to do with when we were all there," Jen said. "You know, the day we took those papers."

"I guess we'll find out soon enough," Anne answered, glancing at her watch. "This day is shot to hell. I need to be alone for a while. I'll see you all at the police station."

Nancy rose from her seat. "Same here."

The two of them left and paused under the shelter of the front porch. The squall line had passed through and the rain had let up.

"Oh, God, this is awful," Anne said. "Since he wants fingerprints, I have to assume they printed the house again. Why didn't we think to wear gloves?"

"Because we aren't professional crooks," Nancy answered. "Let's hope he doesn't remember or connect those books I took, or the journal you found, as belonging to Dorie."

"He will," Anne said. "Sooner or later, when we least expect it, he'll remember. So we'd better come up with explanations fast."

****

Anne sat on a bench in the lobby of the police station with Nancy and Candace while Jen and Rose supplied their fingerprints in a room down the hallway. Gil hadn't come to greet them, not a good sign. The hard wood made her shift positions frequently. A light rain still fell.

*Do I need a lawyer?* She had no idea. To show up with one in tow might be construed as having something to hide. No one else seemed to think an attorney necessary either.

As the minutes ticked by, her fidgeting increased. The normally calm and cool Nancy crossed and uncrossed her legs every few seconds.

Finally she rose. "I'll be just outside. I need a smoke."

When she left, Anne turned to Candace. "Are you all right?"

Her friend offered a weak smile. "What you mean is do I want a drink. The answer is damn straight I do. Your detective scares the crap out of me."

"Don't worry. And he's not my detective. This relationship sank before it even pulled away from the dock. Besides, he'll focus on me being in the house again."

Candace unscrewed the top on her bottle of water and drank. "Did you lie to him?"

"A little."

"I have a feeling the phrase 'a little' isn't in his vocabulary."

Anne twisted a tissue between her fingers afraid Candace was right. Gil had something or they wouldn't be here.

Jen and Rose returned.

"You'd think they'd have something to get rid of this ink," Jen said holding up her gray tinted fingertips. "I must have washed my hand ten times, and it's still there."

Rose pulled another wet wipe from the box in her purse and handed it to Jen. "Here try this. They clean just about anything. With four kids I never go out the front door without them."

"What's next? I guess just leaving is out of the question," Jen said.

"I'd have to say you're right," Gil replied.

Startled, Anne jerked her head toward him. She hadn't seen or heard his approach.

"Hello, Gil. What's this all about?"

"If you'll all follow me, there are some things I want to discuss informally." His gaze raked them. "Where's Ms. Carlyle?"

"Outside," Rose answered.

"Get her."

She hurried to the door and motioned. A moment later, Nancy rejoined them.

"Aren't you supposed to read us our rights or something?" Jen asked. "Should I call my attorney?"

"No one is under arrest, but if you feel the need for a lawyer, then by all means contact one. I just want to talk to you all on an individual basis."

"Well, I have nothing to hide," Nancy said in a firm tone.

He turned and walked down the corridor. Stopping, he opened a door.

"Mrs. Bennett, please have a seat. I won't be long."

He repeated his actions with the rest of them, saving Anne for last.

"In here," he said.

Anne looked around and shuddered. "Gil, what's this all about?"

"I'll be back as soon as I can." He left closing the door behind him.

It was an interrogation room. Anne stared at the

small table; its surface scarred with cigarette burns from Lord only knew how many suspects who relieved their anxiety with a cigarette or two.

Her gaze swept upward where she looked at, and then quickly away from, the camera in the corner of the room. She'd seen enough TV shows to know it was running. Her chin quivered.

Taking a deep breath, she pulled out a chair and sat. The hard plastic seat was as uncomfortable as it appeared. She thought about the others. Nancy wouldn't say anything revealing. And Jen would babble until Gil went deaf. Rose didn't have much information to give up, but might mention the papers they'd taken. It was Candace who terrified her the most. Fragile and already scared to death of Gil, she'd come apart at the seams if questioned too hard, especially about the phone.

Over an hour passed before the door opened again and Gil entered. He walked to the head of the table, pulled out a chair, sat, and leaned back casually.

"I thought you'd like to know what I've unearthed about Irina Petrovsky," he began.

Anne licked her dry lips. "Yes, that would be nice." Her voice sounded hoarse, tense. She cleared her throat. "I'd like to know."

"For starters, we discovered a valid Maryland driver's license and several credit cards under that name hidden in a shoebox on the top shelf of her closet."

"Dorie said she was from Baltimore. She went back every couple of years. I assumed it was to visit family or friends. She never said much."

"The address on the license was bogus and the credit cards were used just enough to establish a presence. People who do that are running—either from someone or something. Any ideas which?" he asked.

Anne shook her head. "The sister said at the funeral she hadn't heard from Dorie in a while."

"Mrs. Sessions confirms it was over ten years and had no idea her sister lived in Florida."

"She also said she and Dorie weren't close."

Gil's eyebrows rose. "Sounds as if Ms. Powell didn't much care for her sister."

"Do you blame her?"

"Irina Petrovsky also had a post office box on the far south side of the city," Gil continued.

"The south side? But that's miles away. We know she had one at the post office two blocks from her house. Jen saw her there, remember?"

"Postal employees at both branches positively IDed the renter as the same woman, Isadora Powell. The workers at the south side station say Ms. Powell—or Petrovksy, if you prefer—came in twice a month to retrieve her mail prior to the fifteenth. Any clues as to why?"

Anne suppressed a shudder and shifted in her chair. Sweat popped out on her forehead. She daubed at the beaded moisture with a tissue, and then stopped herself from shredding it. She knew exactly what Dorie retrieved from that box and why. So did everyone else with the exception of Gil, and that was only a matter of time.

"We also found bank statements from a small bank in Orlando."

"Orlando? She had one in Orlando, too?"

Gil tapped a pencil on the table. "Too?"

"I…I mean…I just assumed she had one here in

224

San Sebastian," she stammered. "What kind of an account?"

"It was a savings account. Once a month she'd transfer funds from her San Sebastian bank to Orlando. Several times a year, she'd transfer those funds to another bank. I suspect somewhere in the Caribbean."

"Why...why would you suspect that?"

"Because the Orlando bank is a branch of the Bank of the Bahamas. It was set up for Bahamian workers in the Orlando area to send funds back home," Gil answered, his eyes cutting through her like a sabre.

"And what did the bank tell you?"

"Nothing. They claimed confidentiality as do a lot of Caribbean banks, but since this bank is located on American soil, we might have a shot at prying the information out of them."

Black dots danced in Anne's peripheral vision. The room swayed in and out of focus. She was going to faint. She knew it. Heat suffused her body. She struggled to breathe.

"Are you all right?"

She leaned over and put her head between her knees. "Water," she gasped.

Gil hurried from the room, returning a few seconds later with a paper cup.

She slowly sat upright and drank. Her head cleared.

"Should I call a doctor?" Gil asked, his cell phone in his hand and concern on his face.

"No, no, I'm fine. I...I think I overindulged on Danish this morning. I avoid sugar and it's catching up to me," she answered breathlessly.

"Breathe deep."

"Thanks. I'm all right now. Just a little shaky from

the glucose. Plus it's hot in here. It'll wear off. Let's continue. What else did you learn?"

*Will this never end? Candace isn't the only one coming apart at the seams. The last time I fainted, I was pregnant.*

Gil cleared his throat. "Are you sure you're all right?"

"Yes, I feel better. Go on."

"We also found another safe deposit box in a bank across town under the name Irina Petrovsky. We got a court order and opened it. It contained several small spiral notebooks with page after page of letters followed by numbers. They date from July four years ago to January of this year." He paused and gazed with concerned eyes at Anne. "Are you *sure* you're okay? You're sweating."

Anne wiped her forehead with the tissue and immediately tore off several strips.

"Please, Gil, ladies do not sweat. They don't even perspire. They glow." She swallowed. "How did you discover all of this?"

"One of the things we tagged as evidence was a folder marked 'paid bills.' Inside were invoices for Isadora Powell and Irina Petrovsky, including two separate cell phones. We can't locate the second phone under Ms. Petrovsky's name. Any ideas as to where it might be?" Gil cast a stern look in her direction.

"Not a clue. And why would someone have two cell phones?" She tried to make her voice sound natural.

*I always said it was only a matter of time.*

Anne had once heard a person could only get so scared, and then calm returned. She experienced that now. Her heart rate and breathing slowed to normal limits, and her sweat glands ceased working on overload. In a strange way, she felt at peace.

"I received the phone records last night. There are several calls after the murder. Kind of odd for a dead woman, wouldn't you say? A couple of outgoing calls show up the night you guys played commando. Others appear the day of the funeral. And one incoming call was from a man at the Bank of the Bahamas who says he talked with Miss Petrovsky." Gil heaved a sigh. "Which one of you has the phone?"

"Why would you think we had the phone?"

"I distinctly remember that night. You were busted and sitting in the living room. Three cell phones were on the coffee table. And later, when I dropped by the bar Ms. Carlyle had a phone in her hand."

"So what? Maybe she was going to check her voicemail when you arrived. We don't have this phone, Gil."

In her mind, Anne distinctly imagined Nancy saying, *And you can't prove we ever did.*

"Withholding and or destroying evidence is a crime. So is lying during a police investigation."

"Is this why you brought us here?" Anne asked.

Someone knocked on the door. A moment later an officer entered, handed a sheet of paper to Gil, and left.

The silence stretched until Gil finally set it in front of him.

"We have a problem."

Anne's heart sank to her toes. *Here it is—judgment day.*

"As a matter of routine, we dusted for fingerprints at Ms. Powell's after the break in. Guess what came up?

We found yours and Ms. Carlyle's, all over the office and the bedroom. We also uncovered another other set of unidentified prints plus a couple of partials."

"Well, we may have gone into the bedroom that first night you caught us," she said quickly. "You know, right before the funeral. You laughed at how Jen was dressed, remember? Everybody did. The waiter at Rafferty's thought she was a terrorist and…"

Gil cut her off. "You're beginning to sound like Mrs. Swanson."

Anne bit her lip and hung her head. She *was* babbling. "I'm sorry, please go on."

"Mrs. Sessions hired Ms. Powell's maid to clean up the mess left from the murder. She cleaned all furniture surfaces last Wednesday."

"Oh." She wanted to kick herself for not thinking of that. "Where was the partial found?"

"On the underside of the banister, about halfway up. We found another on the wall next to the light switch in the office, and a third on the doorknob."

Anne breathed deeply. It would be so easy to give up, confess everything, but something inside demanded self-preservation.

"All right, we went upstairs to see if it had been searched and might have touched a few things."

"You touched a lot of things. What were you looking for?"

"I told you. I had a very important partial manuscript Dorie was reviewing. I'm on deadline for it. I thought I'd picked it up the day you let us in, but was mistaken."

"So you searched in the bedroom?"

"When I couldn't find it in the office, yes."

A surge of heat rushed through her body. That was the trouble with lies. Sooner or later they always tripped up the liar.

"I don't believe you."

"Well, I'm sorry, but it's the truth."

Gil consulted the sheet of paper again. "We only got four points from the partial on the banister, and five from the one near the light switch. The one on the doorknob was too smudged to be of any use. We can't arrest on that few markers. But I can say the markers we have match those of Ms. Swanson."

"Good heavens, Gil, under the banister? Near the light switch? Jen climbed Dorie's stairs on numerous occasions, and may have even turned on the light at some point in time. No maid cleans that thoroughly. Are we finished?"

Gil sighed and rose. "For the moment."

Anne rose and headed for the door.

"Wait a minute."

Anne returned, wary and uneasy. He walked over and placed his hands on her shoulders. His expression was bland, but his eyes held a glint of disappointment mixed with anger. She braced for a lecture.

"I'm free tonight. How about dinner? Say seven o'clock?"

She drew a shaky breath. It was not what she expected. Instinct told her to say no, end all social contact with him immediately. Unfortunately, she wanted to see him.

*But should I?* Her want overruled her should.

"That sounds fine. What should I wear?"

"Casual. I'm not in the mood for wine. Tonight's a beer night. I'll see you at seven."

He walked out the door.

Her friends were not in the lobby. She doubted if any of them had hung around the police station after being interrogated. The first thing Anne did when back in her car was to call Nancy.

"Thank God, I was afraid your detective had slapped the cuffs on you," Nancy said when she answered.

"Not yet, but it was intense. Where are you?"

"We're all at Rafferty's sucking down margaritas."

"Candace, too?" she asked in a worried tone. Candace did not need tequila.

"She's here, but sticking with iced tea. Come join us. We're comparing notes."

Anne hung up and headed for the restaurant that was rapidly becoming their home away from home. She found the others at a table near the front windows. Nancy had a sick look on her face, and the rest of the group avoided making eye contact with anyone. Candace fiddled with the straw in her glass. Rose played with a strand of hair, and Jen's gaze darted around the room.

Before she had a chance to sit, Jen asked, "What did he ask you?"

"What did he ask you guys?" she countered.

"He asked me about Dorie and our relationship. Did we argue, did she argue with any of the rest of us? Where was I the night of the murder? That one scared the crap out of me," Rose said.

"Me, too," Jen piped in. "Said he found some kind of fingerprint on the banister that might have matched mine."

"He made that comment to me, too," Anne replied,

worried their answers might not match. "What did you say?"

"That I had been there a few weeks before and could have left it."

Anne breathed easier.

"But then, he didn't say why they missed it the first time around right after Dorie's murder," Jen continued.

At least, Jen hadn't babbled about nonsense. Her eyes strayed to Candace. She appeared calm and composed as she sipped her iced tea.

"What did he ask you?"

"If I had a cell phone belonging to Dorie."

Her heart stopped. Gil must have asked that question of all of them.

"And?"

"I said, what cell phone."

Anne visibly slumped. Thank God. Candace had kept her cool.

"Of course, when he got around to asking if we had taken anything from Dorie's office that day we were let in, I kind of stumbled. I pretended not to know what he was talking about."

"He asked me about the phone, the calls made and received after Dorie's death, and about my fingerprints in her office and bedroom. Since he had us dead to rights on that, I confessed to having searched it. Said I was curious. I don't think he bought it," Nancy told her, finishing the cocktail in her glass. "What did he ask you?"

"About the same." She gave them a quick rundown of her experience, and then shot a glance toward Nancy.

"Nancy told us she was with you the other day," Rose commented. "Doesn't sound like he has anything concrete on any of us."

"Except that we've been lying, and he knows we've been lying, and he probably suspects one or all of us of murder," Jen said.

"Oh God, what are we going to do?" Candace said, a hint of panic in her tone.

"Keep calm," Nancy ordered. "Just deny taking anything we shouldn't have from the house that day, and forget we ever found another cell phone."

"I'm exhausted," Candace said. "I'm going to go home, take a dip in the pool, have an early dinner, and give Bruno his run in the park. When are we going to critique again? I'm sick of talking about Dorie and this whole mess."

"How about my place next Tuesday, ten o'clock?" Rose said.

Jen drained her glass and rose, tossing a ten-dollar bill on the table. "Sounds good to me. I've got to get home. I have to admit being questioned by the police was unique, but not something I want to do again."

"Especially since we're not telling the truth," Rose replied, also rising and tossing some bills next to Jen's.

Anne, Nancy, and Candace left together.

"I'll talk to you later," Candace said in a curt tone. Without bothering to say goodbye, she slid her sunglasses over her eyes and walked away.

Anne and Nancy strolled to their cars parked side by side in the parking lot. The rain had finally stopped and the sun peeked through the scudding clouds that remained.

"Did Gil tell you about the second safety deposit box?" Anne said in a low voice.

Nancy nodded. "Sounds like Dorie kept a duplicate

of the list I found. It was her hit list. From your detective's information, I'd have to say Dorie kept the old payments received, but didn't have time to start a new one. We found the notes."

"Dorie wouldn't jot anything that incriminating down on a piece of paper and leave it lying around for anyone to find."

"From the timing, she may have been too busy with the new book and screwing her agent and editor."

Anne wet her lips and opened the car door. "Anything's possible. Did you recognize any of the initials?"

Nancy lit a cigarette and took a deep drag before answering. "A few. 'AK' slash 'RR' has to be Alice Kartchman, Ruby Redd. Dorie was holding her up for three hundred a month. 'SM' and 'CH' must be Sarah and Careen. They each had to fork over two hundred. I also saw a 'JS' with a question mark beside it. I have to wonder if it was Jen."

"Jen? What on earth could she have done to fall into Dorie's web?"

"I don't know, but if there was anything worth squeezing, Dorie would squeeze like a python. The question mark tells me the blackmail hadn't started yet."

"I see. Anyone else?"

"There was an 'AJ' down for two hundred a month," Nancy said, blowing a stream of smoke from her lips.

Anne didn't dare look at Nancy. She swallowed and closed her eyes. Of course she was on the list. And Nancy? What did those books she stole have to do with it? She didn't ask and, at this point, didn't care.

Nancy crushed out the cigarette and flipped the butt into the grass.

"Your detective might or might not come up with blackmail as a motive, but as far as I'm concerned that list is just a weird bunch of letters and numbers. I'll destroy it. I'm getting good at destroying evidence. I'll burn it and flush the ashes down the john."

Anne slid behind the wheel, closed the door, and then watched Nancy get into her car and drive away.

*How long? How long before everything comes out?*
\*\*\*\*

Anne sat in the booth nursing a beer. Across the table, Gil did the same. The small talk had dried up and she searched for another topic of conversation—other than Dorie's murder.

She was reprieved when the waitress brought their burgers. Anne dumped the condiments on the bun and ketchup on the plate, refusing to meet Gil's eyes. It was an uncomfortable date, and now she wished she'd said no. She took a bite of her burger, but tasted nothing.

"How long are we going to continue discussing the weather and our kids?" he asked, popping a fry into his mouth.

"Well, the weather's been sucky and I like talking about my kids."

"I like my kids, too, but we need to talk about the case. You're all withholding information. I'd bet my pension one of you has that cell phone. Where is it now? At the bottom of a canal?" He took an angry bite of burger.

Ann almost choked, put hers down, and shoved the plate away. "I'm not hungry. I want to go home."

"I'm violating every police procedure by even

discussing this with you. I could get in trouble. Now, what else did you walk out of there with besides critiques? Officer Watkins did more than just record what was taken. He told me everything, including the verbal trashing of Ms. Powell, and Mrs. Swanson's role as water boy. He was gone less than a minute, but that would be just enough time to shove a folder or papers into one of those suitcases you women carry."

Gil took a huge bite of burger, chewed, and then washed it down with a swig of beer. Anne remained silent, furious the policeman with them that day had been nothing more than a spy.

"I also don't buy that you had just arrived at the house the other day either. I think you came in, found the place trashed, and decided to trash it a little more. What are you looking for? More importantly, did you find it?"

Anne crossed her arms over her chest and stared stubbornly at the table top, her jaw clenched. He could go to hell. Gil dropped his burger onto the plate and shoved it away.

"Dammit, Annie, I want answers. Withholding information is a crime. If I find out you have, I'll arrest the lot of you."

Anne slapped her hands on the table. "You want answers? All right, I'll give you answers. We do not have a cell phone belonging to Isadora Powell or Irina Petrovsky. We've contacted a few of the critique partners, but not all. It's summer. Some of them are up north. Those we talked to said they were sorry Dorie was dead. A few admitted she had broken off critiquing with them. Others confessed they had dumped her. Yes, we went upstairs to check if the intruder had been there.

He obviously had. We came back down and were leaving when that bitchy sister arrived. If you want a suspect, check her out."

She breathed heavily and resisted the urge to pour the remainder of her beer over his head.

"We already did. She's clean. From now on, I want you to level with me. Who talked to Ian Collier from the Bank of the Bahamas?"

"Na…nobody I know of." His abrupt question almost startled the truth out of her before she thought.

His eyes narrowed. "Uh-huh. Did Ms. Powell have overseas bank accounts?"

"How the hell should I know? I'm not her accountant."

He wagged a finger in front of her face. "Anne, I'm warning you. I don't care how much I like you, if I find you've lied, I'll…"

She pushed his finger away. "Get that out of my face before you lose it. I'm tired of hearing your law and order lectures. I have something to say to you, too. Lay off Candace."

"Why?" he challenged.

"She's coming off a nasty divorce and is fragile. You showing up the other day scared the crap out of her. Nancy and I came to pick her up for dinner and found her…sick."

"Drunk, you mean? I remember that night at Rafferty's, and she looked worse than some wino on Main Street at the funeral. She was almost too drunk to stand."

"That's right, and if you'd gone through what she has this past year, you'd be drunk, too."

"I've had my fair share of divorces and drinks."

"Yeah, well, Candace had to put up with the stares and whispers about her husband of over twenty-five years parading his new tribute to plastic surgery all over town. And finding a dead body didn't help. Your stunt the other day frightened her."

"Why? I only asked to see her car. It had front end damage, and the workbench was worse for wear."

"And now she has to take her car back in for repairs!"

"Was she driving drunk?" he asked.

"It doesn't matter. She thought you suspected her of bumping off Dorie. She couldn't handle it and got loaded. Leave her alone."

"Why would she think I suspected her? Because of a dog in a car near the murder scene?"

"That's beside the point. Anyway, what possible motive could Candace have for killing Isadora Powell?"

Gil leaned back, stared at her, and drained his beer.

"That's what I'm beginning to wonder—about all of you."

\*\*\*\*

A frosty silence hung in the air on the ride home. His last remark ripped away her anger. Fear replaced it. Under ordinary circumstances, Anne might have let their relationship blossom, but now it seemed prudent to let whatever had budded wither and die. She clutched her purse in her lap, wondering if he was thinking the same. He hadn't spoken since leaving the restaurant either.

Gil pulled into her driveway and stopped the engine. Anne reached for the door handle when his hand stilled her motion.

"Didn't you leave the porch light on?" he asked.

She glanced at the darkened house.

"Yes. I also left a light on in the living room, but forgot to close the drapes," she said, biting her lip and staring at the now covered window.

Her heart thudded in slow heavy beats and she wanted to run in the worst way. Her eyes trailed up to the second floor. She inhaled sharply.

"There's someone in my bedroom," she whispered, staring at the bobbing light through the sheer curtains. The intruder had not closed the blinds.

Gil pulled out his cell. "This is Detective Gil Collins. Send the nearest unit to 7459 Hamilton Avenue. Nearest cross street Taylor Boulevard. Burglary in progress. No sirens."

"Give me your keys, then get out and go next door—quietly," he told her.

"What are you going to do?"

"What do you think?"

"You can't go in by yourself. What if he's armed?"

He raised his pant leg and removed a pistol from an ankle holster. "So am I."

"Gil, wait for back up."

"I intend to, now go."

Anne cautiously opened the door, wincing with fear when the interior light glowed. She closed it again, but not hard enough to latch. Gil did the same on the other side.

"Go!"

Chapter Fifteen

With a thumping heart and fear clogging her throat, Anne turned and ran for her neighbor's, but didn't ring the bell. Instead, she hunkered down behind a hibiscus bush, which was as far as her shaking legs would carry her. She waited, her heart pounding and fear for Gil uppermost in her mind.

She breathed a sigh of relief when a police cruiser glided to a stop in front of her house and two officers joined Gil, now on the front porch. A second squad car also rolled up. After a brief consultation, those officers headed around the back.

The arrival of the other officers eased her fear for Gil. *Thank God, he has help now.*

Using her key to open the door, Gil and the first two men disappeared inside, guns drawn.

Anne held her breath and counted slowly. When she got to thirty, the lights blazed on in her bedroom window. Unable to stop herself, she leaped from her hiding place and ran to her porch steps crouching behind a huge sellum.

Her heart tripped like a jackhammer. Shouts and the sounds of a scuffle broke the silence of the evening. Then the telltale thumps of something—or someone—falling down the stairs followed by a cry of pain scared her worse than the thought of an intruder.

"Gil!" she shouted. The lights in the foyer and

living room flashed on slicing into the darkness through the open door. Anne broke cover and raced up the steps.

She stopped in the doorway and stared as the men handcuffed a subject on the floor.

"I thought I told you to go next door," Gil snapped wiping a trail of blood from a small cut on his cheekbone.

"I did, but wanted to see what happened. I stayed out of sight. You're hurt!"

"It's just a little cut. He nailed me with his flashlight. Dammit, Anne, for all you knew he was getting away. You could have been hurt or taken hostage."

"But I wasn't. Besides, it's my house."

The officers pulled the burglar upright, patted him down, emptied his pockets, and sat him on the stairs. The man's dark hair was disheveled, and a bruise had already formed on the high forehead of a thin, angular face. His brown eyes glared at everyone. Anne had never clapped eyes on him before in her life.

"What's your name?" Gil demanded.

"Look, this is a big mistake. I thought this was my buddy's house and I was going to play a practical joke. Guess I must have got a hold of the wrong address. I've…I've had a few beers." The man's eyes shifted from Gil to her and back again.

One of the officers opened a wallet taken during the pat down. "It says here, he's Paul Proctor of 2165 Suson Oaks Drive in St. Louis."

Anne gasped and clutched the door frame. Her legs went weak with shock. Dorie's ex-husband? What the hell was he doing in her house?

Gil raised his eyebrows. "Well, Mr. Proctor, we've

been looking for you. Want to try that bullshit story about a practical joke again?"

Anne stepped further into the foyer. When no one stopped her, she walked into the living room and gaped.

Proctor had done a rough search, tossing the cushions from the sofa and chairs. CDs, DVDs, and books from her mammoth entertainment center lay jumbled on the floor. A peek in the dining room showed he'd rummaged through the sideboard. Her house resembled Dorie's a few days ago. She'd have liked to check on her bedroom, but Proctor was still sitting on the stairs. She rejoined the men in the foyer.

"I said, let's try this again. What are you doing here?" Gil demanded.

"Go to hell." He jerked his chin in Anne's direction. "Ask her. She and her band of merry lunatics have been all over Rina's house, according to Tasha."

"Who're Rina and Tasha?" Gil asked.

"Irina, my ex-wife's real name, and Natasha Sessions, Rina's sister."

"But what could you possibly hope to find here?" Anne asked. "I don't have anything belonging to Dorie."

"Tasha told me about finding you clowns in her house the other day. You made off with it or know where it is," he claimed.

"Know where what is?" Gil asked.

"Never mind," Proctor said.

"Get him down to the jail. Anne, I assume you're going to press charges."

The only thing of Dorie's she'd taken from the house that day was the diary. Did Proctor know of its existence? He must—why else search two houses? If she pressed charges, he'd likely spill his guts. On the other hand, if she didn't, Gil would be more suspicious than ever. She chose the lesser of two evils.

"Yes, I'll press charges. How did he get in?"

"Broke the window in the back door," one of the officers reported.

"Same MO as at Ms. Powell's. Get him out of here."

The policemen pulled Proctor to his feet, read him his rights, and hauled him out the front door. Anne headed upstairs while Gil inspected the living room.

Being careful not to touch anything, she hurried to her bedroom. It was tossed, but not as badly as she expected. He'd checked under the mattress and had pulled out her dresser drawers, scattering clothing on the floor. Her closet door stood wide open. Nothing appeared to have been disturbed. Proctor must have been in there when Gil and the other policemen surprised him. A photo frame, its glass shattered, and a smashed vase that had stood on a small table next to her chaise, indicated a struggle had occurred.

She rushed to her office, but everything was in order. He hadn't gotten this far.

Anne returned downstairs and found Gil in the living room.

"He made a mess in the bedroom, but it could have been worse," she said.

"Anne, go outside. This is a crime scene."

"I didn't touch anything." Her gaze swept the living room. It would take hours to clean up the mess. She reached for one of the sofa cushions, and then stopped.

"Should I be touching this?" she asked.

"No." He sighed. "Leave it until later when," he told her. "We'll fingerprint him, of course, but in case you didn't notice, he was wearing gloves. He's getting smarter. I'll bet that unidentified set of prints in Ms. Powell's house belong to him. We have to go to the station. I have a prisoner to interrogate and you have a complaint to file."

"What about my back door? I don't want to leave it open."

Gil searched her garage and returned with a piece of heavy duty cardboard and a roll of duct tape. He taped the makeshift glass over the open windowpane.

"There, not the most secure, but it'll do. Call your insurance company in the morning. Let's go. I want to interrogate Proctor."

Gil locked her front door, handed her the keys, and then walked her to the car. Fastening her seatbelt, Anne gazed at the house now awash with light streaming from every window. Gil backed out of the drive.

"How's your cheek?" she asked.

"Fine. A little first aid when I get to the station will do." His voice was clipped and unemotional.

Anne drew a shaky breath. She knew Paul Proctor was about to be grilled like a burger on a backyard barbeque. She also knew she'd be next.

\*\*\*\*

While Gil had received a small bandage for his cut, Anne filled out the complaint form. Given permission to hear what her intruder had to say, she now stood behind a two-way mirror looking at Gil, another detective, and Paul Proctor in the interrogation room. She found it ironic it was the same room she'd been in just hours before.

"Are you sure you don't want a lawyer?" Gil asked

"What the hell for? You're going to slam the cell door behind me anyway."

"I take that as a no. Your choice. Now, why did you break into Ms. Jamieson's house?" he asked, bracing his hands on the table and leaning over.

Proctor squirmed on the chair. "I thought she had something that belonged to me—something she or her friends had taken from Rina's house."

"And what would that be?"

"Just something. It's personal."

"Personal. Why did you break into your ex-wife's house?"

"Same answer. I was looking for something personal."

"Why not just ask Mrs. Sessions to let you in? She accommodated the ladies a couple of weeks ago."

"She said anything that was Rina's is now hers and to take a hike. Greedy bitch. Just like her sister," Proctor muttered.

"Personal how? Did Ms. Powell have something of value like a watch or a ring? An heirloom perhaps?" Silence. Gil pulled out a chair and sat across from the prisoner. "You know, Mr. Proctor, not answering the questions or lying isn't going to help you. If you cooperate, I may be able to convince Ms. Jamieson to drop the charges. If not, then I'm afraid I'll have to cut this short, and lock you in a holding cell with some— let's say, not so nice people. Now, I don't want to do that, and I'm sure you don't want it either. Do the right thing and come clean."

Anne held her breath. Gil sounded like a nice guy who was sympathetic to the prisoner. Would it work?

*Wish he'd been that conciliatory to me earlier.*

The other detective lounging against the wall with his arms crossed finally spoke.

"Gil, you're too nice. I say throw him in with the gang bangers. Let him take his chances. He's reasonably good-looking and wearing nice clothes. They'll have him bleeding and naked in seconds."

"Now, Chris, don't be so harsh. We're checking with St. Louis to see if Mr. Proctor has any priors or outstanding warrants. I don't see how tossing him in with a bunch of TrueBluds is going to help. You don't have any priors or outstanding warrants, do you, Mr. Proctor? Because that could change things."

"No warrants," Proctor said quickly. "I have a couple of DUIs on my record, but that was three or four years ago. I'm clean."

Chris unfolded his arms and walked over to the table. "I'm tired and cranky, Proctor. I haven't had dinner yet tonight. I want to get home, eat warmed over lasagna, and screw my wife. Don't keep me too long. She goes to bed early. What personal items?"

Anne enjoyed the good-cop-bad-cop routine. Until now, she hadn't known it actually existed. A woman opened the door to the interrogation room and handed Gil a slip of paper.

He read for a moment, and then said, "Now, this is downright interesting, Chris. It seems Mr. Proctor's fingerprints are all over Ms. Powell's house. Since the maid cleaned thoroughly last Wednesday, I'd have to say you paid a visit sometime between Wednesday afternoon and early Thursday evening when the ladies entered. Care to tell us why?"

The prisoner drummed his fingers on the table and

Anne shifted from foot to foot.

*Here it comes.*

"Rina used to keep a journal. She'd write in it every night. When I asked what she was writing, she laughed and said her memoirs."

"A journal? What did it look like?" Gil asked.

"It was one of those artsy-fartsy things with flowers or photos on the cover."

"How big was it?"

"I don't know. Looked like a notebook. I didn't measure the damned thing."

Anne broke out in a sweat and Gil shifted his gaze to the mirror, staring with a stern expression even though he couldn't see her. The shit had hit the fan. She should never have lied, but turned the journal over to him immediately.

"Why did you want it if it was your ex-wife's?" Chris asked.

"Rina never threw those journals away. She must have had five or six of them by the time we divorced."

Chris sighed and leaned in close. "Proctor, I'm hungry and horny, now get to it. What's in this one specific diary?"

"We didn't find anything like that when we went over her office and the rest of the house," Gil said.

Dorie's ex shrugged. "Maybe she finally tossed them or stuffed them up in the attic."

"You didn't answer my question. What's in the diary you're looking for?" Chris leaned further forward, his face inches from the prisoner's.

"About two months before the divorce was final, Tasha came down to St. Louis to visit Rina. One day they crossed the river to gamble on the casino boat and bought a lottery ticket together."

"Let me guess—it won," Gil said.

"They didn't have all the numbers, but enough to walk away with over two hundred fifty thousand big ones."

Chris whistled and Gil raised his eyebrows.

"The drawing didn't occur until after Tasha returned home to Beloit. She forgot all about buying it. Winners have about a year to turn in winning tickets. Rina waited two or three months after the divorce was final, cashed the sucker in, and split."

"Guess we know why she changed her name," he remarked to Chris. "So she took off without informing you or your lawyers of potential community property," Gil said. Proctor nodded. "So, how did you find out?"

"Rina had sold her half interest in the house to me. I still lived there. One day, a letter addressed to Rina arrived from the Illinois Lottery Commission. I was curious and opened it. It congratulated her on the win and gave the date of the drawing. It also asked for more information for tax purposes. I contacted my lawyer. He hired a private investigator who traced her to Baltimore. Then she vanished."

"So, she stiffed you for half of her half of a winning ticket. What about her sister? Did she know?"

"She found out when the PI contacted her. I thought maybe they'd been in touch and had already split the dough. Should have known better. Rina wouldn't share money with anybody. Tasha insisted she and Rina went halvsies, but I only have her word for that. She can't prove she laid out any cold, hard cash, or that it was even the same ticket," he declared.

"And now that your ex-wife is dead, you plan on

claiming the entire quarter million for yourself, huh?" Chris said.

"Why not?" Proctor answered with a sneer. "It's mine. Dorie stiffed me."

"It's yours only if we find a will saying it is," Gil reminded him.

Anne closed her eyes remembering the strange passage in Dorie's diary about them never finding the money. She also remembered the huge total from the overseas accounts Candace had investigated.

*I guess we know where the lottery money ended up.*

"And the journal?" Gil asked.

"I thought maybe she might have said something. She recorded everything."

"And did you find a journal?" Chris asked in a weary voice.

Proctor rubbed his nose. "Yeah, I grabbed it from the bookshelf and ran. It was the wrong one. This one was current."

"Where is it?" Gill asked.

"At my hotel in Melbourne."

"Which one?"

"The Launch Pad Motel and Apartments on U. S. 1. Room one-seventeen."

Gil picked up a phone on the wall. "Contact the Brevard County police. Get a search warrant for The Launch Pad Motel and Apartments in Melbourne, room one-seventeen." He hung up and Chris left the room. "Will we find anything else from Ms. Powell's home there?"

"Naw, I wasn't interested in anything else. My ex did all right for herself," he said in a bitter voice.

"How did you finally find her?"

"Damnedest thing. I remarried six months ago. My wife loves those romance novels. Always got her nose stuck in one. At any rate, she picked up one by Isadora Powell and raved about how great it was. It had a gory cover with some half-naked babe on it. I flipped it over to the back and stared at my ex-wife's face. I hired a private investigator right away."

"When was this?"

"Two months ago. He finally traced her to San Sebastian."

"And you've been down here how long?" Gil asked.

Proctor shook his head.

"How long have you been registered at the Launch Pad Motel?"

"All right! Two fucking weeks, but I didn't kill her. I didn't even know she was dead until I read it in the papers."

"Neighbors saw a man leaving her house the afternoon of the murder."

"Well, it wasn't me. I called and left a message, but she never returned it."

*Oh, yes, she did. She used the other cell phone.*

Anne almost wilted with relief. Here was a real suspect. He was probably lying about being there that evening and for all she knew, had come back later to kill Dorie.

Gil rapped on the closed door. A uniformed policeman stepped inside.

"Take Mr. Proctor to his cell."

"Hey, you said I wouldn't be locked up!"

"I said I wouldn't throw you in with scum. But until we get the warrant and search your motel room, you're going to be a guest of the San Sebastian taxpayers. Besides, Ms. Jamieson filed charges. Take him away."

The cop led Proctor out of the door. Gil followed. Within seconds, he opened the door to the viewing room.

"I want that journal," he said in a tight voice. "And so help me, you had damn well better produce it. Is that clear? Bring it to me here tomorrow morning. If I don't have it by noon, you can join Paul Proctor in a cell, discussing the sins of withholding evidence, and the merits of telling the truth."

"All…all right. We didn't mean any harm, Gil. Honest. We found it in the mess on the office floor. It was old, but not as old as the one Proctor wants. This deals with her life when she first moved to San Sebastian. It says nothing about winning a lottery."

"I don't care. You lied. You've been lying from day one. I'll have someone drive you home."

Anne walked down the hall behind Gil, her conscience stabbing reminders that once, she'd been ethical. The whole ugly business would come out. She was convinced nothing could stop it. The right thing to do would be to tell Gil, but she clung to that last sliver of hope her reputation could be preserved.

She stared at Gil's rigid back. He'd never want to see her again. They'd only had two real dates. Tonight didn't count. They'd both been angry. In spite of her thoughts of earlier about cooling the relationship, Anne would miss him. He was warm, funny and thoughtful.

*Damn. When I screw up, I really screw up.*
**\*\*\*\***

The first thing Anne did when the policeman

finished checking her house and left was to call Nancy.

"Nancy, we've got big problems," she said, and then proceeded to give her friend a recap of the evening's events.

"Oh, crap, this is unraveling fast. I'll go with you."

"God, no, don't do that. He might remember those books you took. I assume they're important to you personally."

The silence on the other end of the line confirmed Anne's suspicions. Whatever Dorie had on Nancy involved those books. She also had a suspicion of what. She couldn't help it when her mind fantasized a furious Nancy in Dorie's office with a Campbell award gripped in her hand.

*Is that what happened?* Had Nancy had enough and snapped? She wanted to ask, but didn't want to know.

Nancy didn't answer, but instead asked, "Does Gil think this Paul Proctor killed Dorie?"

"I don't know. He's not exactly talking to me at the moment."

"It figures Dorie would try to screw both her sister and ex-husband out of the money. We're not doing well with this sleuthing thing, are we?"

Anne sighed and ran her hand through her hair.

"We're doing well enough to get into trouble. He knows or suspects we took something from Dorie's house the day the sister allowed us in. But, I don't think he's connected it with bank statements or the correspondence yet. It might be a good idea to hand them over."

Another silence greeted her suggestion.

"We both have too much to lose by doing that,

Anne. Call the others in the morning, and have them destroy everything. That way we can honestly say we don't have it."

"Like with the cell phone?"

"It's gone, and he can't prove we ever had it," Nancy answered in a sharp tone. "Same goes for the papers."

"Nancy, I don't like it. He's bound to request bank records, and when he doesn't find corresponding statements at Dorie's, he'll *know* who did."

This time the silence loomed longer.

"Anne, a chain is only as strong as its weakest link. Don't be our weak link."

Anne shivered at the tone of Nancy's voice. The statuette in Nancy's hand flashed through her mind again.

"All right. I'll call them in the morning."

"Good. We have to stick together in this."

She had no answer to that, so ended the conversation. "I'll talk to you tomorrow. Right now, I have to clean up."

Anne hung up and began the task of straightening the house. Anything to take her mind off the veiled threat from Nancy. Dorie had blackmailed her for money, but now Nancy was demanding emotional blackmail.

Deep down, she knew everything would be revealed, and she'd rather it was revealed to Gil than to the powers that be at Writers Association of America.

She started with the bedroom, stripping the sheets from the bed and putting on clean. She didn't want to sleep on anything Paul Proctor had touched. The clock struck three when she shoved the last book into the bookcase in the living room.

Trudging upstairs, she crawled into bed, pulling the covers up to her chin. She stared at the ceiling for a few minutes. How much longer would she be able to count any of these women as her friends?

Anne rolled over, buried her face in the pillow, and sobbed.

Chapter Sixteen

Anne called Rose first thing in the morning.

"Hello?" Rose sounded harassed even though it was only eight o'clock. In the background a baby wailed and a TV blared.

"Rose, it's Anne. I need you to do something."

She proceeded to tell her about the break-in.

"So he was the one who broke into Dorie's? God, you must have been scared to death."

"It's not something I'd want to live through again."

"What did he have to say for himself?"

Anne told her about the interrogation at the police station and that Gil knew about the journal.

"I'll take it in to him today. Since we're so far into this now, Nancy thinks it best if we destroy all that correspondence and the bank statements we pilfered from Dorie's last week."

"Right now?"

"As soon as possible."

"I'm on it."

Rose must have taken her literally. The sound of rushed breathing came over the phone. A moment later, a door slammed.

"Anne, do you think your detective will get a search warrant or something for my house? What will I tell the cops? What will I tell Jack?"

"Rose, don't panic. Just destroy everything and

toss it in the trash, preferably not your own."

"Oh, good idea. My neighbors are on vacation. I'll use their garbage can. A warrant wouldn't include my neighbors and the police wouldn't have probable cause to get one either, would they?"

Anne took a deep breath and released it. Suddenly, everyone was a legal expert.

"No, I don't think they'd search your neighbor's trash."

Nearby, Anne heard a paper shredder doing its job.

"There, the first one is history."

More shredding followed until Rose yelped, "Jack! Haven't you ever heard of knocking?…I'm busy. I'll be down in a few minutes…Oh, for Pete's sake, it's scrambled eggs. Make 'em yourself."

She couldn't hear all of the conversation, but sighed again. Rose's husband was a jerk, and in her opinion, her friend should have handed him a frying pan years ago.

"Men! I'm a nervous wreck with this business and if I stopped to think about it, I'd throw up right now. You'd think he'd have a little consideration and just once do something to help around here," Rose grumbled.

Anne had no idea what to say.

"So, do you think Detective Collins will ferret out the blackmail? I'd hate to see Dorie's victims made public."

"Gil is a detective, and a good one. He's going to put it all together."

Anne didn't add she'd hate to see *anything* made public, too. Destroying evidence left a bitter taste in her mouth, but not half as bitter as being exposed to all as a victim herself and the reason behind it. A sudden screeching brought an exclamation from Rose.

"Lousy, cheap piece of shit. The paper's jammed again. I should have bought the more expensive model, but the kids needed shoes and the baby was outgrowing his clothes. However, did that stop Jack from ordering the super deluxe sports package from the cable company? Oh, no, not him!" Her comments were interspersed with grunts as she wrestled with the errant sheet of paper.

Anne didn't want to listen any more. "I've got to go, Rose. I need to call Candace and Jen."

"All right." She paused. "We should never have lied in the first place, but once we got started we couldn't back down. Damn, Annie, I'm scared."

"I know. I am, too."

She hung up and bit her lip. *Nancy suggested I was the weak link in the chain, but what if Gil starts questioning Rose? Would she be the first to admit everything?*

"I wonder how much we're lying to each other?" she whispered.

****

Candace stared at the charred remains of Dorie's bank statements in the kitchen sink. There! They were gone. She gave the faucet a vicious twist and watched the ashes swirl down the drain.

Finished, she turned off the water, and poured another cup of coffee. The one thing she didn't need was Anne's phone call this morning. The news about Paul Proctor and the break-ins scared her almost as much as Detective Collins. If he knew about the journal, what else did he know?

On the other hand, if Dorie's ex was arrested for the murder, maybe Anne's boyfriend would no longer be interested in her. If he questioned her again, she might not be able to lie. She closed her eyes and shuddered. That man and his dog haunted her dreams.

Maybe she should cancel her tee time. Her hand reached for the phone, and then hesitated. No—follow through. She needed the exercise. It was time to rejoin the human race. She'd go early and have lunch. Maybe Bert would be there. In spite—or perhaps because of Eric and the bimbo's presence—she'd had fun the other night.

Candace bit her lip and glanced at the kitchen clock—eight-thirty. Her hands shook and her stomach did nervous little flip flops. She set the mug back on the counter.

*Who am I kidding? I want a drink. I want one bad.*

Bruno scratched at her foot. She picked the little dog up and cuddled him.

"What am I going to do, Bruno? Will I show up for my golf game drunk as a skunk or will I resist the pull of Grey Goose?" The shih-tzu licked her nose. She laughed. "Okay, you greedy little devil."

Candace fed him a treat and set him back on the floor. Dammit, she still wanted that drink.

She eyed her purse and car keys on the table, then whirled and headed for the utility room. Grabbing a bucket, Candace filled it with water, a cleaning agent, and mopped the floor instead.

The ringing phone stopped her halfway through. Caller ID identified Nancy.

"How are you doing? Did Anne call?"

*What she really means is are you sober?* She bit

back a retort. Nancy might be abrupt, but she cared.

"I'm fine, and yes, Anne called this morning. I burned everything and washed the ashes down the sink. What about the list you had?"

"It's gone. Poor Anne. She must have been terrified last night. Thank God Gil was with her. Paul Proctor could be the best news so far. If the police prove he was in the area *and* had a grudge against Dorie, maybe the rest will fall into place."

"We can only hope. How are you holding up?"

Candace suspected Nancy had a secret or two. Her determination to destroy evidence proved it. *But then, we all have secrets, I guess.*

"My agent just called and read me the riot act. Said this latest novel wasn't my best work. I probably could have edited better, but this shit with Dorie is a distraction I don't need."

"I'm so sorry, Nancy. Did she out and out reject it?"

"No, she's e-mailing it back to me. I have one week to clean it up and re-submit. I've never missed a deadline before. Damn, this is book number two of a four book deal. If I don't get with it, I'll end up like Dorie, my contract cancelled."

"We've all been on edge. Maybe you need a diversion—something to take your mind off, well, everything."

"Like what?"

"I'm jittery, paranoid, and still scared. I wanted a drink, but decided to mop the floor. Keeping busy helps. Do you play golf?"

"Not in years."

"I have a one o'clock tee time and no partner.

Would you like to take out some frustrations on a defenseless little ball? I even have an extra set of clubs. We can go early and have lunch."

"That might not be a bad idea. I suppose I can dig a few divots. What time?"

Candace breathed easier. With Nancy around for lunch, the urge to drink anything stronger than iced tea would diminish. "I'll pick you up at eleven."

"See you then."

Candace hung up and looked at Bruno lying in the dining room doorway.

"Mama has a lunch and golf date with a friend." She laughed as the little dog cocked his head and listened. "You know, baby, a few weeks ago the only thing Nancy wanted to do with a golf club was brain me with it."

She resumed mopping the floor. Visions of Grey Goose danced in her head, but she resisted the overpowering urge to have that drink.

\*\*\*\*

"…and I'm sorry. I don't know how often I can tell you that. I found it on the floor and thought it might contain something to convince you to let us continue helping the police."

Anne sat in front of Gil's desk making her plea for leniency.

"I got over mad a long time ago. Do you have the diary?"

Anne fished in her purse and finally extracted the journal, handing it to him.

"It isn't all that interesting. She just goes on and on about moving to San Sebastian, meetings with the Southeast Florida chapter, and forming our little group.

It was her idea to call ourselves the San Sebastian Writer's Support Group, only we dropped the 'support' because it sounded like we were sick or something. In the end we dropped the name altogether. Just called ourselves the group. At any rate, she makes a few nasty comments about some of the members, but…"

Gil held up his hand and Anne ceased talking. Good grief, she babbled worse than Jen.

"I was up until four in the morning. I'm very tired. Is there anything else in your possession from Ms. Powell's I need to know about?"

The lines on his face had deepened into grooves and Anne had an urge to run around the desk and hug him.

"We didn't mean any harm, Gil," she said. "We thought we were helping."

"Right," he said, running his hand through his hair. "This isn't *Clue* or *Murder She Wrote*. There is nothing fun about murder."

"We realize that, and tried to be serious about what we did," Anne stated. "I guess we got carried away."

"Yeah, I guess. What surprised me the last time was finding only two of you breaking and entering. Maybe I should talk to everyone again."

"Gil, please, not Candace. She's easily upset just now. I told you that last night. Nothing's gone right for her in over a year. First her husband dumps her, then she practically gives up writing, and just when it looks like things might settle down, Dorie gets killed. Talk about stress. And to top it off, she damaged her car again. And she'd just gotten it out of the shop."

"Anne, I don't care about the personal lives of your friends."

She took a deep breath to steady her nerves. At least she and Gil were talking in civil tones even though it was in a police station.

"Did you recover the other diary from Proctor's motel room?"

"Yes. That's why I was up so late. I read it. It's only about half full. The entries begin in January of this year and end the day before her death."

"Did you find anything useful?"

Gil gazed at her, but his face and eyes were unreadable. She wondered if all sharing had ceased.

"I have no idea. She used a lot of initials when writing about people or places and spoke of deals and contracts. Unfortunately, she didn't offer any explanations. Must have been in a previous journal."

"Gil, I know we've been a pain in your backside, but if you could lend us the journal, maybe we can figure it out. You know, put names to the initials or know what the deals are about," she suggested in a subdued voice. "I promise we'll report everything we uncover. We probably have a better shot at deciphering it than you do."

Gil closed his eyes. Anne held her breath. Would he let them view the diary?

"I must be going soft in the head." He reached over, lifted the receiver of his desk phone, and punched in a number, while at the same time, pulling the journal from a drawer. "Harris, please come in a moment."

A few seconds later, the office door opened and a uniformed female officer walked in. Gil handed her the book.

"Would you please make a copy of this?"

She nodded and left.

Anne wanted to sag in relief. *Perhaps this is the route to getting back to where we were.*

Gil turned his attention back to her. "I'm going to treat you like any other rookie cop. When you finish reading this, you make a report. And it had better be truthful. I'm done playing games."

"What about Paul Proctor? Is he a suspect?" she asked.

"One set of partials we lifted from the house the day of the murder could be his, but it's not enough to say definitely. Your charges are the only thing holding him."

"Oh. I was going to drop them if he paid for the damages to my door. I don't want to have to call my insurance company. They'll raise my rates."

"Give Mr. Proctor another day in jail. I'd like to ask a few more questions," Gil replied. He tapped a pencil on the desk pad calendar. "That whole crime scene has me baffled."

"In what way?" Anne asked.

He frowned and doodled in the margins of August.

"For starters, we found the victim's, yours, Ms. Carlyle's, and Ms. Warren's prints on the murder weapon."

"Maybe the killer wore gloves," she suggested.

"Then that makes it premeditated. Someone went there with the intent to kill her," he said.

"I'd say a quarter of a million dollar lottery win is a hefty motive, especially if what Proctor said is true and Dorie stiffed both him and the sister," Anne commented. She snapped her fingers. "Yeah, what about her? That sister sounded greedy as hell. Maybe her prints are the unidentified ones."

"The sister has an alibi. She's a waitress and was working at Beloit's Best Steakhouse in Beloit, Wisconsin on the day of the murder. Her employer confirms it."

"And Paul Proctor?" Anne said.

"Claims he was out drinking at several different bars in Melbourne that night. We're still checking."

"So, you really don't have much of anything," she said, shaking her head. "We may never find the killer and if he wore gloves, then he meant to kill her."

"That's it. But…"

"But what?" Anne urged.

"This doesn't smell like premeditated murder. It's a crime of opportunity and passion." He frowned again and ran a hand over his face.

"Passion! You mean like a boyfriend?"

"I know you write romance, but not all passion is sexual. The savagery of the blows—there were five in all—tells me someone was angry—very angry. The killer grabbed the nearest object he or she could find, the statuette, and…"

"A Campbell," Anne supplied, interrupting.

"Whatever…and struck."

"Dorie thought she was alone, hence the headphones and iPod. Maybe it *was* her ex-husband. Maybe he was the guy neighbors saw leaving earlier in the day. He and Dorie could have had an argument. Then he came back later and killed her." She'd expound on any theory to prove Paul Proctor the killer. "Or he and Dorie argued, then she turned her back on him to show contempt. He got pissed and nailed her. He could have used his shirttail or something to wipe the Campbell clean of fingerprints."

Gil shook his head. "Proctor doesn't strike me as being that smart."

Anne had nothing to say to that. Gil's office door opened and the female officer returned with the journal and a sheaf of papers, handing them to her boss.

"Thanks." After she left, Gil handed the papers to her. "Okay, here it is. Look it over and call me with what you find. And I mean everything."

"Oh, I will. I promise," Anne said in a rush. "Although, if this one is as boring as the last I can't see staying awake. For a writer, you'd have thought Isadora Powell would have been more creative in her personal diary." Anne rose. "I'll read it, and give you a call. Maybe you'd like to hear the details over a drink or something." She held her breath. Would he accept the olive branch?

"Just call me when you're finished." He pulled a file folder toward him, opened it, and proceeded to read.

Her heart sank. He was still angry with her. She'd been dismissed like a reprimanded schoolgirl. With a murmured goodbye, she left.

In the car, Anne ruffled through the pages Gil had given her. Their copier could have used a better grade of toner. The writing was faded. Since time was critical, she decided two pairs of eyes were needed for this. But whose?

She couldn't deal with Rose at the moment. And avoiding Nancy had a high priority. For the first time since knowing her, Anne felt uncomfortable in her presence. Candace? *No, I can't put any more pressure on her.*

That left Jen, and while the constant babbling

might prove a burden, she called anyway with a luncheon invite.

Jen was more than willing. "The Palm Court has a great seafood salad."

"Sounds good. We can have a glass of wine, order, and read some of this."

Anne arrived first at the restaurant, and was shown to a table near the front windows. Jen walked in a few minutes later. Both women ordered white wine. Anne divided the sheaf of papers, handing some to Jen.

"So, do you think your detective will call us in again?"

"I wish you guys would quit calling him my detective. It's not true, and after this past week, I doubt if he'll ever ask me out again."

She thought briefly about the books Nancy had stolen. Would Gil remember and question her? How could three historical novels be of any importance?

The waitress brought their drinks and Anne sipped the chilled Pinot Grigio. Did she believe Nancy's reasons for taking the books? On the surface, her explanation sounded plausible, but Anne also knew Dorie's blackmail tentacles ran far and wide. Which could mean those books might have contained something Nancy would rather not see revealed.

*The only thing the books had in common was the sub-genre. One was* The Hills of Home, *Nancy's book of a couple of years ago. The other two are old, probably out of print, and by authors I've never heard of.*

"I still think Paul Proctor's good for it," Jen said, breaking into her thoughts.

"Could be. I hope so. Then this whole mess will be

finished and we can get back to our lives."

"And don't forget Pam Graham. An enraged agent screwed out of fifteen percent of a potential blockbuster could have a huge motive. Claire Chappelle must be pissed, too."

"For all we know, someone on Dorie's hit list may have sneaked into town and done it. She had victims outside of the state." Anne sipped again. "You know, a part of me hopes the case is never solved. I'm afraid I may know the killer."

Jen stared into her glass frowning, and then said slowly, "Anne, do you think the police seriously suspect one of us did it?"

Anne's stomach clenched. The wine burned. She was sure of it.

Chapter Seventeen

Anne was spared answering Jen's question by the waitress arriving. They both opted for the seafood salad. She hoped to duck replying, but Jen didn't let go.

"So, *do* the cops suspect one of us?"

"I...I don't know." She raised her glass with trembling fingers. "Gil hasn't said anything even though he knows we've been less than truthful."

Jen sipped her wine and looked thoughtful. "I agree with you. If Paul Proctor didn't do it, then I hope whoever did is never found. Isadora Powell was a nasty piece of work—insecure, petty, mean-spirited, and greedy as hell."

"Amen." Anne had had enough of Dorie and motives. A change of subject was due. She picked up and riffled through the sheets of paper before pulling some out. "Let's take a look at this. I've got May, June, and July."

"That means I'm starting with the first four months."

They read Dorie's journal in silence for a minute or two before Jen commented.

"Listen to this. 'I can't believe such a great plot came from such a feeble mind. It's a mess, but I can fix it and turn it around.' She must have been referring to her latest book." Jen squinted at the date in the faded printing. "This was written in January—January third to be exact. What on earth does she mean by a feeble mind?"

"We know the creative well was dry for quite a while. Rejections piled up. Some of Dorie's plots and characters during that period were not the best. I read that partial we found in her office. It was like she hurried and wrote without thought."

"It just doesn't sound like a word Dorie would use to describe herself," Jen said, reading on.

"Holy cow," Anne said a few seconds later with a gasp. "Listen to this. 'Had a call from CH today. Told me our deal was no longer in effect. When I replied there was no backing out, the silly bitch told me to sit on it and rotate. She'll be sorry. As soon as I get this book deal done, I'll take care of her.' CH? Careen Holcombe?"

"It must be."

"This is dated May 2nd. So, Sarah was right. Careen hadn't had anything to do with Dorie in months. Wait, there's more. 'Must contact SM. Warn her not to think along those lines, too.' Sarah didn't say if Dorie called her."

Jen snorted. "Of course not. If I was Sarah, I wouldn't admit it either. Oh, boy, this is interesting. 'Have had it with PG. I'm giving her good stuff and she's not doing her job. It's been almost four years. When I get this piece of shit manuscript cleaned up, I'll take matters into my own hands. The same goes for CC. The bitch had the nerve to say *Into the Wind* wasn't up to Orion standards. She'll regret it. I'll get them both.' Just as we thought. She was by-passing both her agent and her editor."

"When's it dated?"

"Ah, let's see, January 15th."

"Something's odd," Anne said, drumming her fingers on the table. "She says she gave Pam good stuff, but in the next sentence refers to her work as a piece of shit. Dorie thought everything she wrote was worthy of a Pulitzer."

"Maybe it was an old manuscript from years ago and she pulled it out in desperation. I did that once, but never got it to gel. The karma wasn't there. But then I'm not as talented as Dorie."

"Don't say that. You're extremely talented."

Anne read quietly for several minutes. The month of May had little else of interest, but June 10th almost made her heart stop.

*AJ is a pain in the ass. Oh, well, at least she's always been on time with what's due. Most of them are on time now. I kind of miss calling AKRR and reminding her. I used to love listening to her teeth grind. God, I love making her grovel. The others are all cowed—except NC and AJ. They have a certain dignity when they let me know in a not so subtle manner that I can go fuck myself. So, they hate me. So what? I'm getting rich and they're not.*

Anne repressed a shudder. What was she going to tell Gil? He was too smart not to recognize AJ as her and NC as Nancy. She swallowed as an invisible noose tightened.

The waitress brought their salads. Anne absently thanked her, but continued reading. By this time, she was afraid to see what else Dorie had penned. She looked up to observe Jen picking idly at the meal while she continued to read also. She stopped what she was doing and gazed at Anne with wide eyes.

"What? Something we should be concerned with?"

Jen shook her head. "No, but geez, this bitch was two-faced. There's not much January through March. I guess she was busy with her book. She got down to personalities in April. On April 19th she says, 'Cannot believe CW is such a moron. Always whining about that stupid husband of hers and his new girlfriend. I could have told her ages ago the guy was looking to bolt. The aging Lothario came on to me once. Luckily, I had someone else on the line and told Eric to go stick it in himself. Of course, if CW had any brains at all, she'd have never bought that bullshit I gave her about her last book.' I can't believe Eric Warren came on to Isadora Powell."

"Do you think Candace *knew*?" Anne asked.

"I doubt it. If she did, she'd have killed…" Jen stopped short and stared. "Oh, God, you don't think…?"

Anne's thoughts raced back to Candace's ramblings of last Friday and to other comments made regarding Eric in the past few months.

"I don't think so. She'd have said something, especially with how much she's been drinking. No, her bitterness is centered on Missy What's-Her-Name." Anne speared another forkful of seafood and ate. The salad was delicious and the light vinaigrette dressing perfect. Shame she couldn't enjoy it more. "I wonder what she meant about bullshit and Candace's last book."

"Knowing Candace, she probably asked for advice and Dorie gave her a hunk of crap about plot or characters. She'd get a kick out of Candace taking the advice, and then failing again."

"Come across anything else?"

Jen shook her head and scanned the rest of the diary. She ate and read several pages in between bites.

"Just the usual, although she does comment on contacting the publisher she eventually sold to, Fulbright Press. Anything else in your pages?"

"Not really," Anne lied. "Wait a minute. Here it is, July 1st. 'I did it! I sold *Death Becomes Him* on my own. As soon as I have the contract signed, I'll dump that asshole Pam. My contract with Orion is up on July 15th. I'll tell BP not to release any announcement until after that and to date the contract accordingly. I'll get rid of two assholes at the same time.'"

"Wow, there really is a hell of a legal battle forming over this, isn't there? Who's BP?"

Anne sipped her wine. "Brian Preston, the head of Fulbright. I can smell lawsuit a mile away. I'll bet Dorie even managed to convince Brian to go along with delaying until after the 15th. I've met him. He's not above screwing a rival."

"Don't you just love this business? It's full of such upstanding people."

"Most of the people I know are nice, hard-working, and friendly. It's just a few manipulators and bad apples like Dorie that grab the attention of the public."

"I suppose you're right. Remind me to tell Pam to never submit my work to Fulbright Publishing. Are you finished reading?"

"Almost."

Anne skimmed the entry dated July 13th while Jen continued eating.

*Got nasty call from CC at Orion. Heard rumor that Fulbright would be my new publisher. Threatened lawsuit. Told her to cram it. Also talked to PG. She's furious about being canned. Called me a lot of nasty names and said she didn't need me anyway. Said she just sold a book by JS and claimed she would be the next Isadora Powell. HA! Guess maybe it's time to call JS and have her play the game, too.*

Jennifer? Jen was about to join the list of blackmail victims? Why? What did Dorie have on her? She wanted to ask, but then thought better of it. She really didn't want to know.

Anne put away the pages and cast a glance at Jen who smiled before pushing her bowl away.

"That was great. I love this place. The food's never disappointed me," Jen said.

"You know, some of what Dorie wrote is damned explosive. She makes veiled references to blackmail on several occasions. How much of the truth do we tell Gil? He probably suspects it anyway."

Jen shrugged. "As much as will make him happy, but not enough to hang the victims."

"I guess that makes sense. I can say some initials refer to people in other chapters. I just hope he won't want to talk to them."

"Tell him some of them moved away and you have no idea where they are. People like Careen. She may be pissed enough to spill the beans about everything if he were to talk to her. So, do we talk to Gil together or would you like to get him one on one?"

Anne didn't miss the gleam of humor in Jen's eyes, but ignored it. "I'll talk to him. Should we make up a plan?"

"What kind of a plan?"

"Matching names with initials in case Gil wants to

verify what I tell him with one of us."

"Pretend ignorance. We're all in too deep with the lies for anything else. I'll just say I'm not very good with remembering names," Jen said airily with a wave of her hand.

The waitress arrived with the check. After splitting the bill, Jen left wishing Anne good luck. She assumed Jen referred to meeting with Gil and not lying, although by now, the two were intertwined.

Anne rehearsed what she'd tell Gil on the drive home. It had to sound convincing and yet not give anything away.

*Which means I'm lying to him again. And does it really matter? He's more or less dumped me anyway.*

It angered her that the first man to spark her interest since the divorce was also the one man to whom she couldn't tell the truth. Even from the grave, Dorie reached out to screw up her life.

****

Anne tweaked a curl into place, and then hurried to answer the door.

"Hello, Anne," Gil said stepping inside. "Thank you for calling. I didn't expect to hear from you so fast."

She tried to ignore the cool, professional tone of his voice.

"I read most of it over lunch." She led him into the living room. "Can I get you something to drink?"

"No, thanks, I won't be staying long." He sat in a chair while Anne perched on the edge of the sofa. "What have you got for me?"

"Well, it was vintage Isadora Powell. She had the tongue of an adder, but I guess you know that."

"I know." He pulled a notebook from his jacket pocket. "What can you tell me about SWFWAA and Frolic on the Beach? What are they? She made a couple of comments in the diary about them."

"SWFWAA is Southwest Florida Writers Association of America. I'm a member there also. They cover the southwest coast from Naples up to Sarasota. Frolic on the Beach is their annual conference. It was held last February on Marco Island. I read that passage. She called the co-chairs a couple of inexperienced boobs, and said the workshops were uninspired. I attended the conference. Neither is true. What she really meant was nobody fawned all over her."

"I'm interested in the initials. For instance, CW— as in Candace Warren?"

Anne heaved a sigh. "I'm afraid so. Dorie didn't like Candace that much. Said she was too stupid to read let alone write. I just hope none of this is made public. Candace liked her and considered her a good friend. She'd be terribly hurt by what Dorie wrote."

"And CH and SM?"

"CH, I'm not sure. I think she may be referring to a former member who left town several years ago. I can't remember her name—Carol? Cathy?"

"Why would she tell Ms. Powell to kiss off?"

"Oh, Dorie could be persistent, especially if she wanted something."

"Like what?" Gil asked with a raised eyebrow.

Being vague wasn't going to work. She'd have to come up with more details.

"Critiquing for one. She went through a lot of partners. I think we told you that. Maybe she wanted to form another online group."

"And SM? Who's that?"

"I kicked this one around all afternoon. It may have been a lady named Sally. Her last name eludes me, but I think she moved to Sacramento two or three years ago. I didn't know her that well."

He shot her an unreadable glance and Anne immediately tensed. She had the feeling he wasn't buying this.

"How about AKRR?"

"I have no idea."

"PG and CC?"

"Probably Pam Graham and Claire Chappelle, her agent and editor."

*Let Pam and Claire answer for themselves.*

"I'm interested in NC and JS. Could that be Ms. Carlyle and Mrs. Swanson?"

"Jen said no when I asked. Ours is a large chapter—close to a hundred and ten members. We have a Nelda Conway, and a couple of other JSes. I also belong to the chapter that covers the Tampa area. They have several members with the same initials. Dorie belonged to more than one chapter, too. A lot of us do. She could have been talking about someone from a different group."

"You're just a fountain of information. The initials AJ piqued my interest the most."

Anne laughed nervously. Better to admit it. "Yes, I confess, the pain in the ass AJ is me."

"What did she mean by being on time?"

"Some critique partners are lazy about sending in their stuff. Dorie hated that. Figured if she was ready, then everybody else should be, too."

"Any idea what she meant by an increase?"

"We usually limit ourselves to twenty-five pages per session. It used to be twenty, but when Dorie was in a hurry, she bullied the rest of us until we agreed. She often wanted to critique more pages."

Gil flipped the notebook closed and smiled.

"Thank you. I guess that answers most of my questions. You were right. For a bestselling author, Isadora Powell wrote a lot of boring stuff in her diary."

Anne relaxed, relieved he seemed to be thawing.

"So, what's going on with Paul Proctor? Do I drop the charges or let him rot for a few more days?"

He hesitated for a moment before answering. "Paul Proctor. A very interesting man. I talked to him. He admits Ms. Powell called him back. The records for the missing phone confirm it. He also admits the two of them met that afternoon around five-thirty and argued. According to Proctor, his ex-wife said he couldn't prove anything, but changed her tune when he waved the letter from the lottery under her nose."

Anne nodded. "The date of the winning draw would be in it. So, if she won prior to the divorce, he has a legal claim of the winnings being community property. I can't understand why Dorie would risk having her photo on the back of her books if she was hiding from her ex."

"Proctor admitted the only thing he ever reads is the sports page."

"And the sister didn't strike me as a book lover. I'll bet the thought of coughing up two hundred fifty thousand big ones had Dorie damned near choking."

"Proctor said she almost turned purple, cussed a blue streak, and threw him out. But he also swears he never came back later that night to kill her. We found one bartender who can confirm Proctor's story from seven until about eight-thirty, which still leaves time to drive down to San Sebastian and commit murder at ten or thereabouts."

"He could have left Melbourne at eight-thirty, driven here in an hour, killed Dorie, and then raced back to Melbourne hitting another bar at say ten-thirty to establish an alibi," she said.

Gil smiled and shrugged. "Anything's possible. And rarely are eye witnesses, like bartenders, accurate regarding time. Eight-thirty could have been eight-fifteen and ten-thirty could be eleven."

"In other words, he's still a suspect."

"Let's just call him a person of interest. Give me another day to verify his alibi." He paused and stared into her eyes. "The phone records for the missing cell also show Paul Proctor's number was called after Ms. Powell's death. I don't suppose you know who made that call do you?"

"Not a clue."

Gil's expression sent a creeping sense of unease slithering up Anne's spine. He knew something, but wasn't sharing. She decided to probe.

"Have you uncovered anything else?"

"Her agent has been cleared. She was definitely on the four-thirty plane to New York from Orlando on the day of the murder. Her editor also was in New York that night. It was confirmed by several dinner guests."

Anne was glad neither Pam nor Claire was involved, although it brought the attention right back to the five of them and Paul Proctor.

"I never suspected Pam or Claire. They were pissed and likely to sue Dorie, but that was all. Well, that and a lot of character assassination along the way." *If the contract with Fulbright Publishing didn't work out, they'd have made sure she never sold another book to a reputable house again.*

Gil stared at her with an inscrutable expression. "Her bank statements are predictable."

"Predictable? How?"

"The Bank of the Bahamas branch in Orlando decided to release the information we wanted. Every month Ms. Powell made deposits between the fifth and the fifteenth. The totals were always within the fifteen hundred to two thousand dollar range and in cash. Then once every three months, she transferred between two and five grand to the main bank in Nassau."

Anne licked her lips and swallowed. Gil stared like a tiger about to pounce. She refused to wipe the faint dampness forming on her forehead.

"So, the Bank of the Bahamas is cooperating?"

Gil uncrossed, and then re-crossed his legs.

"Just the one in Orlando. They're in US territory," he told her.

"Then how do you know that's where she sent this money?"

"Everything leaves a trail. People get away with hiding income because the government doesn't look until they have a reason. Even then, it's still possible to cover the tracks by routing money through five or six countries."

"Well, Dorie hated giving up a dime to anyone, so I can see how she'd do that."

"This pattern suggests something else. As a cop, I'm naturally suspicious, so I asked the south side post office to let me know if anything arrived for Irina

Petrovsky's box. The supervisor called yesterday. Two letters showed up. I dropped by this afternoon. Guess what?"

A trickle of sweat slid down Anne's temple and her heart rate increased. He knew. He knew everything. She waited like a Thanksgiving turkey for the axe to fall.

"What?" she asked in a hoarse voice.

"The envelopes contained two hundred dollars each. That's all. Just cash. No notes, no explanations, and no clue as to the sender. Not even a return address."

"How...how odd."

"It's not odd at all. I think Isadora Powell was a blackmailer."

The room spun for a moment. Sickness churned in her stomach. He'd been toying with her—a cat to a mouse. He had connected the dots.

"Blackmail? I don't believe it. She was a bestselling author. Why would she blackmail people? It makes no sense."

"It does if she was greedy. And you've told me on several occasions she was. Plus, she hadn't sold a book in quite some time. Did I mention the bank account in Orlando was opened exactly three years ago? One of you also stated that Ms. Powell was a master of research. Dig deep enough and it's possible to find anybody's secret."

His blue eyes pinned her to the back of the chair like an insect in a collection. Her stomach turned. *It's all over.*

Still some sense of hoping she could escape the inevitable prevailed. She tried to look and sound incredulous.

"I'm sorry, but I just don't believe it," she stated in

a shaking voice.

"I think you do. I pulled Ms. Carlyle's and your bank records for the past year. Every month you both withdrew two hundred dollars in cash. Isadora Powell was blackmailing you. Why Anne?"

She licked her lips and inhaled an unsteady breath. "That's…that's crazy."

Gil leaped to his feet and pointed a finger at her.

"No, it isn't. Dammit, why can't you for once since I've met you, tell the goddamned truth! What did the woman have on you?"

Anne flinched at the harsh tone. She closed her eyes. *I'm tired of the lies. I'm tired of wondering which one of my friends might be a killer. And I'm tired of being scared all the time. He knows. At least give him this before he walks out for the last time.*

She rose, walked on shaking legs to the bookcase and stared at the family photo on the shelf. Tears slid down her cheeks.

"Those first few months after my divorce were rough. I was alone, dealing with two kids, and had bad coping skills. My ex was regular with his alimony and child support payments, but somehow it wasn't enough. I'd never paid a bill or balanced a checkbook during my married life. He did all of it. To take my mind off my problems, I volunteered to judge the Writers Association of America Campbell awards."

"That's the name of the murder weapon, right?" Gil hadn't moved, but his voice was hard.

She nodded. "I received a box of books to read, and when I opened it found Dorie's. Judges are supposed to return any book they feel they can't judge for whatever reason."

"But you didn't."

"I meant to, but the next day was my turn to host the critique meeting. I put the box in the corner of the dining room. Dorie was the first to arrive. While I was in the kitchen, she snooped. She stayed after the session and made me an offer I couldn't refuse. She'd pay me five thousand dollars if I gave her book a perfect score and assigned the others in her category a low one. Five grand meant a lot to me, so I agreed. She left and returned a while later with the money in an envelope."

"And that's how she won an award she didn't deserve. I remember one of you telling me about this rumor."

"I had no idea such a rumor was floating around. At any rate, the next day I regretted my decision and tried to pay the money back, but she refused. Said a deal was a deal. I got angry and told her I'd report her to the National organization."

"What was her response?"

Anne heaved a deep sigh. "She said she'd tell them I came to her and solicited a bribe, and that she'd refused. She also added that she'd better win or she'd do it anyway."

"Were you the only one to judge her book?"

"No. I think each book had three judges. A fourth would be called in if there was a tie."

"So, she had no guarantee of winning on just your word alone," Gil said.

"Dorie's book was good, but not great. I gave her a perfect score. I guess the other judges also scored it high."

"When did the blackmail start?"

"The week after she won. If I didn't pay, she

threatened to tell the committee it was all my idea, that she'd said no, and since she won, was only telling them now as a moral obligation. Moral obligation. Those words out of Dorie's mouth. My reputation would be ruined and my publisher would drop me like yesterday's news. Same with my agent. My career would be over. When I asked where I'd get the two hundred a month, she said she didn't care. I should eat hamburger instead of steak."

"Why didn't you tell me this a long time ago?"

"I was afraid you'd think I did it—killed her I mean." She looked him straight in the eye for the first time since beginning her confession. "And I was afraid you'd think less of me. I enjoy being with you, so I lied. And once I started, I had to continue. Lie after lie after lie. Gil, I'm so sorry."

Gil sighed and ran a hand through his hair. "What about Ms. Carlyle? Is she also on the list? What about the others?"

"I don't know. You'll have to ask them. All I ask is that you don't tell them about this."

"No reason why I should unless it turns out to be relevant to the case. Of course, when we make an arrest, you may have to testify about all of this in court."

Testify in open court? Her stomach cramped. *How on earth do I get out of this? Oh God, please let it be Paul Proctor.*

"You do realize blackmail gives you a motive, don't you?"

"I know, but I swear to you, I had nothing to do with Isadora Powell's murder."

He blew out a breath. "Your actions have thrust

both of us in a bad situation. A woman I'm very fond of has just officially put herself on the suspect list." He glanced at his watch. "I'd better go."

She trailed behind as he walked to the front door. To her surprise, he turned and placed his hands on her shoulders.

"Anne, I'm sorry you got involved with this. I'm a hardened cop who still gets sick when he sees a corpse. I can imagine how you must have felt finding Ms. Powell's body. And I'm sorry you've had such a rough time."

Before she could answer, he pulled her into his arms and covered her lips with his. A hot surge of pure desire shot through Anne from head to foot. Her knees went weak and her heart beats pounded in her ears. She wrapped her arms around his neck and kissed him back. For the first time in years, her body reacted, coming alive, and responding to a primitive urge.

The kiss went on and on—hot, wet, and incredible. He tasted of breath mints with a hint of coffee. The hair sliding through her fingers was soft and thick. He gathered her closer until not even a slip of paper would fit between them. She was both shocked and excited to feel his erection growing. Anne leaned into him thanking the goddess of laundry she had changed the sheets yesterday.

But when she moaned deep in the back of her throat, Gil stepped back. Slowly, she opened her eyes and stared. The expression on his face was part passion, part sorrow, and part pity.

"Gil?" she whispered, confused. "What is it?"

The conflicting emotions still swept across his face. "Did I mention that Ms. Powell's neighbor across the street finally came home? She had a lot to say about that night. I was especially interested in the redheaded woman knocking on the front door the night of the murder. We need to talk. My office. Tomorrow at eight sharp." He pulled her back into his arms for a brief hug. "I'm sorry, Anne, but that's the way it has to be."

He released her, opened the door and walked through, closing it with a soft click.

Anne stood rooted to the foyer floor in stunned amazement. *I was seen that night? And he knew. From the moment he walked into the house, he knew. I'm in deep trouble.* Like the actions of an attacking shark, she'd never seen it coming.

Another trip to the police station called for serious measures. Anne whirled and ran to the kitchen where she grabbed her address book and her phone. With trembling fingers, she fumbled through the pages for a number and dialed her attorney.

Chapter Eighteen

Anne walked behind her attorney into the police station. At the front desk, she stood still, biting her lips and trying to hide the tremors in her hands.

"This is Anne Jamieson. I'm Thomas O'Dell, her attorney. We have an eight o'clock appointment with Detective Gil Collins."

The man behind the desk ran his finger down a sheet of paper on a clipboard, and then made a check mark next to a name—hers, she supposed.

"Have a seat. I'll let Detective Collins know you're here."

Anne stumbled to a vacant chair and sat heavily. Her night had been sleepless, and even the thought of coffee this morning had churned her stomach. It growled now, demanding food.

"Relax, Anne," Thomas told her. "Just tell him what you told me. You'll be fine."

"Yeah, but what I told you could get me arrested."

"I doubt that, but the fact you withheld the information isn't good."

Her divorce attorney had recommended Thomas O'Dell, a colleague from the same firm. A quick call along with an explanation of why she needed him had produced instant results—not cheap, but instant. She hadn't told him about the blackmail. She'd do that only if she was actually arrested for murder.

A uniformed officer stopped in front of them. "Ms. Jamieson, Detective Collins will see you now. Please follow me."

She rose on shaking legs. The fact that Gil hadn't come to escort her back personally didn't bode well. She swallowed and kept her eyes trained on the officer's broad back. Inside the interrogation room, she took a seat on the far side of a Formica topped table. The tiny room stank of sweat and the lingering scent of fear from numerous suspects, guilty and not guilty alike. She was certain she'd add to the miasma.

Thomas sat next to her and opened his briefcase. Extracting a file, he read silently. Her gaze fixated on a clock on the wall. It was eight-oh-two. She then looked toward the large mirror to her right knowing exactly what it was. Only a few nights ago, she'd been standing on the other side watching Paul Proctor's interrogation. Anne wondered who stood behind it now watching her.

The door opened and Gil walked in followed by the same detective from the other night. Thomas rose and introduced himself. The men shook hands and Gil took a seat opposite them. The other man leaned against the door, his arms crossed. Her almost-boyfriend messed with some papers and set up a small tape recorder before raising his head to stare at her.

"Good morning, Ms. Jamieson. Thank you for coming in."

Unable to think of anything to say, Anne nodded and twined her fingers together on the table top as if in prayer, but in reality to hide the trembling.

"This shouldn't take too long. Before we begin, I want to inform you this proceeding is being both video and audio taped. This machine is strictly for my benefit.

Are you ready?"

Anne nodded and let her gaze slide toward the second detective—Chris? Was that his name? He didn't smile, but just stared, a blank expression on his face.

"On the morning of July 21$^{st}$ of this year, you and two others ladies discovered the body of your friend and critique partner, Isadora Powell. When asked for a statement, including your whereabouts the night before, you stated…" Gil opened a folder and read from a sheet of paper. "'…I was home all evening reading one of the last critiques and making comments before our meeting the next day. It was nothing special. My children were staying with their father in Orlando. I had dinner, did the critique, and worked on my work in progress until around midnight, then went to bed.' Would you say that was accurate?"

His brusque, businesslike tone didn't instill confidence. Any thoughts of him cutting her a break disappeared. To compensate, she kept her tone cool.

Casting a glance at Thomas who nodded, she replied, "No, it wasn't."

"Would you care to amend your statement?"

She licked her lips. "Yes, I would."

Gil switched on the tape recorder. "Please begin."

"Dorie called around five o'clock to remind me about the meeting. She also insisted I…I repay some money I owed her. The amount she mentioned was more than the debt, and when I protested, she said we'd talk about it the next day."

"Why did you owe her money?" Chris asked.

"I…I had some unexpected expenses pop up. Kid oriented. Dorie lent me the money. When she called, she said she needed it repaid immediately."

"How much was this loan?" he continued.

"Two hundred dollars. She told me three hundred."

Anne swallowed again hoping this was close enough and that Gil wouldn't officially pursue the blackmail angle. She shuddered remembering her anger at Dorie upping the payments to three hundred a month.

"I thought about it for a while, and then decided not to wait until the next day. So, I left the house and went to Dorie's. I knocked on the door for several minutes, but she never answered. I finally gave up and came back home."

"And what time was this?" Gill asked.

"Eight, maybe eight-fifteen."

"Detective, the coroner's report states that the victim died between ten and two o'clock, considerably after the time my client was there," Thomas said.

The Chris detective answered. "Doesn't mean she didn't come back under the cover of darkness and whack her over the head. Why didn't you tell us this in the first place?"

Thomas answered for her. "Because she didn't think it was of any importance. Plus, finding the body of her friend was traumatizing."

"I…I forgot about it—really. I didn't remember until much later, after I'd given my statement. I'm sorry if I've created problems."

"At least your times coincide with the neighbor across the street," Gil said.

"I guess Dorie must have been busy writing and didn't hear me ringing the bell or knocking."

Gil turned off the recorder and shoved the papers into the folder.

"The coroner's report states Ms. Powell had

consumed dinner approximately two hours before her death. Stomach contents revealed the meal had consisted of heavy sauces reminiscent of French cooking. There's a French bistro a few blocks from her home. When we questioned the staff, they stated she arrived about seven-thirty, ate, and then left before nine. Her credit card receipt confirmed it." He rose. "Thank you for coming in, Ms. Jamieson. I'll have this amendment typed up and added to your statement. It won't take but a few minutes. Please, wait here."

Both men left the room and Anne sagged back in her chair.

"Exactly how much trouble am I in?" she asked.

"Enough to drag you down here in an official capacity, but the time frame isn't a match and so far, no one has put you at the scene of the crime when it occurred."

Time dragged. She drummed her fingers on the table. *What is taking so long? I want to get out of here and home. I've seen enough of the inside of police stations to last a lifetime.* While she waited with ill-concealed impatience, her attorney read files.

To occupy her mind, she tried to focus on her work in progress, but failed. Dorie's grotesque, bloody body kept intruding and she couldn't help but wonder about the woman's last moments on earth. Had she felt pain or was the first blow the killing one? Had she sensed someone behind her? Perhaps a brief reflection of her attacker in the monitor screen—just enough to give her a hint of what was to come? Anne could think of a lot of ways to die. Being bludgeoned wasn't one she'd choose.

*Maybe I should switch from vampires and*

*werewolves to suspense. God knows I'm accumulating
a butt load of firsthand knowledge.*

Finally, a policewoman entered with the newly
amended statement. Anne signed and rose. One last
look at the clock told her the whole ordeal had lasted
less than an hour.

While walking through the lobby, she glanced
toward the far side of the room and stopped in her
tracks. A woman stood beside a man, her body
language tense.

"Nancy?" she said with a gasp.

Nancy looked up, anger and fear on her face.

Before either woman could speak, Thomas guided
her through the station doors.

"Don't talk to her in the middle of the police
station," he advised. "Save it for later."

Nancy had also been brought in? She assumed the
man with her was a lawyer.

*Oh, my God, what kind of information does Gil
have on us? Is he going to tackle her about the
blackmail, too?*

And what about the others?

At home, Anne finally choked down a piece of
toast and some coffee. Every few minutes she looked at
her watch. Nancy would call. She knew it.

Her cell rang at ten-fifteen. It was Nancy.

"Nancy? Did Gil call you in to talk about…about,
you know?"

"You mean blackmail? Oh, he asked if I was being
blackmailed, but I denied it. Told him I withdrew
money because I like to pay cash. No. He called
because some nosy neighbor saw me at Dorie's that
night."

Anne gasped. "You, too?"

"Oh, damn, let me guess, you also paid the bitch a visit that night."

"Oh, God, can this get any worse?"

"I think it can. When I was leaving the police station I spotted a familiar red minivan parked not far from my car. I looked in the window and saw four child seats, assorted empty fast food containers, and a passenger seat full of books."

"Rose? He called in Rose?"

"Looks like it."

"I wonder if he's calling us all in. My appointment was for eight. You obviously had a nine o'clock time. My guess is Rose bought ten. That leaves Jen and…oh, crap, Candace. She's scared to death of him. I have to call her."

"If he called her last night and she's upset, she'd have called one of us. Look, let's not talk about any of this on the phone. Meet me at my house this afternoon. Is three all right? I'll call the others."

"Three's fine."

She hung up wondering how much trouble they were all in. And why would Gil want to talk to Rose? Unless, she'd been at Dorie's the night of the murder, too.

Anne hung her head and cried. The solution was clear. If Paul Proctor hadn't killed his ex-wife, then one of her friends did.

****

Anne arrived early. She wanted to talk to Nancy privately. A pale, clearly shaken Nancy answered the door and showed her into the living room.

"Did you say anything to him about blackmail?"

Nancy asked.

Anne nodded. "I told him, but I didn't mention you. He had it figured out anyway. Said the journal writing combined with her financial records confirmed it."

"Thanks for nothing."

"Look, we're in deep trouble here. He strongly suspects you're on the list and that Jen was about to be. And I just couldn't lie anymore—at least about my end of it. I'm tired of doing that."

Nancy ran a trembling hand through her dark hair. Anne noticed she needed a trim. The normally short, precise style was ragged. *Guess we all have other things on our minds.*

"All right, all right. Sorry I snapped. Have a seat. I don't care why Dorie was blackmailing you, and I have no intention of telling you why I forked over two hundred bucks a month. It's none of your business. Besides, it's all over now."

Anne settled on the sofa. "I agree. Did you get a hold of the others?"

"Yes. Rose is terrified and even Jen's beginning to show signs of stress. But get this—Candace wasn't invited to the party."

"He didn't ask to interview her again? But she was with us when we found the body."

"But apparently no neighbors saw her at the house the night of the murder. Would you like some iced tea?"

"Yeah, fine," Anne muttered. "Well, that's one load off my mind. I'm not sure Candace could have survived Gil questioning her, especially with an attorney present."

The doorbell rang.

"Get that, would you. I might as well pour tea for everyone."

Anne answered the door and let Jen in.

"Oh, God, Carl almost had a cow when I told him I needed to go to the police station with a lawyer. He's demanding answers I haven't got."

"Did he go with you this morning?" she asked leading Jen into the living area.

"Yeah, he sat there with me and the lawyer while your detective asked me questions about the night of the murder."

The doorbell pealed again. Anne opened up to Rose and Candace standing on the porch. As they took seats, Nancy walked in with a tray of iced tea glasses and set it on the coffee table. They all grabbed one and gulped at the same time, not looking at one another.

The women resembled characters in an Agatha Christie novel. *I've gathered you all here to tell you the killer is...*Anne had the strangest feeling this group would never critique another page together.

"Why are we here?" Candace asked.

"Because other than you, we were all questioned— with lawyers present—about the night Dorie was killed," Anne said.

"From what I understand more than one neighbor saw cars and people arriving at her house," Nancy added.

"Why were you there?" Jen said staring at Anne.

She wasn't about to admit to being blackmailed to the rest of her friends.

"I was in the neighborhood and needed to talk to her about something personal. She didn't answer the door, so I left."

Jen's gaze slid to Nancy. "And you?"

Nancy's gaze was riveted on the floor. "I showed up around eleven-thirty. I wanted to tell her I would no longer be critiquing with her. I'd been driving around for quite a while. I often do that when I'm having a problem with a story only this time the problem was Dorie. I'd had it with her nastiness, her demands, and everything that was Dorie. I pulled up in front of her house under the street light, got out and went up the walk. But I never made it to the porch. I decided it was too late to have any kind of discussion with her, so I left. I guess one of the neighbors saw my car and remembered."

Anne could understand how a neighbor at that time of night would remember a white Toyota Prius. Then she caught the look Jen sent her way.

*She knows. She knows we were on the list with Careen and Sarah.* Did she suspect she was about to join them?

"Did you tell the police this?"

"Of course. The neighbor never saw me go in or come out of the house because I didn't." Nancy took a long pull of tea. "Rose? Why were you questioned?"

Rose sniffled and searched in her purse before pulling out a travel-sized package of tissues.

"I can't afford a lawyer, so when Detective Collins called I was so scared I spent practically the whole night throwing up." She wiped tears from her eyes.

"But why were you there?" Jen insisted.

"You guys aren't going to believe this, but *I* had the best motive for blackmailing *Dorie*."

Anne choked on her iced tea. "You?"

Rose nodded. "Last fall I was at a conference in Atlanta. Dorie was there, too, but I didn't see much of her. She was too busy with Pam and other pubbed authors to talk to me. At any rate, I'd submitted a manuscript to one of the editors attending and I had a pitch session with an agent. I was in the bar late one night practicing my spiel when the editor and agent came in and sat at the table next to me. They started talking about the pitches they'd heard and comparing schedules for the next day. When the agent mentioned my name, the editor said she'd talked to Dorie earlier and Dorie, who knew I'd submitted, told this editor she was my critique partner, and to be careful because I plagiarized some of my work. The editor said she'd considered giving my book a green light, but now didn't think she'd take a chance."

Anne stared. *Plagiarism? Stinking bitch.* How like Dorie to use the setting of a conference to screw Rose.

"Did you set the record straight?" Nancy demanded.

Rose shook her head. "No. I was too embarrassed and upset. I wanted to talk to Dorie first. I cornered her at breakfast the next morning and demanded answers. She denied everything at first, but in the end had to admit it, so she said she'd talk to the editor and make it right. She apologized and said she was drunk at the time."

"That's a load of crap," Candace said. "If she'd been loaded, the women wouldn't have given her information so much as passing consideration."

"Obviously, she didn't do what she promised," Jen replied.

"I waited a couple of months, and then Dorie was

gone for the holidays, so I didn't tackle her about it until January. Her excuse was she was busy, but would get right on it. Only, she never did." Rose blew her nose. "Naturally, during this time, I received a rejection letter. That night I had to run to the convenience store about nine-thirty or so. I stopped by her place and parked in the drive. I knocked, but she didn't answer, so I came home."

"What was it about Dorie that she couldn't stand to see other people succeed?" Candace said almost to herself. "She took pleasure in giving them the wrong advice, and then watching them fail."

"Did you tell Gil all of this?" Anne asked.

Rose nodded. "I was so scared and don't have an attorney. If I'd used the guy Jack does for his business, he might have told him, and then I'd be in deep trouble at home, too. I guess someone must have seen my van that night."

"Dorie had obnoxiously observant neighbors," Nancy commented. "So, everyone showed up. I'm surprised we didn't trip all over each other."

"I wasn't there," Candace said. "I was home tying one on. I got stinking drunk early and woke up at six in the morning on the sofa hung over as hell. I almost canceled going to the meeting, but had some errands to run and decided why not go. Wish now I hadn't."

"That leaves you, Jen. When and why were you there?" Rose asked.

"Dorie called me around four or four-thirty that afternoon. Said she wanted to talk to me about our mutual agent, and then congratulated me on my first sale. Told me Pam mentioned how having two critique partners as clients was a plus for her, and thanked Dorie for the letter of recommendation. Dorie instructed me to come by around ten-thirty that night for a private chat. I tried to put her off, but she was damned insistent. I knew what she wanted to talk about."

"What?" Candace asked sipping her tea.

"I lied to Pam Graham at a conference. I pitched my book to her, and then when I saw her in the bar later, bought her a drink. I...I told her Dorie and I were good friends, and that she suggested I talk to Pam. I even gave her a letter from Dorie praising me. I typed and printed it out myself, then forged Dorie's name from an autographed book I had. A month later, I had an agent."

*And Dorie was about to add you to the list of monthly payments.* But would Pam have dumped Jen because of a little subterfuge? Anne doubted it. Agents dealt in that every day. But then, perhaps Jen hadn't considered that.

"Ten-thirty?" Nancy said. "Did you go?"

Jen nodded. "I told Carl I had to run out for some milk. He was up to his ears in the Asian markets on the computer and didn't pay any attention to me. His SUV was parked in the drive. I grabbed the keys and headed for Dorie's. I took a couple of wrong turns, so it was closer to eleven when I got there."

"Oh my God, did you see her?" Anne asked, sick at what the answer might be. Jen could very well have been the last person to see Isadora Powell alive. Had they argued? Did Jen get so angry she nailed her critique partner with the Campbell?

Jen put her glass down on the coffee table with shaking hands, and then covered her eyes. Her shoulders shook with sobs.

"Yes," she said in a choked voice. "The front door was ajar, so I walked in. The place was dark except for a faint light from the kitchen. I called her name, but when I didn't get an answer went upstairs. The office door was wide open. I remember there was this odd smell, but couldn't place it. I walked in, flipped on the light, and saw her. God Almighty, there was blood all over." Jen shuddered, uncovered her eyes, and reached for one of Rose's tissues.

"Did you check to see if she was still alive?" Nancy asked.

"Hell, no. She was dead. Her eyes stared at nothing and the back of her head was all caved in. I knew it was fresh kill. The blood slid in little paths down the computer screen and large chunks of...stuff...was splattered all over. That's what I smelled—the blood. All I wanted to do was get the hell out of there. I stumbled to the door and for some reason turned the light off again, ran from the room, slammed the door behind me, raced down the stairs, and out of the house. I went home and straight to bed. That's how my partial prints got on the light switch and doorknob. I was so panicked, I didn't think.

"The next morning I deliberately waited until I was certain someone had found the body before picking up Rose. That's why I was so late."

"Why didn't you call the police?" Anne questioned.

"Because I was scared," Jen wailed. "I had no reasonable explanation for being there at that hour of the night. You know me. When I get nervous, I babble and say all kinds of things."

"God, no wonder you were talking a blue streak

when you pulled up," Anne commented.

Jen nodded. "I couldn't shut up. I also know people tend to shut me out after a while. I counted on it."

"Did you tell this to the police today?" Candace asked.

"No way, but I damned near died when he told me a neighbor had seen a woman in an SUV peal out of the driveway and down the street. He checked DMV and found out we own an SUV. There are a lot of dark-colored Trailblazers around. I told him it wasn't me. I don't think he bought it, but I swear I didn't kill her."

Anne hoped Jen was telling the truth. She took a long drink of tea and said, "Other than Paul Proctor, we are the list of suspects. Does anybody know of someone else who may have hated Dorie enough to want her dead?"

"Well, Alice Karchman—Ruby Redd, hated her guts," Rose said. "After Detective Collins called last night, I did some research. Pam Graham was in Orlando at a one-day workshop for the chapter up there."

"I know. Gil told me she caught a late afternoon plane and was home at the time of the murder," Anne informed them.

Rose nodded. "But the speaker for the day was Alice Karchman."

For a moment Anne couldn't breathe. "You mean Alice was in Orlando, an hour's drive away the day Dorie was killed?"

"Looks that way," Rose said, nodding again.

"Did you tell Gil?"

"Of course I told him."

Anne thought hard. Gil had asked her about the initials AKRR in Dorie's diary. Now he had a name to go with them.

"Rose, did he ask you anything about initials?" she asked.

"He asked about CH and SM."

"And?" Nancy prompted with a stern look.

"I said I didn't know," Rose returned in an injured tone.

"Oh, good grief," Candace said. "As much as we'd love to put all of Dorie's victims on the suspect list, the chances that Careen and Sarah would show up for a one-day workshop in Orlando *and* that one of them would take the time to kill Dorie is not a probability."

"I agree," Jen said with a shake of her head. "Let's just forget both of them."

"I wonder what Dorie had on Alice," Anne commented.

"I think I know," Rose replied. "Alice wrote some incredibly graphic male/female sex. Unfortunately, she was flaming and into whips, chains, and lots of leather. Things got out of hand at some conference—lots of noise, and one of the other guests called in a complaint at three in the morning. My guess is Dorie was attending and found out."

Jen snorted. "Bitch probably called it in herself."

"And if her publisher found out then Alice's career could have been over. Publishers don't like authors who make them look bad," Nancy said.

Anne sighed. She didn't want to hear any more of this.

"Ladies, I have to get home. Rose, Nancy, and I admitted to the police about being at Dorie's. Jen denied it. I have the feeling Gil is working on this as we speak. He may even be having us followed."

"Getting a little paranoid, are we?" Nancy suggested in a snotty tone.

Anger bubbled in Anne's chest. She was tired of constantly defending herself and of Nancy's sarcasm.

"Getting to sound a lot like Dorie, aren't we?"

"Let's not fight with each other," Rose begged.

"Divide and conquer," Jen added. "Maybe that's what Anne's detective is doing to us."

"He's not my detective," Anne answered automatically. "But you could be right. I'm calling it a day."

She rose and headed for the foyer with the others close behind. Nobody said goodbye. Everyone just drifted to their cars and left.

Later, while picking at an unappetizing frozen dinner, Anne realized that Nancy's chain analogy of a few days ago had been correct.

The chain had broken and the damage was irreparable.

Chapter Nineteen

After dinner, Anne took her time cleaning the kitchen, wiping down already sparkling countertops, scrubbing spotless appliances, and scouring a gleaming sink. Anything to keep from thinking. It didn't work. Conversations floated through her head.

She poured a glass of wine and settled into the corner of the sofa. If she continued to think about Gil, the interrogation this morning, his abrupt departure the night before—including the kiss, and the developments with her critique partners this afternoon, she'd go nuts. Instead, she concentrated on the information gleaned from their meeting.

She was pretty sure Rose and Candace had no motive for killing Dorie. Their names never appeared in any kind of notebook or such. And Rose was right. She had more of a reason to blackmail Dorie than the other way around. *At least in her own mind.*

The question mark in one of the notebooks next to Jen's name made her think. Jen had just signed a contract, and planned on announcing the good news at the meeting. And now that the effervescent Jen had something of value, Dorie had pounced. Had Jen also pounced with a Campbell in her hand? Anne shook her head. She just couldn't see her scatterbrained friend doing that. But then, neither could she visualize Jennifer actually finding the body. Nor could she believe how good Jen had become at lying.

*Two months ago, I wouldn't have believed any of us capable of doing what we've done.*

So, Jen lied to get an agent. It was harder to land an agent than to have an editor read a manuscript. Many publishing houses now required authors to have agents. They refused to consider any unagented work presented. New authors had to impress more than one or two people, which was why pitching a work at conferences was so important. An otherwise unapproachable editor became very available.

Nancy, however, was another story. Those damned books bothered her. Why would Nancy risk going back to Dorie's for a bunch of books? She'd stared at the covers when Nancy had showed them to Gil that day. Anne remembered one as being Nancy's, but the other two author's names eluded her.

*Maude Something. Began with an "L," didn't it?* And the other name was Cassandra. That she remembered, but not the last name. *Moore? Marshall? An "M" for sure.* The first initials had been elaborate with curlicues.

She wished she could ask Nancy outright, but then Nancy was rapidly becoming withdrawn and secretive. *Not to mention snarky,* she thought, remembering the snide comment about being paranoid.

The stress was getting to all of them, and with Nancy's temper hanging by a slender thread Anne didn't want to unleash it. Besides, her friend might ask a few pointed questions in return. She wasn't about to discuss judging and the Campbells at this stage of the game. She'd have to figure this one out on her own. *Gonna be tough. I don't often read historical novels.*

And then, she remembered who did—Marian Tyson. Marian was a long time chapter member. To the best of Anne's recollection, the woman had never written a word of fiction, but was a certified historical junkie. Plus, she wrote the occasional online review. Maybe Marian could help. She knew everything there was to know about historicals.

A quick glance at the clock showed it to be only nine. Marian wasn't likely to be in bed this early.

Running upstairs to her office, Anne searched her files until finding the chapter roster. She thought for a moment to get her questions and story in order, and then dialed. Marian answered on the fourth ring.

"Marian, this is Anne Jamieson. Did I catch you at a bad time?"

"Heavens, no. I was just about to send in a review. You delayed me from having to really hose this poor author. What can I do for you?"

"Well, a couple of us were talking about historical novels and had a problem remembering authors. I thought you might be able to help."

"Shoot."

"Now, no one remembered the plot, but one gal thinks the author's name may have been Maude, and the last name could have started with an L." Anne recalled the cover of the book Nancy had taken didn't look too out of date. "I don't think it was written that long ago."

To her amazement, Marian chuckled. "Maude Lofton?"

*How does she do it?* "Yes! I think that's it."

The chuckle turned into a full-blown laugh. "My dear, Maude Lofton was the pen name of Nancy Carlyle when she first started writing."

Anne damn near dropped the phone in astonishment. "What? I never knew Nancy wrote under a pseudonym."

"Had to be fifteen years ago. She only used it once or twice, I believe. Her maiden name was something long and hard to pronounce. She switched to Carlyle after getting married and before the Lofton name was branded."

"My God, I had no idea." In fact, Nancy had specifically told her she'd written her first book after her marriage. Another little lie from her friend.

Anne's mind wrapped around Marian's information. Nancy had stolen two of her own books? Why? *God, don't tell me she's this Cassandra person, too.*

"I reviewed it, lo those many years ago. The title eludes me at the moment, but the setting was London, I believe. I guess that's why she chose the name Maude, it sounds British and mature. It was pretty good, but not as good as the author she's become. I don't recall reading the second book."

"There was another book being discussed," Anne said. "Once again, no title, but the author's name was Cassandra. The last name may have been Moore or something like that."

"Moore, Moore, Cassandra Moore. That sounds familiar, too. I'm sure I must have read it. Let me think for a second."

Anne tapped a pencil in a notepad while Marian thought.

"Oh, yes, of course. I remember now. My goodness, you are reaching back for a golden oldie. She was English and wrote in the late fifties or early sixties. Seems to me the title had something to do with meadows and valleys. Very British and not very good, if memory serves. Her stuff's been out of print for decades."

"How do you do that? I mean remember some obscure book from so long ago?" she asked in an awed tone.

Marian chuckled. "When you love a genre, you tend to read as much as you can of it. The bad ones stick out as much as the great ones."

Anne had nothing to say to that. If she remembered correctly, that particular book cover had been tattered.

"Marian, I don't know how to thank you. You've been a tremendous help."

"Glad I could be of service," Marian said with a laugh. "You know me—a fountain of useless information."

"You are a fountain of information, none of it useless. Have a good night, and I'll see you at the next chapter meeting."

Anne hung up and added ice cubes to her rapidly warming white wine. Okay, getting a hold of a Maude Lofton book might take some time, but could be done. The Cassandra Moore novel was another story.

"I wonder if Patricia Wales could help," she said out loud.

Pat owned a bookstore in Kensington Beach, a town twenty miles down the coast from San Sebastian. Her shop contained over five thousand used books, most of which Pat had read. With what amounted to a photographic memory, her ability to remember each book was legend among her fellow chapter members.

On a roll, Anne once again consulted the roster and dialed Pat's home phone.

Pat answered on the third ring. "Hello?"

"Hi, Pat, this is Anne Jamieson. I'm sorry to be calling so late, but I just learned that Nancy Carlyle, wrote a couple of books years ago under a pen name. I love her work and wonder if you had them in stock or could track them down for me."

"No kidding, she did? I never knew that. What's the name?"

"Maude Lofton. I have no clue as to the titles."

"Nancy is Maude Lofton? I had no idea." Anne held her breath when Pat paused. "Let's see, the last time I looked I think I had two copies of two books. How many did she write?"

"I'm not sure. But I think only two. Do you have them?"

"Yes, and if I'm remembering right, they were pretty good. One is titled, *Goodbye Is Not Forever*, and the other is *Cottage By the Sea*."

Anne let her pent up breath out in an audible whoosh. "Pat, that's terrific. I knew if anyone had them, it would be you. Would you put one of each aside for me? I'll be by in the morning to pick them up."

"Sure, no problem. Anything else you'd like me to hold?"

"Actually, yes, if you can find it." She went into her spiel about Cassandra Moore. "The title might have the word meadow or valley in it. It was written in the late fifties or early sixties."

"H-m-m, that name rings a bell, but I don't have anything here that she wrote. Maybe Walt Patterson does. He owns a used bookstore down in Seaview. Part of his merchandise deals with hard to find and out of print books. The last time I was there, he had a book written by an obscure author from the 1920s. Wanted a small fortune for it, too, considering it was only about a hundred pages long. *Love in the Meadow*," Pat said suddenly.

"What?"

"The title of the Moore book. *Love in the Meadow*. I did have a copy years ago when I first opened the store. I'll check with Walt. He might remember it. Walt never forgets a book."

This was high praise coming from Pat.

"Pat, you're the best. I'll see you tomorrow, and thanks for your help."

Anne hung up. At least part of her quest would be realized. She crossed her fingers that this Walt person would have the Moore book, and that it wouldn't bust her budget.

She wandered into her office, wine glass in hand, and sat in front of the computer. With a click of the mouse, she brought up the Google search engine and typed in Maude Lofton. Only a brief paragraph appeared with the names of the books and the dates of publication. So, how did Dorie make the connection? On a hunch, she pulled up Nancy's website. She rarely visited author websites, and this one was no exception. She skimmed the five pages and found what she sought at the end of the biography. Nancy's books were listed, the bottom two clearly stating, "writing as Maude Lofton."

Why would Nancy steal her own books from Dorie? And what connection did a long forgotten novel by an even more forgettable author like Cassandra

Moore have to do with any of this?

*And why would Dorie have them in her bookcase?*

\*\*\*\*

Anne entered The Book Nook at ten the following morning just as Pat hung up the phone. She came from behind the counter with a wide smile.

"Anne, it's so good to see you. How have you been?"

Anne hugged the woman. "Fine. Haven't seen you at any chapter meetings lately."

"I know. Hope to rectify that next month. My assistant, Ruth, has been handling books sales at the chapters for me."

"Well, we've missed you. Did you find the books?"

"Sure did. And I just got off the phone with Walt Patterson. Your karma must be fabulous today. He's got the Cassandra Moore book."

"Hallelujah!"

Pat laughed. "Why do you want such an old book?"

"Oh, an online critique partner of mine mentioned it as having inspired her to read as a kid. I just thought I'd see what was so inspiring."

Pat gave her a funny look. "Inspiring? That thing is a piece of crap. I read it when it first came into the shop." She poked a finger toward her open mouth. "A real gagger. At any rate, here are the Lofton books."

Anne wanted to grab Nancy's books and head for Seaview, but forced herself to remain and chat with Pat for another ten minutes. Finally, with the books in hand, she said her goodbyes and headed thirty minutes further south to Books-A-Plenty.

She entered a small, narrow store where the smell of old paper and dust gave off a musty odor. A short, balding man greeted her.

"Mrs. Jamieson? I'm Walt Patterson. Pat just called to say you were on your way."

"A pleasure to meet you. Do you have the book?"

"I certainly do. To the best of my knowledge, this is the one and only book written by Cassandra Moore."

"Oh, really? I guess I'm lucky to find it. How much are you asking for it?"

"Twenty dollars."

More than Anne wanted to spend, but less than she had anticipated. He reached beneath the counter and withdrew a slim book, placing it in front of her. The creased and torn paperback cover showed a woman standing on what appeared to be a moor-like setting and was the one she'd seen in Nancy's possession.

Rather than haggle over price, Anne forked over a twenty. Then Patterson asked the same question as Pat as to why she wanted the book. She gave the same response.

Patterson's eyebrows rose as he echoed Pat's comments of earlier. "This inspired her? There's a reason why the author only wrote one book. It's not very good."

Anne waved her hand dismissively in the air. "Who knows what inspires any of us. My friend was young and impressionable."

She thanked the man and hurried back north. By one o'clock, following a quick drive through a fast food joint, she was curled up on her sofa chomping a spicy chicken sandwich and trying to decide which book to read first. Anne recognized the thicker volume of

Nancy's as having been the one in Dorie's possession. A check of the publishing date in the front confirmed it was book number two.

*Save Cassandra Moore for last. Concentrate on Maude Lofton.* She chose the first book, the slimmer novel to begin. She liked to get a feel for the author's style and voice, both of which could mature with experience.

A fast reader, by four she'd read the last word on Nancy's first book. It wasn't bad for a debut novel. She riffled the pages with her thumb. Probably about fifty-five thousand words. But she'd read nothing of much consequence. It was a straightforward historical romance taking place in the mid-nineteenth century in London. It contained no love scene per se, just a few chaste kisses.

After eating leftovers for dinner, Anne settled in for round two of marathon reading with the second Lofton book, *Cottage By The Sea.*

The locale in this one was still England, but the setting was rural Kent with the time more toward the turn of the century. Anne liked this one better. The writing was tighter, more cohesive, and the voice crisper, similar to the Nancy of today. The major love scene, however, left a lot to be desired. It was vague with stiff dialogue, the prose overblown and frankly, boring. Nancy had improved over the years.

At eleven o'clock, Anne retired upstairs with the Cassandra Moore book. The spine cracked when she opened it, and the pages curled up slightly at the corners. The first chapter had her yawning.

*Good thing I'm in bed. This thing is better than Valium.*

She closed the cover and placed the book on the nightstand. She'd finish it tomorrow after several cups of coffee.

She turned off the light, but couldn't turn off her mind. Why on earth would Isadora Powell, no fan of historical romances, have one of Nancy's first two novels and that of an author no one had ever heard of in her bookshelf? The bigger question was why would Nancy risk getting caught to steal them?

*The answer's there. I just haven't found it yet.*

Chapter Twenty

Anne sat at the kitchen table sipping her third cup of coffee with Cassandra Moore's book open in front of her. It had taken her four hours to wade through the morass of a contrived plot, over-the-top and stilted dialogue, along with some of the worst purple prose she'd ever read. And she still wasn't done. Maybe a lunch break would help her concentrate. Or more coffee. Anything to keep her alert and focused. This came close to being the worst book she'd ever read.

*No wonder this was the poor woman's only novel. I can't figure out how it got published in the first place. She must have had a relative in the business.*

Sighing, Anne forced herself to read on, her mind occasionally straying from the words. She didn't bother to re-read them. As far as she could tell, there was no connection between this book and the other two.

With only one chapter to go, Anne finally came to the love scene. So far, the novel hadn't even titillated the reader with so much as a kiss.

Her mind wandered again, and then snapped back with suddenly refocused attention. She reread the passage. *No, it can't be.*

Anne hurried into the living room and riffled through the pages of *Cottage By The Sea*, until finding the insipid love scene.

*"Lord Windermere, I implore you not to impugn*

*my honor. I am a maiden and wish to remain that way until my wedding day," Sarah said. "You are so rich and powerful, you can have any lady. Why pick on me, a lowly servant girl in the employ of your uncle?"*

*"Sarah, my dear girl, have you not noticed your beauty? You do not have an aristocrat's blood in your veins, but you have the heart of a queen. I can no longer keep my love for you a secret. Marry me, and we will live in Windermere Manor forever."*

Anne quit reading, ran back to the kitchen, and scanned the Cassandra Moore love scene again. Here was the reason for the blackmail. With the exception of the names and a word here and there, it was identical.

*Oh, my God! That's Nancy's secret. She plagiarized. But why the hell would she plagiarize this crap?*

Perhaps Nancy, not the most demonstrative of people, had had a hard time writing a love scene. Some authors never mastered the careful balance between overwhelming emotion and keeping it realistic. In her present writings, Nancy saved her one and only love scene for the endings of her books. The build-up was some of the best sexual tension ever written.

But how the hell had Dorie discovered it? She had no clue, but given Dorie's insatiable appetite for research it wasn't surprising. Maybe she recognized the style as not being Nancy's. At some point in time, the bitch might have read the Moore novel and remembered the horrible prose. Then, she found out Nancy had used a pseudonym, read that book, and made the connection.

*A really bad book can be just as memorable as a good one. And Isadora Powell remembered a lot of things.*

Now, what the hell should she do? The blackmail, and the reason for it, gave Nancy motive. The means was available in Dorie's office. And the opportunity? Any time that night around ten o'clock.

*We only have Nancy's word for it that she arrived at Dorie's at eleven-thirty. And the neighbor might have been wrong about the time. Plus, the time of death was stated as anywhere between ten and two in the morning.*

Anne had the sinking feeling Nancy Carlyle was a murderer. Even with a temper supposedly under control, if Dorie had demanded more money, the demand might have triggered a killing rage.

*Thanks to my admission the other night, Gil knows about the blackmail. I'm also a prime suspect. I have to tell Gil. If I don't, I'm likely to be arrested.*

On the other hand, with everybody denying everything, Gil would have a tough time proving who did it unless the murder scene had yielded forensic evidence—other than the fingerprints. And Gil had said nothing to her, even when they were getting along, about finding anything significant in Dorie's office.

Trying to keep the sick feeling from growing in her stomach, she paced only to be interrupted by her ringing cell. Caller ID showed it was an unknown number. She was tempted to ignore it, but even talking to a telepromoter beat thinking about her friend.

"This is Anne."

"Ms. Jamieson, this Sam over at San Sebastian Auto Repairs. Just calling to let you know your car's ready."

"Oh, thank goodness. How much do I owe?"

"The total is fourteen hundred sixty-five dollars

and eighty-seven cents."

"What? That sounds awfully high." Damn! This would set her back a small fortune for a ten-year-old car.

"It had a lot of other problems, plus you've got a little over a hundred thousand miles on the car. Things begin to break at that age, and you did say to just fix it."

"What kind of other problems?"

"The rattling sound you'd been hearing off and on was the water pump going south. The spark plugs also needed to be replaced, and we found a small radiator leak. All of that plus labor adds up."

Anne inhaled a deep breath. What he said sounded logical. However, she wasn't feeling logical at the moment. No way could she write a check. Her credit card would have to sizzle for another month. *Damn!*

"All right, I'll be over in a little while. I have to turn in my rental."

She hung up. "Why is the world conspiring to drive me nuts?"

The walls didn't answer. *Might as well get this over with. Maybe after getting my car I'll go talk to Nancy. See if I can't draw her out about the Moore book.*

Grabbing her purse, she slammed the front door behind her and walked to the black rental in the driveway. At least she'd get her metallic maroon-colored car back. She slid behind the wheel, inserted the key, started the engine, and put the car in gear. Twenty feet later, Anne jammed on the brakes as a thought crossed her mind.

*Rental cars. Colors. Oh my God, why didn't I think of this before?*

She clapped a hand over her mouth and swallowed to stem rising nausea.

*No, no, it can't be true.*

Her logical mind, however, told her it was. She backed into the street and took off with squealing tires.

****

Anne rang Candace's doorbell, and then smoothed her skirt. *Please, please let there be a reasonable, if not logical, explanation.*

The door opened. Candace stood in the entryway. She led a glass of clear liquid in a small tumbler, not unlike the night she and Nancy had found her. It wasn't even noon yet. Anne's heart sank.

"Well, well, well, it's Annie the mystery solver," she said in a slurred voice. "Come on in."

"Candace, I need to talk to you. Now. It's serious." Was her friend capable of carrying on a conversation?

Candace drained her glass, hiccupped, and smiled. The lines on her face deepened. She looked ten years older than her fifty-three years. "I've been expecting you."

"What do you mean you've been expecting me?" she asked, a knot forming in her stomach.

"Can I get you something to drink or would you prefer iced tea?"

"No thanks, nothing."

She followed Candace into the family room and took a seat on the sofa unable to look her friend in the eye. Candace sat in the chair. Bruno immediately jumped into her lap.

Anne took a deep breath, not sure how to begin.

"Why were you expecting me?" she finally asked.

"You have great deductive reasoning. You should

really write romantic suspense. The minute I saw the folder, I knew you'd been through it."

"The one on the loveseat with the repair and rental receipts in it."

Candace nodded. "I chucked it there after picking up my car from the body shop the morning we all went to Dorie's. I knew someone had read it. The papers were all straight—and neat. You were the only one in the house who could have done it." She rose, walked to the bar and refilled her glass. "Like I said, great deductive skills. Sooner or later, you'd put it all together."

Anne's hands trembled. "You killed Dorie. Why?"

"Because she was a fucking bitch, that's why!"

Anne sat in stunned silence. Sucking in a deep breath, she fumbled for words—any words. *This has to be a bad dream.*

"Candace, please tell me what happened."

"It's all so complicated, and yet so simple."

Her mind still had a hard time grasping Candace's words. "But you…you were as shocked as Nancy and me when we found Dorie's body."

Her friend drank deeply from her glass again, tears filling her eyes. "Let's start at the beginning. Do you know what it's like to spend twenty years of your life pursuing something you know in your heart is never going to happen? Do you know what it's like to realize your friends pity you and sometimes ridicule your work? No, of course you don't. You're Miss Perfect. Well, *I do*.

"I tried so hard to put the things I learned from my precious critique group and from conference workshops to good use. I acknowledged years ago that I didn't have the talent the rest of you do, but I kept hoping that one day I'd get lucky."

Tears overflowed, trickling down her face. She sniffed, rubbed them away, and then poured again refreshing her drink. Anne remained silent hoping she could understand the slurred words and explanation of a drunk.

"In spite of my shortcomings as a writer, I enjoyed the creative process. I had all these ideas floating around in my head begging for an outlet.

"Then, Eric—that stinking bastard—decided he wanted a divorce so he could be with someone younger, more glamorous. The miserable son of a bitch squired that silly bimbo around to the country club, and other places we used to go as a couple. Invitations from people I thought were my friends dried up. I'd been replaced by a twenty-two-year-old redhead with unbelievable titty implants." She raised her glass in a salute. "This eased the pain.

"I can't tell you the number of times I cried myself to sleep. Then one night I didn't cry. I got angry. I wanted him dead. And that's how the plot came to me."

Candace paused and, confused, Anne asked, "What plot? To kill Dorie? What did she have to do with Eric and the bimbo?"

"Nothing. My plot was to kill Eric. I played the 'what if' game."

The what-if game. They all played it. Authors loved taking ordinary circumstances, then bending and twisting them into sometimes bizarre book plots.

"You mean literally kill Eric or did you think of a book plot?"

Candace nodded and blinked owlishly before

resuming her seat on the chair. "Oh, I thought about killing him and his bitch often, but in this case it was a novel. What if a woman going through a painful and humiliating divorce kills her philandering husband and gets away with it? She keeps everything, and the girlfriend is left out in the cold because the husband hadn't transferred assets yet. That's how it worked between Eric and me. We had just begun talking about the settlement.

"Suddenly, I was visualizing entire scenes and conversations. I wrote for eighteen solid hours, slept for four, and then wrote for another twelve. I finished the rough draft in three weeks—a hundred thousand words of verbal revenge."

Candace paused to gulp more vodka. Anne marveled at her friend's drunken, but calm demeanor. How did a book plot morph into Dorie's murder?

Candace frowned. "Where was I?"

"You just finished a hundred-thousand-word manuscript in record time." Anne couldn't keep the amazement from her voice. Candace had pulled off an incredible accomplishment.

"Just about. At any rate, I spent the next two weeks editing. I was going to spring it on everyone at the next critique meeting."

"But you didn't. How did Dorie become involved?"

"I was hosting the critique group the week I finished it. Dorie called to say she couldn't make it. Before I could stop myself, I was telling her about my new book.

"She said it sounded like an interesting premise, but that sending it through critique would take forever.

She offered to do it. Said she was at loose ends and would take a look.

"I know she'd said some horrible things about my writing in the past, but I was anxious to see what she thought. That afternoon, I e-mailed the first three chapters, the last chapter, and the synopsis."

"Your first mistake—trusting Isadora Powell," Anne murmured. "Did she ravage it?"

Candace shook her head and sniffed. "Not really. A few days later, she called and asked me to send the full, so I did. She didn't get back to me until just before Thanksgiving. Said that while the premise was interesting, it wouldn't fly in the romance publishing world. Plus according to her, it needed work. She suggested I put it away for four or five months, clear my head, and then read it with fresh eyes before doing major re-writes. Claimed I needed to take my time to think over plot and characterizations."

"Dorie being helpful? That doesn't sound right. Dorie didn't put herself out for anybody," Anne replied. "What did you do?"

"Sounded reasonable, so I did it. The holidays helped. Didn't touch the damned thing until the end of March. I took it slow, but finally finished the revisions. Last month, I decided it was ready. I called Dorie and she said she'd take a look at it in a few weeks."

Anne knew why the revisions had taken so long. Candace's divorce had turned nasty over the settlement and become final only a month or so ago. And then there was all that drinking. Editing while in an alcoholic coma was not recommended.

Candace swallowed the rest of the glass's contents. Anger poured from her eyes. Her hands trembled. She slammed the empty tumbler onto the coffee table, doubled up her fists and briefly pressed them to her lips before continuing. Sick to her stomach, Anne had an inkling of what was to come.

"Then came Dorie's good news about selling a book and how she wanted to celebrate. The day before our meeting, I got an e-mail from my critique partner up in Jacksonville giving me a couple of agent's names. She told me a friend of hers who critiqued with Dorie online said that Dorie told her the new book was a sure-fire bestseller. It was all about a woman who, going through a painful and humiliating divorce, kills her philandering husband, and gets away with it."

Anne's suspicions were confirmed. "She stole your book. Did you confronted her?"

Candace curled her lip, relaxed her fists, and leaned back. "I was in shock to think that anyone, especially an author of Dorie's ability and reputation, would stoop so low."

Anne had no problem seeing Isadora Powell doing something so underhanded. "Dorie was desperate and stooped lower than you might imagine."

Candace eyes fixated on the white crown molding around the ceiling. Anne followed her gaze and registered that it had a rope pattern.

"I sat on the sofa crying for hours, then got up, popped a microwave dinner in the oven, ate, and took Bruno for his walk in the bark park—all routine. It wasn't until we finished and I was behind the wheel that I began to shake. I was so…" her voice choked and she swallowed…"so furiously angry, I'm not even sure I knew what I was doing. The next thing I remember is ringing Dorie's doorbell. She answered, took one look at my face, and said, 'I see you've found out.' She had a glass of red wine in her hand and this smug smile on her face."

Candace stood and paced with slightly staggering steps, her trembling hands pressed to her cheeks. "I came in, closed the door behind me, and asked how could she do this to me? The bitch laughed. Laughed and said my version of the story would never have gotten past a semi-educated beta reader, much less published. The writing was grade school level and the characters boring. She, on the other hand, had no problem selling it."

"I told her I'd sue. She laughed again saying no author had an exclusive on plots. She changed the title, the character's names, and the setting, and who was going to believe me? I was an unpublished nobody, and she was Isadora Powell, *New York Times* bestselling author.

"I think I was crying because she told me to stop sniveling and go home. She had work to do, and I was bothering her. She opened the door. I walked out and it slammed behind me."

Candace ceased her pacing and inhaled several deep breaths as if trying to sober up. Anne didn't speak.

"This is where things get hazy. I'm not quite sure what happened. I know I stopped at a liquor store, bought a bottle of vodka, drank some, and then drove around for a while. I don't know where or for how long. I kept hearing her laughter and seeing that smug smile. I looked up and realized I was cruising in front of her house again. I pulled around the corner, parked, and walked back to her place."

Candace's face had a look of pure loathing on it.

Her breathing accelerated.

"The front door was unlocked. I opened it and walked in. The only light came from the kitchen. I knew Dorie would be in her office, so I went upstairs. I had no idea what I was going to do. Talk some more, maybe. Beg. Plead. It was strange, like another person inhabited my body, my mind.

"The next thing I remember is waking up in the morning on my kitchen floor, an empty vodka bottle lying next to me. I was covered in dried blood. At first, I though I'd injured myself, but couldn't find any wounds. Bruno was licking my face, so he was all right. I was terrified. It wasn't my first experience with a booze-induced blackout, but I'd never looked like this before. I kind of remembered having a weird, crazy dream about Dorie.

"I ran to the car. The keys were still in the ignition and a bloody towel lay on the passenger's side floor. It wasn't mine. I was scared I'd had an accident and that someone had been hurt real bad or was dead. I didn't know what to do, so I showered, threw the bloody clothes and towel into the trash, took the car back to the rental agency, got mine, and came to the meeting."

She emitted a strangled sob. Anne stood and put an arm around her shoulders, guiding her back to the sofa.

Candace sat, hiccupped, and continued. "The instant I saw Dorie's body, I knew I'd had no dream. I remembered bits and pieces—grabbing the Campbell, swinging it—but that's all. I must have made some kind of effort to clean up. I guess the towel came from Dorie's bathroom. I tried to touch as many things as I could in the house that morning to explain any fingerprints I may have left behind. I know enough about romantic suspense to do that."

She finished her story and looked at Anne with pleading eyes.

"Candace, I'm so sorry." The words sounded lame, but Anne could think of nothing else to say.

"She stole from me the only thing I would kill for. I don't have one ounce of remorse. I'm glad I did it. I'm glad I killed her."

Anne wanted to cry. Candace, the least talented of the group who tried so hard and persevered through bad contest scores and tons of rejections, had been victimized by a *New York Times* bestselling author. She understood her friend's anguish completely.

*Dorie, wherever you are I hope it's hot and the flames are licking your ass.*

"Candace, I don't know what to say."

Candace rose, walked behind the bar, and smiled. "So now you know. What are you going to do?"

*Maybe a diminished capacity plea will work. A good lawyer could get her a reduced sentence or something.*

There was only one thing to do. She couldn't let this go. As a prime suspect herself, she had to clear her own name.

Anne rose and headed for the hallway. "Come on, we'll go talk to Gil. He might understand the circumstances. Call your lawyer to meet us there."

"No."

She turned. Candace stood behind the bar, her face set in determined lines.

"But, Candace, you have to tell the cops. Otherwise, an innocent person might be charged with murder."

"Like you? Or maybe Nancy? One of the others? It doesn't take a genius to figure out Dorie was blackmailing one or all of you," she said in a soft tone.

A chill raced down Anne's spine. The soft voice, coupled with the slurred words and curiously sad look in Candace's eyes, made her aware she was in the room with a killer.

Her friend walked with a halting step from behind the bar, a bottle of champagne in her hand.

"I was saving this for when my book was published. Too bad, I can't share it with you. At least not in the usual way. I'm sorry, Annie, I really am."

She raised the bottle over her head and charged.

Anne turned and ran for her life, visions of Dorie that fateful morning streaming in front of her eyes. The foyer was just ahead. She tripped over a rug and stumbled against the door.

Candace was right on her heels, but in her drunken state ran into the small table under a mirror. With an oath, she swung the bottle, hitting Anne on the shoulder. Pain radiated down her arm and up to her neck. She screamed and shoved her friend in the chest sending her back several steps where she slipped and fell. It gave Anne an extra second to reach for the doorknob.

From behind, she heard sobbing curse words. She fumbled with the latch. Candace would regain her footing and be on her in seconds. Finally, the door opened. She ran outside and into the arms of Gil Collins.

Chapter Twenty-One

It was almost eight o'clock when Rose, Nancy, and Jennifer arrived at Anne's. She'd called them as soon as she returned home from the police station, but didn't enlighten them to why she wanted to see them. A lot of things needed to be discussed.

She poured wine for all except Rose who declined, requesting water instead.

"I'm on the wagon for another seven months. I'm pregnant."

"Not again," Nancy said.

"Yes, again, and I told Jack this morning he was cut off from all sex until he gets the operation."

"I guess that explains why you were puking all the time," Jen commented. "Are you okay with it?"

Rose shrugged. "Do I have a choice? And before you say anything, the answer is no, I don't have a choice."

"Congratulations, Rose. There's always love for one more," Anne told her.

"Okay, Anne, why are we here?" Nancy asked. "And where's Candace?"

She took a deep breath and spent the next twenty minutes telling them what had occurred earlier. They all stared back with stunned expressions.

"Dorie stole Candace's book?" Jen said.

"Poor Candace," Rose sobbed.

"I can't believe Candace had it in her," Jennifer commented, shaking her head.

Anne wasn't sure if she referred to the book or the murder.

"Who knows what's in any of us if pushed too far," Anne said, wiping tears from her cheek. She wished with all her heart the killer had been someone from the outside.

"Thieving sack of shit," Nancy replied. "I know exactly how Candace felt. If it had been me, I'd have killed the bitch, too. We should give her a medal. She actually tried to kill you?"

"Sure as hell looked like it to me. She was drunk, scared, and beyond rational thought."

"I can't believe you went there to confront her," Jen said. "No offense, but that didn't sound too bright."

Anne shrugged. "I know that now. I went to a friend's house hoping I had come up with the wrong solution."

"I was really convinced Dorie's ex-husband had offed her," Rose said.

Anne shook her head. "A lot of things make sense now that didn't earlier. Like that partial we found. It wasn't Dorie's, it was Candace's. Remember? I said it wasn't her usual style. Can't think of why I didn't recognize the author."

"Because none of us expected it to be Candace's," Nancy replied. "She must have put a lot more emotion into this manuscript than in previous works."

"Dorie probably printed out the first three chapters, edited, rewrote the full Candace sent, deleted it, and forgot about the partial in the credenza," Jen said.

"No wonder Candace went on a drinking binge,"

Nancy said. "That night we found her drunk *was* a kind of confession, only she was confusing events. The nights at the bars and the murder blended into each other—especially the parts about the men walking their dogs. Geez, why didn't we see it?"

"Because none of us ever took poor Candace seriously as an author," Rose said. "We rolled our eyes and tried to be kind at her efforts. Who could have guessed she'd have written something Isadora Powell would want? See, even now I used the adjective 'poor' in front of her name."

"Remember the comment that stumped us in Dorie's diary about a great plot coming from such a feeble mind?" Jen asked Anne. "Even while stealing it, Dorie was contemptuous of the author. I've got to wonder how many roadblocks Dorie tossed in front of all of us, masking bad advice as critique."

"I just can't see Candace bashing in Dorie's head with a Campbell," Rose commented. "She was always on the quiet, passive side. It showed in her writing. We always harped about her use of passive voice and telling."

"Little of which got through," Nancy said. "The diminished capacity plea might work, but it's a long shot. Juries don't always buy the 'it's not my fault' defense anymore."

"I'm sure she'll do jail time," Anne told them. "Maybe they'll slap her in a sanitarium for a while. I'd say her writing days are over, unless she decides to write about this."

"What kind of evidence did your detective have to seal the arrest?" Jen asked.

"He's not my detective and I wish you all would

stop referring to him as such. I have no idea what brought Gil to Candace's this morning. Never had a chance to talk directly to him at the police station and he hasn't answered my voicemails. He arrested Candace on the spot for Dorie's murder. I'm just glad he showed up when he did. I suppose it'll all come out during the trial."

"If there is one," Nancy said.

Rose drank from her water bottle. "Why wouldn't there be a trial?"

Nancy shook her head. "She'll have to plead guilty by reason of mental defect in order for the defense to be accepted. Then comes plea bargaining. The judge can go straight to sentencing from there."

"I really wish the killer had been Paul Proctor, too," Jen murmured. "I'm going to miss Candace at our meetings."

Nancy drained her wine and set the glass on the coffee table, and then shot a keen glance toward Anne.

"What I told you about my motive for being at Dorie's the night of the murder was the truth. I had decided to drop out of the group. It still applies."

"But why?" Rose cried, her eyebrows rising.

"Do you honestly believe we can still get together and discuss our work knowing what we know? Will we ever see each other in the same light?" Nancy shook her head. "No, it's over. I'm at the point where I might try to submit without critique. I found myself using fewer and fewer of your suggestions."

Anne bit her lip to keep it from trembling, and then released it.

"I understand. I came to the same conclusion a few days ago."

"What?" Jen said, astonishment on her face.

"It's true. Dorie's ghost will always be sitting on the sofa next to one of us. And we'll always see Candace taking our criticism with an earnest expression." She sighed and blinked to keep tears from welling. "If we had been honest, we'd have told Candace the truth years ago—that her writing hadn't improved and maybe she should find another outlet for her creative side." She looked from one to the other. "We all had secrets, but if we were true friends, we'd have come clean—trusted and supported each other. We didn't."

Rose sighed. "I guess if we had, none of this would have happened."

Nancy rose. "I'd better be going. I have revisions to finish. There's no reason why we can't still be friends. And we'll see each other at chapter meetings; maybe even have lunch together now and then."

The others also came to their feet and drifted toward the foyer. There Nancy surprised Anne by hugging everyone.

"Thank you for all the years you helped me." She took a deep breath and smiled. "Goodbye. I'll see you at the next chapter meeting." Nancy walked through the door.

Rose turned to Jen. "Do you still want to critique with me?"

Jen hesitated, and then shrugged. "Why not? We'll give it a try."

Rose hugged Anne and also departed.

At the door, Jen stalled before saying in a low voice, "You and Nancy were being blackmailed by Dorie weren't you?"

Anne stiffened her spine, but said nothing.

Jen nodded as if understanding. "Once we discovered *Dorie's* secret, I was sure that's why she wanted to see me that night. To add me to the list. She said her name, even on the bottom of a letter, had value. Funny, Candace did what I would never have had the guts to do. I should be feeling horror and condemning her actions, but you know, I can't. See you at the next meeting."

She turned and left.

Anne closed the door and leaned back against it fighting tears.

Alone, she wandered into the kitchen. The Cassandra Moore novel was on the table where she'd left it this morning. She picked it up, opened it, and ran her hands over the yellowed paper, then deliberately tore the pages from the flimsy binding. One by one they drifted to the table. Finished, Anne tore them into little strips and threw them away. It was her last foray into destroying evidence.

She poured a glass of wine and returned to the living room. Curled up in the corner of the sofa, she sipped and fought the tears again. She needed a shoulder to cry on—someone who would tell her everything would be all right.

She needed Gil.

Chapter Twenty-Two

Anne had never visited anyone in jail. She'd endured the search and the wait before being led into a large room. A long counter ran approximately thirty feet down the center of the space. Glass partitions separated one side of the counter from the other. Telephones were the only form of communication between prisoner and visitor.

She sat in a hard plastic chair covertly looking around. From her left came the voice of an angry woman, the receiver clapped against her ear. A quick glance showed the prisoner shaking her head and sobbing. To her right and further down the row, a man sat talking to another female inmate.

In the back of the room, a door opened. Candace emerged being led by a female deputy. She took a seat, her lips curving into a tremulous smile. Anne reached for the phone. Candace did the same.

"Hi, Candace. How…how are they treating you?"

It was a dumb thing to ask, but what else could she do? She was still trying to figure out why she'd come in the first place. She should have been filled with outrage at Candace trying to kill her. Instead, the only emotion she felt was intense sorrow that a friend had been driven beyond the edge.

"As well as can be expected, I guess," she replied, her eyes downcast.

"Is there anything I can get for you? Books? Magazines? Anything?"

"No. No, I'm fine." She finally raised her eyes to Anne. "I…I'm really sorry for what happened. I didn't want to hurt you, but I felt so trapped, so scared."

Anne refrained from rubbing her shoulder. It still hurt. "I understand, and I…I guess I didn't want to believe you had killed Dorie. Have you been arraigned yet?"

Candace nodded. "Yesterday. My lawyer is going with guilty by mental defect due to the booze." She raked a hand through her hair. "God, that booze will slowly eat your mind. I drove drunk one night and almost hit a man walking his dog. And then Gil paid his visit talking about a man and his dog. I got all confused about the two men. In my mind, I wondered if perhaps I had hit him, maybe even killed him. I thought that's who your detective was talking about when he came to see me that day we were supposed to go out to dinner. Then I realized he was talking about the night of the murder.

"I didn't remember a lot of things when I drank. Sometimes I'd wake up in the damnedest places, like slumped over the kitchen table or half-undressed on the floor of my closet. Once I came to in the bathtub. An empty bottle was always with me. I'd try to remember what happened, but everything was a blank. I found out later that blackouts aren't uncommon to heavy drinkers."

"But you're getting help now."

"No liquor available, so I have no choice." She sighed. "It's all for the best."

Anne cleared her throat. "Is there any news on

sentencing?"

"Not yet, but my attorney is working on it. He thinks I'll get sent to a rehab facility for a while, and then a medium security prison. Two maybe three years is his guess." She shrugged. "I'll leave it up to him. By the way, thank you for taking in Bruno."

"My pleasure. He's a sweet little thing. Keeps me company. Maybe I can arrange to bring him to visit you sometime."

Her friend smiled. "I'd like that. He must be horribly confused."

"He is, but seems to be rolling with the punches. The kids are due home next week. I'm sure they'll play with him."

"Good. That's good. Um, Anne, how did the others take to the news? They must know by now."

Anne gave Candace the reactions of the rest of the group.

"Rose is pregnant again? Good heavens, how does she find the time to write? And good old Nancy. I can see how she'd lose no sleep over Dorie's death."

"None of us did. They're all planning on visiting soon."

"That'll be nice."

The conversation well had dried up. For the life of her, Anne couldn't find anything else to say.

"I've got to be going, Candace. I've got a deadline."

"You don't really, but I understand. It's kind of hard to make casual conversation with an inmate of the San Sebastian County Jail, especially one who tried to brain you with a champagne bottle." Her voice sounded remorseful, while her expression showed horror at her actions.

She shook her head. "That's over and done with. You acted under, ah, diminished capacity."

Candace sighed and blinked tears from her eyes. "No, under the influence is more like it. Goodbye, Anne. See you again soon, I hope."

"Goodbye. I'll be in touch."

They both hung up and Candace was led back through the door. As Anne walked from the jail, she promised to visit her friend at least once a week until she was released from prison.

*Candace did what I wanted to do, but never had the courage. It may have been wrong, but I can't blame her one iota.*

\*\*\*\*

Anne sighed and massaged the back of her neck. Another chapter down, she thought with satisfaction. The plot was finally coming together. A glance at the clock showed it to be almost six. Time for dinner.

A small tongue licked her ankle. She looked down and gazed into sad, and slightly confused, shih-tzu eyes.

"Hey, Bruno. Want to share some dinner with me?" she asked scratching behind his topknot.

He was a cute, loving little guy. No wonder Candace had set such store by him. Her kids, Ken and Lisa, were due home from her ex's this coming weekend. She hoped they liked the thought of Bruno staying.

She rose, descended the stairs, and walked through the foyer into the kitchen. Bruno's nails on the porcelain tiles tapped behind her in a comforting rhythm. Staring into the freezer compartment, Anne reached for a chicken parmesan entrée when the doorbell rang.

Retracing her steps, she walked back to the foyer. Through the sidelights, she saw Gil. She hadn't spoken with him since the day Candace had been arrested. He hadn't answered her voicemails nor had he bothered to call. She had assumed whatever they'd had was over. Now, seeing him on her doorstep gave her hope.

Anne's heart beat in slow, hard thumps and her legs moved as if trying to run in water. She took a deep breath and opened the door with a shaking hand.

Gil smiled. "Hello, Anne. May I come in?"

"Of course."

He entered and she led him into the living room. Bruno, hiding under the coffee table barked. Gil crouched and tickled the little dog under the chin.

"Bruno! I wondered what happened to you. I see you've found a new home."

"Yes, I offered to take care of the poor thing. He's still confused, but getting used to me. I'm hoping the kids will help when they come home. Please, have a seat. Can I get you something to drink?"

He sat in one of the chairs. "No, thanks, I just dropped by to bring you up to date on things. The judge sent down her ruling late this afternoon on the sentence."

"And?"

"Candace Warren is being sent to a rehab and mental health facility for six months, after which she'll go to a minimum security prison for two years. The charges were reduced to involuntary manslaughter from murder two."

Anne breathed a sigh of relief. "Thank goodness. Candace really wasn't in her right mind when she killed

Dorie."

Gil shrugged. "She killed her all the same, and over a book of all things."

"You have no idea what Dorie did to her. An author's book is like a child. Dorie kidnapped that child and sold it to the highest bidder. Given the circumstances, I might have done the same thing," she replied with indignation.

"For a while there, I was afraid you had."

Anne bit her lip and sat on the arm of the sofa. "I heard where Orion Publishing is suing Dorie's estate over the book. I'll bet Candace's computer hard drive will show she wrote it, not Dorie. If they ever straighten the mess out, maybe Candace will get the credit she deserves."

"I'm sure Paul Proctor and Miss Powell's sister will also be involved. The last I heard they were fighting tooth and nail over the lottery winnings," he replied with another smile.

"Gil, now that this is all over, why did you show up that day? I assume it was either to arrest or interrogate her again. I seem to remember a couple of female officers with you. What evidence did you have that led you to Candace?"

He sighed and shook his head. "Our computer gurus found a deleted manuscript with Candace Warren's name on it in Isadora Powell's hard drive. That caught my attention, but the real clue came from you."

Her mouth gaped. "From me?"

He ran his hand through his hair. "If it's any consolation to you, I hoped the killer was Paul Proctor, too. There was enough hate and anger in the attack to kill three people, let alone one. Just the kind of thing an ex-husband who'd been screwed out of a large sum of money might do. But we found no forensic evidence that he'd ever been in her office. We did, however, find dark brown, red, and blonde hairs—both long and short—in the office. The short blonde hairs, Mrs. Warren's length, outnumbered the others by a huge margin. I went back over everyone's statements and realized all of you gave me the clue I needed to solve this case."

"We did? What did we say?"

"Remember that man walking his dog the night of the murder? He said he saw a small dog in a dark-colored car parked around the corner from Ms. Powell's about ten o'clock. Only one person has a small dog—Candace Warren. But her car is white. I saw that for myself. It had front-end damage from where she hit the workbench.

"And from comments made by everybody, including Mrs. Warren, she'd just gotten her car out of the shop. While looking through the papers confiscated from Proctor's motel room, I came across a car rental agreement. The light bulb lit. What if Candace Warren had a rental?"

Anne rubbed her finger over the hem in her shorts. Apparently, cops played the "what if" game, too.

Gil shook his head. "By this time I was checking credit card transactions from all of you. Ms. Warren's showed both a body shop and a car rental agency. I called and found out she had taken her car in for repairs to the back bumper the Wednesday before the murder. Quick Rentals also confirmed she'd rented a black sedan with black leather interior the same day. It was returned the morning after the murder. That was one of the errands, Mrs. Warren mentioned in her statement.

"The agency let us examine the car. They had washed it and vacuumed the interior, but we found traces of blood on the upholstery, the carpet on both the driver and passenger sides, and on the steering wheel. We also found some on the underside of the driver's side door handle. Very few people think to clean under there. The guy who washed the car just gave it a quick spray and wipe down. We analyzed the blood. It's a match to Isadora Powell's—type AB. I'm sure DNA will confirm it's hers."

"I was taking my rental back when I remember having seen repair and rental receipts in her office. I finally put it all together."

"And you still went to her house. Not a smart thing to do. She tried to kill you."

Anne shook her head. "I know, but Candace was always so quiet, so compliant. I never dreamed she'd come after me. Besides, she was wasted."

"No excuse. Plus, we found Ms. Powell's blood on the hardwood floor and the rug runner in the upper hallway of her house. The bathroom also yielded blood evidence."

"She really didn't know what she was doing, Gil. I'd bet my life on it. She was furious, confronted a contemptuous Dorie, killed her, then went home and drank herself into a coma. When she woke up the next day, she didn't remember a thing. What she'd done was so horrific her brain blocked it out."

"As a cop, I find it hard to make excuses." He rose. "I'd better be going. I thought you'd like to know how it went down."

She also stood. "Gil, would you like to stay for dinner?"

His gaze softened. "No, I don't think so. Not yet."

Anne bit her lip. "I've missed you."

He stroked a finger down her cheek. "I've missed you, too."

*Have dignity. Don't beg.* She did anyway.

"Gil, can't we just pretend none of this happened? Can't we start over?"

He dropped his hand to his side. "Anne, I'm not one to try to fit the pieces of anything that's broken back together and call it whole again. That includes relationships."

"But, Gil…" He held up a hand and she stopped.

"I expect criminals and the scum I deal with to lie, but not the woman I might be falling in love with. You lied to me—not once, not twice, but on numerous occasions. You only admitted to it when you had no other choice. And I know one of you found and took the cell phone.

"You destroyed evidence and hindered an investigation. Both are felonies. I should have arrested the lot of you. And then, I'd look into those big blue eyes and wanted to believe with all my heart I was wrong. Remember that night you made dinner and how abruptly I left?"

She nodded. "You were looking at family photos and thought I couldn't let go, but that's not true."

He shook his head. "I left because I wanted to stay. I wanted to drag you upstairs and make love all night. But you were a suspect in a case I was investigating, and you hadn't come close to being truthful. I had the feeling that underneath all the so-called sharing of information, you had an ulterior motive. Picking my brain to see how close I was coming to the truth."

"You didn't tell me everything either," she replied in a low voice.

"Because I couldn't give evidential details of an ongoing investigation, no matter how much I liked you."

She didn't have an answer to that.

"It's about trust, Anne, and right now, I don't trust you."

Anne blinked tears from her eyes and whispered, "Can you ever?"

"I don't know. I just don't know. I need time." He leaned down and brushed his lips over hers. "Goodnight, Annie."

He walked out the door, closing it behind him with a soft click.

She made her way into the kitchen and poured a glass of wine, letting the tears flow. It would be so easy to make Dorie the villain in all of this, but realized she had only herself to blame.

*I should have told Dorie to go cram it up her ass at the first demand for hush money. No, from the instant she suggested the bribe. I should have said no and stopped critiquing with her immediately. But I didn't. I let fear rule my common sense. And God knows Dorie could sniff out the weaknesses of others and take advantage. There was so much I could have done but didn't.*

Bruno licked her ankle again. She picked the little dog up and cuddled him, her tears wetting his fur.

"I really botched it, Bruno. What do you think? Will he ever be able to trust me again?" He licked a tear from her cheek. "He's got to. I can't just let him walk out of my life."

She set the dog on the floor and snatched the chicken parmesan dinner from the freezer. Later, she'd work on her newest project again. Anything to keep from thinking.

But she couldn't stop thinking as she ate. Gil admitted he may have been falling in love with her. Now, she could admit the same. Somehow, someway, she had to regain the trust.

"And come hell or high water, I'll do it. That's a promise, Bruno."

## A word from the author...

I was born in Indianapolis, Indiana, but lived for many years in Memphis, Tennessee which I now consider home. I have two adult children and seven grandchildren. At present, I reside in Ft. Lauderdale, Florida with my husband, Bruce, and as many pets as the house will accommodate.

I've been a serious writer since 2002 and belong to Romance Writers of America, Florida Romance Writers, and River City Romance Writers. Without these organizations and the wonderful people in them, I would never have succeeded.

I love writing and hope readers enjoy the many journeys and adventures my imagination creates.

~*~

Other Suzanne Rossi titles
available from The Wild Rose Press, Inc.:
*A TANGLED WEB*
*ALL IN THE FAMILY*
*ALONG CAME QUINN*
*DEADLY INHERITANCE*
*DEATH IS THE PITS*
*HEAR NO EVIL*
*NEARLY DEPARTED*
*THE REUNION*
*THROUGH MY EYES*

Thank you for purchasing
this publication of The Wild Rose Press, Inc.

If you enjoyed the story, we would appreciate your
letting others know by leaving a review.

For other wonderful stories,
please visit our on-line bookstore at
www.thewildrosepress.com.

For questions or more information
contact us at
info@thewildrosepress.com.

The Wild Rose Press, Inc.
www.thewildrosepress.com

Stay current with The Wild Rose Press, Inc.

Like us on Facebook

https://www.facebook.com/TheWildRosePress

And Follow us on Twitter
https://twitter.com/WildRosePress